A life or death choice . . .

The man's eyes opened wide, and he clawed for his gun. It was just clearing the holster when he looked up at the business end of Joshua's Colt Peacemaker, and he saw flame stab out from it twice in an instant and immediately felt two bullets slam into his chest and pass through his body. He could not breathe, and he felt his body roll backward over his horse's rump as he fell face-first onto the ground behind his dun. He was dead before he hit the dirt with a loud thud.

Joshua swung the gun toward the leader and held it on his chest. It was cocked.

"Now," Strongheart said, "if you boys decide to kill me, it will be with bullets and not a rope, but I am shooting, too, and it starts with you, partner. You die with me no matter what. Now, I have done nothing wrong and am not going to be strung up by a bunch of vigilantes just because you do not like half-breeds. So, mister, it's your turn to make a decision . . ."

Titles by Don Bendell

BLOOD FEATHER
STRONGHEART
CROSSBOW

The Criminal Investigation Detachment Series

CRIMINAL INVESTIGATION DETACHMENT
BROKEN BORDERS
BAMBOO BATTLEGROUND
DETACHMENT DELTA

BLOOD FEATHER

A Sequel to Strongheart
A Tale of the Old West

Don Bendell

BERKLEY BOOKS, NEW YORK

THE BERKLEY PUBLISHING GROUP
Published by the Penguin Group
Penguin Group (USA) Inc.
375 Hudson Street, New York, New York 10014, USA

USA I Canada I UK I Ireland I Australia I New Zealand I India I South Africa I China

Penguin Books Ltd., Registered Offices: 80 Strand, London WC2R 0RL, England
For more information about the Penguin Group, visit penguin.com.

BLOOD FEATHER

A Berkley Book / published by arrangement with the author

Berkley Books are published by The Berkley Publishing Group.
BERKLEY® is a registered trademark of Penguin Group (USA) Inc.
The "B" design is a trademark of Penguin Group (USA) Inc.

For information, address: The Berkley Publishing Group,
a division of Penguin Group (USA) Inc.,
375 Hudson Street, New York, New York 10014.

ISBN: 978-0-425-24791-4

PUBLISHING HISTORY
Berkley mass-market edition / August 2013

PRINTED IN THE UNITED STATES OF AMERICA

10 9 8 7 6 5 4 3 2 1

Cover illustration by Bruce Emmett.
Cover design by Diana Kolsky.

ALWAYS LEARNING   PEARSON

DEDICATION

My sister Bette Ann (Bendell) Lunn is eleven years older than me, so became like a number-two mom to me. Bette was loving, protective, nurturing, and although I am now in my sixties, she tries hard not to baby me still. What I appreciate most about my sister is the love of music she passed on to me. Now retired, she studied and then taught music her whole life and is an inductee into the Colorado Music Educators Hall of Fame. Besides rock and roll, I was exposed to piano and organ concertos by her when I was small, and she took me to concerts where I developed a love for symphony, opera, and all music.

My brother Bruce Bendell passed away several years ago and was nine years older than me. We were always close, but when I was a boy he made sure I would not grow up a sissy. For one birthday, he gave me two pairs of boxing gloves, an army fatigue uniform, an M1 cap rifle, and a pair of six-shooter cap guns. He and I did American Indian fancy dancing starting when I was barely out of kindergarten, and he was a tremendous artist, singer, and hilariously funny.

I had several stepbrothers and stepsisters, but I had just one who was very close to me and close to my age. She became like a sister to me and still is. Kathy, known as Roberta Kathleen (Magenau) Schmitt was one of the hottest girls at Coventry and Kenmore High Schools. We shared secrets, and she taught me how to fast and slow dance and told me that knowing how to dance would always get me women. She was right. She has been through a very rough life, but like me, she is a survivor who is determined to always land on her feet and never give up. Kathy always has had a sharp wit, a ready laugh, a twinkle in her eye, a love of God, and a sensitivity which will bring a tear if I just say something slightly sentimental.

My wife's aunt, Joyce Ann (Kittenger) Edwards, is a retired art professor, but more importantly, she introduced my wife to me more than three decades ago. Joyce is like another older sister and shares my love of art. She was a professor at the University of Akron (Ohio) and was my art director and still photographer when I made the feature film *The Instructor*. We became like siblings even before she introduced me to Shirley. Like Shirley and me, Joyce loves God, and is a consummate *drama queen*, and I say that with a loving smile on my face.

Last but not least, my younger sister is actually my sister-in-law Jan. Janice Lee (Ebert) Guy is so much like my wife, her big sister, in so many ways, I could not help but love her. A beautiful blonde, she is a successful small business owner partnering with her husband Jerry, to whom she is totally devoted. Like Shirley, she can outwork (or outdance) anybody and everybody and has to be told to slow down, turn out the lights, and go to bed.

This book is dedicated to these five siblings. I love each of you very much, and each of you has positively touched and helped form my life in different ways.

Thank you,
Don Bendell, 2013

To be feared is to fear: No one has been able to strike terror into others and at the same time enjoy peace of mind.

Seneca

FOREWORD

Strongheart was my first new Western for Berkley Books, and I am very happy to be back in the saddle again. In fact, my ranch south of Florence, Colorado, is named the Strongheart Ranch, and I am a real cowboy with a real horse. My own horse is named Eagle, although I have another horse, Gabriel, who looks identical to Strongheart's horse Gabriel, but I found him and bought him after *Strongheart* was released. I hope you will enjoy this sequel to *Strongheart* and escape with me back to a time when a man's word was his bond, women were ladies, and men were men, and you survived only if you were hardy. These were the people who made America.

I hope you like Joshua Strongheart's further adventures as much as I do and come with me on an escape from computers, television, news stories, traffic, and our fast-paced society, to a time when our country was simpler, tougher, and more natural. Let's take a journey back to the Old West, to the real America.

ACKNOWLEDGMENTS

No author has influenced my writing more than the late great Louis L'Amour. Louis L'Amour was born March 22, 1905, and grew up in Jamestown, North Dakota. To me, he has always been the premier storyteller of the American West. Many of Mr. L'Amour's Westerns were made into very popular motion pictures. For example, *Hondo* and *Apache Territory*. Sadly, he passed away from cancer in June 1988, and a great light was extinguished in the halls of Western literature. Shortly before his death, he was told he had sold more than 200 million books worldwide.

Like the late Louis L'Amour, I ride on every piece of ground I write about as much as I possibly can, and now also do so with Gabriel (Gabe), who is as I said identical to the mount of Joshua Strongheart but was found and bought after *Strongheart* came out. In that way, you, the reader, get a truer vision of the mountains and valleys, the countryside, the smell of the sagebrush, the heat from the sun baking a rocky canyon, and you hopefully will almost hear the clicking of horses' hooves on rocks and can escape into my world for a little bit. Enjoy the ride, partner.

Don Bendell

1

THE PREDATOR

The eyes were intelligent but lifeless and were very dark brown, almost black. They carefully followed the movements of the small tribe of Minniconjou Lakota moving far below the large cottonwood where the predator remained motionless. He had taken one of their band and carried the body high up in the branches of the majestic tree. A single drop of blood dripped off his chin and landed on the branch below him. His eyes went down in response to an imperceptible sound then refocused on the band of Sioux. He had just eaten the last bite of the prey's heart and wanted to close his eyes and nap.

His appetite sated for now, the predator would awaken in a few hours with his mind wondering about a new hunger to kill again, another two-legged animal that would challenge his predatory instincts so much better.

The mutilated body of the young Sioux woman lay across a branch nearby. She was no longer a challenge and therefore of little further interest to this muscular predator. She could not run or thrash around, but now just lay still, unmoving, her ears not attuned to the whistling of the meadowlark, her eyes not seeing the super-busy wings of the ruby-throated

hummingbird, air-balancing in front of the bright crimson
area of her left breast, where her heart had been torn from
her body.

The band of Lakota had missed Sings Loud Woman, but
nobody was really alarmed yet, as she was wont to wander
off while gathering firewood if something tickled her fancy.
Considered a dreamer, she was not a hard worker but was
exceptionally beautiful. Many men in the circle of lodges
had watched her walk, a natural movement of curves and
symmetry that stirred the imaginings of all men, the young
and the elders. But not anymore. Now she was a bloody, lifeless mass high in the branches of a cottonwood tree along
the banks of the Greasy Grass.

In just two years, members of this tribe would take part
here in the Battle of the Greasy Grass, which the *wasicun*
would be calling the Battle of the Little Big Horn or
Custer's Last Stand. Now though, it was a shallow, glacial
water–clear, rock- and sand-bottomed, small river with little brook trout streaking to and fro and, when the sun was
just right, giving it the look of occasional energy in an otherwise lazy summer afternoon. The thick green foliage of
the surrounding cottonwoods and hardwoods made the
twists and turns along the waterway obvious to any traveler
at a distance, as the rest of its surroundings were large rolling ridges covered with long green prairie grass.

The predator had slept high in his perch, and the red-
skinned creatures below were gone. Satisfied for now, he
climbed down to the ground and drank deeply from the clear
waters of the Little Big Horn River. The trees, the river and
its small grass-walled canyon would provide good cover as
he began his migration. He started on his slow lope, always
heading south, toward his southern hunting grounds, many
weeks' travel away. His hunting area was much larger than
that of any grizzly or male cougar. As he had so many times
before, he'd struck and fed in his northern hunting grounds

and now would move hundreds of miles to the south, from the Montana Territory to southern Colorado Territory. Keeping to the shadows and draws, he was seldom if ever seen. When he was seen, it was usually a fleeting glance, often a shadow. The thought of his next stalk and kill, this time of a white-skinned two-legged creature, kept him moving, kept him alert.

The big Concord stagecoach headed east on Road Gulch Stage Road. The road had many years of use as a trail before becoming an offshoot stage route in southern Colorado. The rules for travel on the leather-strap suspension stage came directly from Wells Fargo and were posted inside most Wells Fargo coaches:

- Abstinence from liquor is requested, but if you must drink share the bottle. To do otherwise makes you appear selfish and un-neighborly.
- If ladies are present, gentlemen are urged to forego smoking cigars and pipes as the odor of same is repugnant to the gentler sex. Chewing tobacco is permitted, but spit with the wind, not against it.
- Gentlemen must refrain from the use of rough language in the presence of ladies and children.
- Buffalo robes are provided for your comfort in cold weather. Hogging robes will not be tolerated and the offender will be made to ride with the driver.
- Don't snore loudly while sleeping or use your fellow passenger's shoulder for a pillow; he or she may not understand and friction may result.
- Firearms may be kept on your person for use in emergencies. Do not fire them for pleasure or shoot at wild animals as the sound riles the horses.
- In the event of runaway horses remain calm. Leaping from the coach in panic will leave you injured, at the mercy of the elements, hostile Indians, and hungry coyotes.

- Forbidden topics of conversation are: stagecoach robberies and Indian uprisings.

The coach was crowded, and the passengers were all anxious to get to Cañon City, several days' travel to the east. This coach had left Poncha Springs near the Arkansas River, which ran through a long, winding, high-walled canyon for forty-some miles to Cañon City, where the white-water river poured out onto the prairie and headed through mainly flatlands on its winding journey to the mighty Big Muddy.

The passengers saw a small herd of white Rocky Mountain goats high up on the ridge on the north side of the river shortly after leaving the Poncha Springs area. Then they ran into several large herds of bighorn sheep on the rocky cliffs north of Cotopaxi, named for a mountain in South America.

After a night there, in which the passengers were entertained by the dry humor and colorful stories of white-haired, pipe-smoking Zachariah Banta, the stage had turned south, and within a mile, all six passengers had to get out and walk, as it was a long, winding stagecoach road heading uphill and the driver wanted to take it easy on the horses. Sarah Louise Rudd, visiting relatives in Cañon City, was breathing heavily, struggling against the altitude and her arthritic hips, and felt relieved when the tall Pinkerton agent took a gentle hold of her left arm and helped her up the inclined grade. Finally back in the confines of the relatively roomy stage, they eventually turned east on Road Gulch Stage Road and crossed the north end of the big, beautiful Wet Mountain Valley.

It was on this winding stage road with piñon-covered ridges and outcroppings where the predator came down from his lair on Lookout Mountain. It was the ideal hideout and observation point for both mountain lions and outlaws. To the west lay the beautiful Sangre de Cristo and Collegiate mountain ranges, thirteen- and fourteen-thousand-foot snowcapped peaks stretching skyward from northern horizon to southern horizon. To the south the Sangre de Cristos stretched deep into New Mexico. Lookout Mountain was not that tall, but it stood as a lone rocky sentinel on this, the southeastern end of the Wet Mountain Valley. It overlooked piñon- and stunted-cedar-covered sandy ridges going off in every direction and was a natural vantage point from which to observe all that moved for miles.

This predator had a hunger for human flesh, and more importantly, it had been many days since he had made the kill on Sings Loud Woman. He knew where to make another stalk, testing his skills, moving quietly and unseen among the two-legged creatures.

The stage went slowly through the twisting narrows as it climbed uphill five miles toward Copper Gulch Stage Road. The road wound its way like a granite-scaled serpent, and the predator moved quietly and swiftly over the rocks toward a rendezvous with the upcoming Concord. His eyes seemed empty as his gaze swept back and forth in wide arcs, looking for unseen potential enemies under rocks, behind bushes, and in the shadow of every tree and rocky overhang.

He had watched the stage from his rocky lair and knew that it stopped at this spring to let the passengers fill their canteens or soak their kerchiefs in the cold spring water, to wrap around their necks to help in the sweltering summer heat. It would be here that he would take down his prey, and he could already taste the blood. Like always, he would select one prey out of the herd of passengers. It would be one that stood out as strong, almost *worthy* of being killed. He would soon carry the body up into the rocks to feast on this hot day.

The predator found his hiding place under a rock and between two thick bushes right near the spring. Passengers would walk within a few steps of him, and like before, he would patiently wait for the prey he picked out of the herd.

Jack "Blackjack" Colvin was an outstanding Pinkerton detective and was riding the stage to courier a message to fellow Pinkerton Joshua Strongheart. Blackjack was a tall, slender man with wiry muscles and a leathery face from many years in the saddle, the sun beating on his face, the wind chapping his rugged countenance.

Someone had dubbed him Blackjack because of his black handlebar mustache and because he was an outstanding cardplayer. Actually though, he was great at five-card-stud poker not blackjack. He thought about becoming a dealer and dreamed about owning his own gambling house in one of the big western towns. However, his father was a trapper, a mountain man, and Blackjack had a penchant for the high lonesome. He loved the wilderness and everything about being out in the mountains, desert, or prairie. His ideal roof at night was the Milky Way.

The Pinkerton man loved the black, steep Grand Tetons west of Jackson Hole country, far to the north, and he really loved the Wind River country, but this area was special. Southern Colorado Territory in many places, such as Pueblo and Cañon City, got less than a foot of snow per year and over 330 days of sunshine, yet less than one day's horseback ride away, plenty of snow could be found in the bordering mountains and mountain valleys. There was plenty of wildlife, water, and fertile growing land, and there were also plenty of railroad and stagecoach routes and hearty, self-sufficient residents.

His grandfather was from England and had taught Blackjack as a child the fine art and many nuances and pleasures of tying flies and fly-fishing. The Arkansas River, which emptied its giant bladder out onto the prairie at Cañon City, had the finest brown trout fishing in the world, stretching west from Cañon City all the way to Poncha Springs. There was also great rainbow and cutthroat trout fishing in the area, and Blackjack had told his friend Joshua by wire that he wanted them to spend a day fishing west of Cañon City along the Arkansas. Joshua had made his home in the area and operated out of there, receiving regular telegraphic communications in regards to assignments from his boss, Lucky, in Chicago.

At that moment, Joshua was making arrangements for a friend and excellent fly fisherman from Cañon City to take the two men out along the Arkansas to fish the best pools in the churning, foamy river.

The driver reined in the horses, and Blackjack exited the stage first, to help the ladies down. Clarabelle Sicher had traveled many miles to see her son, daughter-in-law, and grandchildren in Florence and was very excited that they were getting so close. Her legs and back ached from years of hard work and many travails. This final stagecoach ride was especially hard on her, but she was glad they were riding in a large, comparably comfortable Concord stage. Behind her was Joanne Rivers, who was either a dance hall entertainer or, occasionally, a prostitute, depending on her financial straits at the time. Sarah Louise Rudd was the last lady off the stage. Also aboard were the storyteller, Zachariah Banta, and an old cowpuncher, Luther Burrell, riding the grub line, as he had done so many times in the past. He had worked on cattle ranches for years in the Montana and Wyoming territories, but he was tired of snow and cold, another rider motivated by arthritic conditions. He had decided he would head to the Cañon City, Colorado, area and wrangle for his cousin's spread in the Red Canyon locale.

Clarabelle thanked Blackjack and immediately went to the spring, soaking her hankie in the cold water and rubbing it along her neck and face, the breeze running through the gulch cooling the skin as it gently blew across the damp

skin. At the same time, she washed away some of the dust
and grime of the trail.

Joanne batted her eyes at Blackjack almost automatically
as he helped her down, but his mind was on fly-fishing with
his good friend Joshua Strongheart. She had looks and a figure that enabled her to ply her trade anywhere, but a horrible
four-year marriage to a wife-battering miner in Leadville
had sent her packing, disheartened again about romance but
determined to survive.

Blackjack waited until all the others had refreshed themselves at the spring and had moved over under a thick bunch
of young cottonwoods along the stage road. This is what the
predator wanted: to see his prey heading toward him. Lying
under his camouflage layer of branches and grasses by the
spring and water tank, he had lain perfectly still when the
others came over to the spring. Clarabelle Sicher's left foot
actually touched up against his leg, but she thought it was
just a branch under all the leaves. Disciplined after years of
stealthy stalking and killing, the predator patiently did not
move, his mind made up to wait on one prey—Blackjack.

The tall, slender Pinkerton agent came forward unsuspecting. The predator looked at the gun on his hip and the
belly gun he carried as backup, knowing that those things
could kill and wound him. He had been shot years before
by one prey, bruising a rib and feeling the burning pain of a
bullet crease along his side. It taught him to be more cautious. His eyes looked over at the others, and none were
paying any attention to Blackjack, as Clarabelle was passing out sandwiches to the other passengers and the driver.
The prey got closer, and he slowed his breathing, muscles
tensing and ready to strike as the Pinkerton got closer. Only
a few more steps.

Blackjack automatically noticed that there seemed to be
more foliage around the spring this trip, and he felt that the
stage line should have somebody clear such places, as they

could provide great cover and coolness for rattlesnakes. The predator tensed up, breathing slowly, carefully.

Blackjack stepped forward, canteen in his gun hand, ready to dip it into the spring. He was now straddling the predator, and he leaned forward to cup a hand and drink directly from the spring. It was time.

He saw a blur as a giant hand shot up out of the green and clutched his windpipe like a vise, while there was also the movement of another hand coming out of the green lower down and something slammed into his stomach. The pain was unbearable and the power of the stroke knocked the wind out of him. He struggled to get air, but panicked as he could not, and he could not cry out either, such was the grip on his throat. He was able to see that the arm below was very large and muscular and was holding the handle of a large, very large, knife, now penetrating his intestines and stuck all the way into his spine. He saw the predator's face as it came out of the green, and the eyes were unforgettable. In an instant Blackjack flashed back to his brief stint as a seaman on a fishing trawler out of San Francisco. A large great white shark had gotten entangled in a big net, and although his shipmates marveled at the fish's size and gigantic mouth, Blackjack was fascinated by the dark, lifeless, untelling eyes. He was staring into such eyes now, as the life drained out of him, the pain and shock preventing him from reaching for either gun. He died thinking of the entrancing and haunting eyes of the shark, not knowing his heart would soon be taken from his chest, and eaten raw by this Lakota Sioux serial murderer, *We Wiyake*. *We Wiyake* meant "Blood Feather," and after eating the now dead Pinkerton agent's heart, he would follow his pattern. First, he would dip a feather of an eagle or red-tailed hawk into the blood of his victim's chest cavity and then place the bloody feather on the victim's lifeless face. This would be the fate of the late Jack Colvin in less than an hour, in the rocks up above, after *We Wiyake* carried the body effortlessly slung over his right shoulder without detection. This was part of the exhilaration that made him feel alive each time he made a kill, carefully planned to be red-skinned one time and white-skinned the next time. Not only did he carry Jack's body up to his hidden lair among the ledges and boulders above, but Blood Feather only stepped on rocks, not wanting to leave moccasin prints.

As always, feeling he had taken the spirit and the strength of another prey by eating Blackjack's heart, *We Wiyake* would sleep for hours over several days. He would then start thinking about his next kill, and would head back up north to hunt a red man or woman.

2

JOSHUA

The rider dismounted and walked in the narrow doorway of the Western Union office. His shoulders were so broad he had to turn at an angle to fit through the narrow door. The jingle-bob spurs over his tan rough-out boots made a loud tinkling sound in the small room as he walked over to the counter. The Western Union telegrapher had never seen anybody wearing Levi's before, and they could not hide the man's leg muscles. His antelope-skin shirt did little to hide the bulging muscles of his chest, abdomen, shoulders, and arms, and the neck came together in a V-shape, with fringe dangling down and accentuating the chest muscles even more so. The man's face was chiseled and dark coppery, with high cheekbones and very intelligent dark brown eyes that always had a hint of a smile. His hair was shiny black in a long ponytail, and his head was covered by a black, flat-brimmed hat with a round crown and wide, beaded headband. What stood out as well was his gunbelt and holster, in which rode the pearl-handled Colt .45 Peacemaker with the miniature marshal's star on the grip, left him by his stepfather, a quiet, respected town marshal. Then, on the left side of the tooled, brown gunbelt, was the fancy, fringed, porcupine-quilled, and beaded knife sheath and the Bowie-sized, elk antler–handled knife left him by his late father, a mighty Lakota warrior named Claw Marks.

The telegrapher said, "Howdy, Mr. Strongheart. Have a short message for you from the Pinkertons."

Joshua, a friendly smile on his handsome face, said, "Thank you. I want to send one, too." He read the message:

Blackjack bringing msg for you STOP Assignment change STOP Meet my stage Fort Lyons next Friday STOP Lucky END

The tall Pinkerton agent wrote out a message and handed it to the telegrapher. The man transmitted the message the Pinkerton detective had written.:

Lucky STOP Blackjack missing from stagecoach STOP I will find him STOP Blackjack and I will be at stage STOP Joshua END

"Is that what you want, sir?"

Joshua smiled, saying, "Not quite. My pa was sir. Please call me Joshua."

He shook hands with the telegrapher, paid him, and left the office.

François Luc Des Champs, better known as Frank Champ and even better known as Lucky, was the boss of Joshua Strongheart and his staunchest supporter. Reading the message, Lucky became very concerned. The phrase "Blackjack missing from stagecoach" really concerned him. Blackjack was extremely reliable. The only relief was the other phrase "Blackjack and I will be at stage." Of all the people Lucky had ever known, Joshua Strongheart was the one man who would be willing to die keeping his word.

He proved that when he made a promise to a beautiful young widow after a stage holdup, that he would track down the robbers and get her ring back. He did just that, going through a series of shoot-outs and life-threatening situations. The young woman, Annabelle Ebert, was the lady that Joshua now loved. Joshua almost died, but he kept his word and got her ring back.

Joshua Strongheart walked into the café on Main Street in Cañon City as the two cowboys sitting at the far table were placing their orders for lunch. Their waitress was ravishing. She was Annabelle Ebert.

One of the cowboys said, "Look at thet. I hate when these uppity blanket niggahs think they can jest go inta any white man's place they want. They oughta."

He was interrupted by Annabelle pouring a pitcher of water on his head.

Through gritted teeth she said, "Mister, I will not have that kind of talk in my establishment. You and your partner, leave now."

Drenched in water and shocked, the puncher jumped up with fists clenched. Joshua started forward, but Annabelle's hand held palm out stopped him. She wanted to handle this.

She spoke very quietly but firmly. "This is my business and I said leave. I will not speak again."

The puncher glared at her, and his riding partner grabbed his upper arm, guiding him toward the door. There was something in Annabelle's beautiful eyes that made the cowboys feel like she had the upper hand, even if they could not figure out what that was. They turned and stormed out the door, brushing against Joshua on the way. He grinned across the room at Annabelle.

He walked over to the table and picked up the men's dishes and headed toward the kitchen. Annabelle cleared off the glasses and tablecloth and followed him. In the kitchen, he swept her into his arms and they kissed long and softly.

Joshua briefly told her about Blackjack being reported missing from the stage, and that he had told Lucky he would find him.

She jumped up and walked to the stove, saying, "I will make you up some food to carry. You go saddle up Gabe and get your saddlebags and clothes ready."

The sixteen-and-a-half-hands-tall red-and-white overo paint gelding Gabriel ate up the miles on Copper Gulch Stage Coach Road with a floating trot as Joshua rode toward the rest stop where Blackjack Colvin had disappeared. The road twisted and turned through a rocky piñon and stunted cedar canyon, climbing steadily for five miles. Finally, at almost eight thousand feet elevation, the canyon opened out into a wide mountain valley, and at the west end the majestic, towering snowcapped Sangre de Cristo Mountain Range rose up into the sky, rocky sentinels against angry storm clouds attacking from the west. The granite sentinels had clouds stack against them almost daily, releasing their bladders over the San Luis Valley on the other side. Joshua Strongheart, like many travelers who came this way, never tired of this view. Sangre de Cristo means "blood of Christ," and the mountains were so named for the red hue on the many snowcapped peaks in the early morning, when the sun came up over the Wet Mountains, which rose up on the east side of the valley, though nowhere nearly as tall as the thirteen- and fourteen-thousand-foot peaks of the Sangre de Cristos. Many were already describing this as the most beautiful mountain range in the entire world.

This route brought back many memories and was the place where several major scars had been born on the

Pinkerton's body. It was also where Annabelle and Joshua had first spoken to each other, riding another stage up this hard-packed canyon road.

Shortly after the valley opened up, the land spread its arms in welcome to the majesty of God's sculpturing of the Sangres, or the Big Range, as the locals called them. It was here that Road Gulch Stage Road branched off to Strongheart's right, and he trotted in that direction across a small prairie section a few miles wide. Now, to his front, in the northwest, was the Collegiate Range, towering over distant Poncha Springs. Joshua trotted Gabe downhill on Road Gulch, a stage road very similar to Copper Gulch but with shorter ridges on both sides. To his right front rose the lone sentinel of Lookout Mountain, where Joshua had had several gunfights the previous couple of years and where *We Wiyake* had laid out his ambush plans and taken his prey.

After four miles, Joshua came to the spring where Blackjack had disappeared. First, he watered Gabe, then he ground-reined him under the tree where the passengers had eaten lunch. He had read the statements of each passenger and was familiar with the area, so Joshua knew right where to go. The area where the spring was had an S-curve which wound between a couple major rock outcroppings. Joshua lay on his belly studying the undergrowth around the spring and branch by branch started pulling the thick green foliage away, tossing it to the side.

In a half hour, he had carefully removed all greenery where *We Wiyake* had lain. He saw the indentations in the sand where the predator's body had been, and by positioning himself next to it, he discovered that the man was close to seven feet tall and well over two hundred pounds, probably close to three hundred. He got up and saw where the upward thrust of the knife had caused a great deal of blood and greenish bile to spill through the greenery and onto the dirt. He hung his head, certain now that Blackjack was

dead, and that his friend had been stabbed in the stomach
or intestinal area. He saw the giant moccasin prints in the
ground leading up to the spot and could tell they were Plains
Indian moccasins, possibly from his own nation, the Lakota,
or its close friends the Cheyenne or Arapaho.

He knew the arduous task of tracking an expert at con-
cealment and stealth lay before him, as he had given his
word he would meet Lucky along with Blackjack. Now he
understood it would be Blackjack's body and him, but his
word had been given, so that was that.

He found his first two prints leaving the scene, and they
were much deeper than when the killer had come. The right
one was especially deeper, so he knew that the killer had
picked up Blackjack and carried him over his right shoulder.
He was probably right-handed.

Strongheart moved up slowly over the rocks, finding a
drop of blood here, a scuff there. His eyes swept in arcs left
to right directly in front of him, moving out in ten-foot
increments. He would stop every ten steps and look behind
him, all around, and overhead if he was near large trees or
rocks. He lost the trail. He continued to walk in the same
direction, sweeping back and forth left to right again, his
eyes scouring the rocks and ground for more sign. Soon, he
spotted a faint scuff on the edge of a rock, and he looked to
where the next left or right foot might have stepped, and in
four paces he found where a dry stick had broken under a
left foot and there was a deep impression from a heel in the
ground between rocks.

Joshua stopped and did not move. He listened intently,
his eyes now carefully sweeping the terrain before him in
wide arcs. This went on for five minutes, then he slowly, very
slowly turned around to face the way he'd come, always
checking his backtrail. He sat like this, unmoving, for five
minutes, then slowly moved upward and onward and continued this pattern.

The Pinkerton was amazed that the killer had not obviously stopped yet to set the body down momentarily and take a break. *He must be incredibly strong*, Joshua thought.

After another hour, he spotted what he'd hoped he would not see: Two birds took off from the rocks maybe two hundred feet above him. Both birds were large, and one circled higher then swooped back down. The other rose higher, with large wingspan, and soon started soaring on the cliffside thermals. By the way both birds soared when their wings were not flapping, a slow, steady gliding, but with a slight wobbling of their wings side to side, told him at a distance that these were not eagles, but buzzards. The higher bird descended again and disappeared as had the previous one, in the rocky perch.

Joshua let down his guard a little and moved up the mountain ridge faster than he had been traveling. He was certain he would find what was left of his friend there in the rocks. It was a mistake on his part that he did not often make, but it was human nature that he wanted to avoid having the vultures feeding on his remains any more than they already had.

Gabe patiently fed on grasses down below. He was ground-reined and would not move very far from where Strongheart had left him.

The half-breed crawled up over the rocks where needed and scrambled up the rest of the time using his hands and knees. So anxious was he now that he was really letting his guard down, while the large brown eyes stared at his movements. The rapidity of movement now away from the predator made him more interested in attacking this seemingly fleeing prey. Joshua stopped looking again for new tracks, and the big boar grizzly now stood on his hind legs testing the wind.

The nose of the bruin was incredible, and his mind automatically catalogued what he smelled on the mountain breeze: a porcupine over the next ridge; a rotting winterkill elk carcass a mile away; the bacon and eggs Joshua had eaten for breakfast, as well as coffee; Joshua's human smell, and the smell of his horse on Joshua's legs; pine and cedar; the rotting carcass of Joshua's friend; and a variety of other smells.

Bears have horrible eyesight, but this bear could tell that this prey was moving rapidly away from him. This excited his pursue-and-attack instinct, and he immediately dropped to all fours and began his uphill charge. Bears cannot run downhill well, but uphill, with their powerful leg muscles, they can move like a runaway freight train. That is exactly how this monster bruin charged for Joshua Strongheart, who now was seeing his friend's decomposing body for the first time. Strongheart was visibly upset as he got to the body of Blackjack Colvin, now simply decaying meat with some semblance of his handsome features.

Joshua was thinking about his next course of action. First, out of respect, he removed Blackjack's gunbelt with his giant knife, and stripped off his antelope-skin shirt. After removing the shirt, he placed it over the head and torso of his buzzard-scavanged friend. He would wrap him up in the bedroll from his saddle down below and deliver the body as promised to Lucky.

No sooner had he placed the shirt over the body than he heard the movement behind him and spun around, reaching for his pistol, which was ten paces away. Shocked, he saw before him the blur of the charging grizzly; it was well over seven feet long and over a half a ton in weight. Joshua had no time to do anything or react in any way. A grizzly bear can outrun a thoroughbred race horse for short sprints, and this bear was no exception. The twelve-hundred-pound bruin slammed into Strongheart, sending the big man flying back, breaking Joshua's left forearm as it slammed into a rock. In an instant the bear was covering Joshua's body with his massive hulk and trying to bite Joshua's skull, but Joshua tried to ward it off with his broken left arm and his right. The weight was crushing, and he could barely breathe. He punched the bear in the nose several times with the heel of his hand, as the nose is the most sensitive part of a bear's body.

Strongheart was pinned to the ground and knew he was in for the fight of his life. The bear, whose breath reeked of a rotten carrion smell, opened its mouth and almost swallowed Joshua's face. He felt the canine teeth crunch down on his head and felt the warm flush of blood as it rushed over his face. He fought to maintain consciousness and bit down on the bear's tongue with his own teeth.

The bear let up on the face, not liking getting bitten at all; nor did it like the taste of human flesh, which was quite typical of bears. Now the bear grabbed the broken arm in its jaws and shook Strongheart violently like a ragdoll. The half-breed reached down into his right boot and grabbed the handle of the sharp, short knife sheathed and strapped to his leg. He brought it out and fought to stay awake and alert. He waited, and the enraged monster now tried to close its jaws on Joshua's throat, but Strongheart plunged the knife deep into the bear's right eye, and it stood straight up, popping its teeth, and roaring in pain. The knife handle protruded from the eye, and the bear rolled and growled trying to grab the blade with its paws. It pulled the knife out and bit down on Joshua's right leg, its fangs going deep into the calf and shin. Blood streamed from the bear's eye, and it seemed even more enraged than before.

It paused and stood on its hind legs, bent forward at the waist and growling, ready to fling all twelve hundred pounds back down on top of Strongheart, who was going in and out of consciousness, but he came wide alert now. He knew the

bear was probably about to go for his throat or head again,
and he pulled up his left leg, ready to kick-stomp up with his
heel.

Suddenly, the bear screamed in pain and wheeled around.
Tears literally flooded Strongheart's eyes, and he weakly
smiled ear to ear, as he saw his magnificent red-and-white
overo gelding pinto horse, Gabriel, biting the back of the
bear's neck. Gabriel's legs were oozing blood out of cuts
from scrambling full-gallop up the mountain over the many
rocks and boulders.

With a faint voice Strongheart tried to yell, "Gabe!"

The horse wheeled and kicked the bear full-power in
the chest with both rear hooves, then as the bear meekly
lunged again, the horse kicked again, then spun and bit the
bear on the front shoulder. The grizzly raked Gabe with a
swipe of its mighty paw, and blood appeared in four crimson streaks across the horse's muscular chest. Gabe bit the
bear again, spun, and kicked five times in rapid succession,
and the bear backed away.

Joshua saw his chance and pushed his body forward
hard with his left foot, grabbed his pistol, just as the bear
charged in on Gabe. Strongheart shot quickly and put five
Colt .45 rounds into the bear, one low behind the left shoulder and four under the bear's left ear. It fell on the ground,
kicking its legs rapidly, gave out a mighty death roar, and
then lay still unmoving. Gabe bit the bear's rib cage, and the
bear did not move. It was dead.

Joshua passed out.

His eyes opened, and he saw millions of stars over his
head, smelled the putrid smell of a rotting human body,
and fainted again. He heard Gabe whinny softly nearby
and smiled in his unconsciousness. He knew the horse was
alive, so far.

Strongheart opened his eyes and blinked at the bright
sunlight, then realized he could barely see. He reached and

felt dried blood all over his face and neck. Something pushed his back and startled him, and he grinned realizing that Gabe had nuzzled him with his nose. He smiled and reached up to pet the wonderful horse's jaw and neck. Strongheart looked at the horse's chest and saw dried blood where the bear had raked his chest. It would be too late to do anything, and there would surely be proud flesh later. There was also dried blood that had been obviously running down Gabe's left foreleg.

The monstrous bruin lay nearby, and only then did Joshua realize the true size, the enormity, of his foe. He also was starting to realize the enormity of his predicament, and then it grew even worse because he saw that Gabe could barely walk. Joshua crawled slowly and grabbed a stirrup with his good hand, and pushing on his good leg, he slowly stood. This took several minutes. Before checking himself out, he checked Gabe's leg, and saw that the grizzly had smacked the leg and maybe bit it, too. There was dried blood all the way down the leg. Strongheart felt and massaged the muscles and checked the joints. He then collapsed in a faint.

When he opened his eyes, he could tell only a few minutes had passed. He raised himself up again holding the stirrup, and knew he would have to doctor himself first or he could do Gabriel no good. He reached his canteen and swished water around in his mouth, recalling biting the bear's tongue. His mouth had a putrid taste. He then swallowed water, and it had never tasted so good, and he poured some also on the back and top of his head.

Joshua pulled his shaving mirror and his razor out of his saddlebag. He looked at his face and was shocked. It was completely covered in dried blood, his own. He knew that facial wounds bleed a lot, so he did not get too concerned. Joshua pulled materials out of his saddlebags and grabbed several nearby sticks for splinting his broken forearm. He tried cleaning his leg as best he could and then bandaged it and did the same with his head. After getting his face cleaned off a little, he saw giant bite marks; his nose was broken, and both eyes were swollen almost shut. He had bites and claw rips all over his torso and arms, as well as much biting on the leg.

Fortunately, this ridge ran off Lookout Mountain, which he was intimately familiar with. Strongheart knew that if he could make it along this ridge and down one draw, there was an active spring with plenty of green grass around it for Gabe, as well as some rock overhangs. There, he could try to nurse Gabe and would have plenty of fresh springwater to clean both him and his horse, and he'd also be able to make a sufficient shelter.

Several of the fangs had gone in deep, and the pain in his leg was excruciating, but he was not sure if it was broken or not. He did not find by feel or probing any place where the bone was broken all the way through, so instead of splinting, he tried wrapping it tight with bandages made from the big towel he carried in his bedroll. He then tried putting his weight on it and promptly fell down in excruciating pain. To be safe, he gathered a few more stout sticks and crafted a splint for the leg, too. Although his left arm was broken, he was able to use his hand and fingers since he had set the bone and placed the splint on it. Joshua found a stout green branch, which he chopped up with his razor-sharp knife and made a crutch with.

Leaving his antelope-skin shirt on what was left of Blackjack's face, he got his spare elk-skin shirt from his bedroll and put it on, then took it off, opting for the sunlight and fresh air to help heal his wounds. He packed his belongings and started leading Gabe slowly, very slowly, along the ridge. He was only able to walk five minutes at a time, then sit down and rest, before several more minutes later, he and Gabe would limp along again.

It took the rest of the day and several naps to travel the one mile to the spring. Joshua, exhausted, fell asleep by the spring while Gabriel grazed on the tall, lush green grass.

When Strongheart awakened, the morning sun was in his eyes, and he looked at the red hue on the snowcapped peaks of the Sangre de Cristos across the valley from him. He understood fully why they had gotten their name from that crimson reflection complemented by the clear blue sky above. He had a pounding headache and realized his whole body felt like a giant toothache. A good sign, though, was that he was starving. The Pinkerton grabbed some beef jerky from his saddlebag and chewed on that, while he pulled out his small coffeepot and made some coffee.

After seeing how badly he needed nutrition, he grilled some biscuits and cut a slab of bacon into the pan from his saddlebags.

Afterward, he spent most of the day cleaning and treating his wounds and Gabe's. The Lakota would use witch hazel, derived from the witch hazel bush, which Joshua carried in his saddlebags, mixed with smashed acorns to treat poison ivy and poison oak. They also used just straight witch hazel to treat a variety of ills, such as sore muscles, aches, and pains.

Joshua found some acorns, mashed them up, and made poultices by mixing them with the witch hazel, figuring that adding the acorn mash would help the mixture serve as an antiseptic and astringent. He then applied the poultices to Gabe's wounds and his own. Gabe's were then covered with more poultices, these ones made of moss, which Joshua easily found on the north side of trees. He bandaged his own wounds with bandaging cloth he also carried for emergencies.

He cleaned his pistol and sharpened his knife, then, grabbing his crutch, he made the relatively long trek back to Blackjack. He was perplexed to find a bloody eagle feather placed atop Blackjack's face. Next, he went through his friend's pockets to retrieve what he could. This would all be turned over to his boss, including his fellow agent's Pinkerton badge. Knowing now that the body was too far gone to return to Lucky, Strongheart then gathered a great deal of firewood and built a giant woodpile around Blackjack's body, then cleared the perimeter for a good distance and began the cremation process.

With darkness approaching, and while the fire raged, he removed the bear's claws and cut some meat from the hindquarters to cook later. Joshua did not particularly like bear meat, and the cleaning process was very messy as the meat was very, very greasy to the touch.

Satisfied that the fire would not send showers of sparks or spread any farther, he departed for his own campsite. By the time Joshua made the mile hike back to his camp, his eyesight was blurry and the whole scene spun around. He collapsed to the ground and splashed water on his face. After looking over at Gabe, who was standing in the tall grass, napping, he fell asleep and slept until morning.

Strongheart awakened the following morning very sore and headachy, plus his eyesight was bad, as both eyes were still swollen almost shut and very black and blue. His right leg and left arm both ached horribly. He made it to Gabe, and the big horse was now limping around the small glade. He walked up to Strongheart when he saw him coming. He wanted to have his head rubbed and held. Joshua gave his lifesaver plenty of loving.

Still standing next to Gabe, he turned his head and was amazed to see three mule-deer does standing in the grass, one of them drinking from the spring. He glanced at his fire, and the wind was blowing his smoke away from them to the west. The two lookouts stared at him, and the larger doe lifted her head up in alert. The first two started to bound off, and he drew his Colt and fired from the hip, hitting the water drinker right behind her left shoulder in mid-bound. She hit the ground in a heap, dead from the quick heart shot. As was the habit of the Lakota, Joshua meditated and communicated with the soul of the animal, thanking her for her sacrifice, and then he prayed and thanked the Lord for the bountiful supply of venison.

Three days later, Joshua was much stronger and had a solid camp built for himself and Gabe. Gabe was moving around now without as much difficulty, and Joshua had made himself another crutch identical to the first. Miles to the east, at Fort Lyons, Lucky was very concerned and knew something was wrong. So Annabelle was not shocked when the Western Union man came in to hand her the inquiring telegram from Joshua's boss.

She sent a reply explaining that she had no idea what the problem might be. Annabelle wanted to cry, so instead she went back to work and kept herself as busy as could be. In 1874, the Denver and Rio Grande Western Railroad had just completed a new line into Cañon City from Pueblo to the east, and Lucky was on that train, having come in from Fort Lyons, farther out east.

Joshua was so glad that Annabelle had packed him a lot of good substantial food. With the deer he'd shot and her food, he had one major thing in his favor. However, he was far from safe, and so was Gabriel. Joshua could tell he had fever now, and some of his fang bites and claw marks from the grizzly were an angry red and obviously infected. Gabriel had blood oozing from several spots in his wounds, and Strongheart tried his best to keep a fresh poultice on those spots. He was getting weaker by the hour and knew he was in for the fight of his life just to survive, let alone have his horse survive. Neither he nor the horse could begin to think about making it down the mountain over the rocks.

Over the fire that night, he took paper and pencil from his saddlebags and wrote two letters. One to Lucky and one to Annabelle:

Lucky,

Blackjack was murdered with a knife by a very large Lakota, 7 feet tall, very powerful. He was carried up the mountain and his heart was cut out. Bloody eagle feather left on his face. I cremated him. If I am dead, give any money owed and belongings to Annabelle.

All respect, Joshua

Annabelle,

If you are reading this, I am probably dead. I have loved you and wanted to marry you from the moment we met. I held off because your husband was not gone that long. I wanted to be sure you felt the same in your heart. Since meeting you, I have grown more deeply in love and worship everything about you. Please smile when you remember me, but you be a survivor and live on with a grin on your face and song in your heart.

Your devoted servant forever,
Joshua

Joshua finished and titled both letters and placed them in his saddlebag. He felt everything whirling around and wondered where he was as he collapsed at Gabe's feet in a faint.

3

CAÑON CITY

Joshua opened his eyes and blinked against the sunlight. He looked around in a daze. He was in a room with sunlight streaking in the windows, and outside the window in the distance were snowcapped peaks. A nurse walked into the room carrying a basin of water.

"So, I see, Mr. Strongheart," she said, nonplussed, "I see you have decided to come back to the land of the living and refrain from such shenanigans as ancestral walks."

He was in a total fog.

Joshua said, "Where am I? What happened?"

The nurse said, "I am not sure except that you were almost killed by an enormous brute of a grizzly bear, which you killed. You were brought here on a train, closer to St. Peter than the gates outside the Union Pacific Hospital."

Strongheart shook his head and tried to make sense of what was happening.

"Union Pacific Hospital? Where?"

She replied, "Denver, Colorado, sir. Near the corner of York and Fortieth Avenue."

Smiling, she stepped from the room, and Annabelle

Ebert, eyes red-rimmed from lack of sleep, stepped in and rushed to Joshua's bedside. She kissed him deeply and stepped back, her eyes glistening.

"Joshua," she said happily, "they all said you would surely die, but I knew you would not leave me. I knew you would live!"

"Annabelle! What has happened?"

She sat down, and the nurse who had left unnoticed returned and handed her a cup of hot tea.

Annabelle smiled and nodded.

"Joshua, Lucky came to Cañon City and organized a posse, and the Fremont County sheriff even rode with him. They went up Copper Gulch Road, then Road Gulch Road, then found where you climbed toward Lookout Mountain. They found you, the bear, Gabe, and where you burned your friend. You had a horrible infection, a broken arm, broken leg, had lost a lot of blood, and were very near death."

"What about Gabe?"

Annabelle smiled. "Two men who used to serve in the cavalry volunteered to stay with him and led him down the mountain two days later. He is doing fine. He has some scars to be certain, and you have some more yourself."

"Anna, he saved my life. He attacked the bear while it mauled me," Strongheart said. "He scrambled where a mule would fear to go to come up there and save me."

A tear rolled down her cheek as she smiled softly.

"The doctor said that he thought Gabe would be dead if not for your poultices and care of him."

"How did I get to Denver?"

Annabelle said, "Lucky had you brought here by train because they felt you would surely die down south. This is a new hospital."

"How long have I been here?" he asked.

"Three weeks."

"Three weeks!" he said trying to sit upright but was too weak.

"Yes, Joshua," she said and smiled sweetly. "I told you that you almost died."

Suddenly it hit him and he blurted out, "I am starved!"

She said aloud, "Nurse?"

The nurse came in, and Annabelle said, "He is very hungry. I told you."

Smiling, the nurse disappeared, then reappeared minutes later with a steaming bowl of stew, biscuits, and butter. Joshua ate several helpings and a large slice of fresh apple pie. He washed it all down with several large cups of steaming hot coffee.

Smiling and recalling things now, he said, "Are we going to spend the rest of our lives with you nursing me back to health?"

"If we have to, I will," she said and smiled. Then she paused, and continued, "I read your letter . . . and I am happy to report you are not dead."

Getting serious, he said, "I meant every word. Hey, what about your restaurant?" he asked, his mind now flooding with thoughts.

Annabelle responded, "I left it in good hands. Sarah Rudd and Elizabeth Macon are running it for me."

"Where is Gabe?"

She said, "He is in my stable. I have the Canterbury boy, you know the one who is so good with horses, working on him and taking care of him."

Joshua said, "Come here."

He reached up with his good arm and pulled her to him, and their lips met with a long-lingering kiss. He pulled her onto the bed next to him and held her in his arms, and she started sobbing on his chest, as he stroked her hair. The nurse came in the door again, saw them, and turned around, exiting. He just held Annabelle like that for a good ten minutes, while she shed tears of relief.

Joshua brushed her hair back and said, "I have to get out of here now. Do you understand?"

She hopped off the bed and called for the nurse, who came in the room immediately.

Annabelle said, "Mr. Strongheart needs his clothes and belongings."

The nurse replied, "Ma'am, the doctor said that he needs rest and attention addressed to his nutritional deficiencies right now. On top of that, his tibia, the shin bone, and his radius and ulna, both forearm bones, need to properly heal. If Mr. Strongheart is taken now—"

Annabelle interrupted, "We thank you for all you have done, Mrs. Hair, but he needs his clothes and belongings now."

The nurse looked at Joshua while he struggled to sit up, and he grinned at her, saying, "Ma'am, I tried to argue with her once."

An hour later, they were on a train headed to Pueblo, and from there would head to Cañon City.

Now, on the trip, Joshua had time to think as Annabelle napped with her head on his shoulder. He watched out the window and thought about her taking care of him more than a year earlier as she nursed him back to health from numerous gunshot wounds. Vastly outnumbered in a gunfight, Strongheart was shot to doll rags, while single-handedly cleaning out a gang of outlaws and would-be shootists in Florence, not far from Cañon City. He really loved Annabelle, but his life was just too dangerous. He did not want a marriage wherein she was constantly nursing him back to health from near-death experiences.

Now he had to turn his attention to the killer of Black-jack Colvin, and what was the meaning of the bloody feather on Jack's face? Had he pulled the feather out of the hair of a Lakota warrior? If so, why was it bloody, and why did the sign show that he was stabbed and had bled to death quickly? Could the feather be another sign of some sort?

It was nightfall when they arrived in Cañon City and headed to Annabelle's café, where they entered through the back door. The beauty fired up the oven and made them a great dinner.

Joshua walked her to her house just a few blocks away from the Main Street café, and they immediately went to the stable. Gabe was happy to see Joshua, and the half-breed shook his head looking at the raking grizzly claw marks across his horse's chest. He wondered how his own new scars would look and wondered about his father, whose name was Claw Marks, from a giant plains grizzly that attacked him. Joshua was conceived in a covered wagon when his mother was nursing his father back to health from the wounds.

They went into the house, and he thought about this and about growing up without ever meeting his pa. He got up to leave, and Annabelle stood, walked over, and melted into his arms.

"Stay tonight," she said.

"No," he replied. "This is a small town and you have a sparkling reputation. It will stay that way."

"I love you, Joshua Strongheart."

He kissed her again and said, "I love you, too, Miss Ebert, and as much as I hate to say this, I am heading down to the Hot Springs Hotel."

After a few more futile protestations, Joshua saddled Gabe and headed toward the popular hotel with the hot springs bath, near the egress of Grape Creek into the Arkansas River at the west edge of town.

The waters felt good again, as he had soaked there often when he was shot to doll rags before and was healing. He had wrapped his arm and leg casts with oilskin, simply because it made sense to him. Joshua decided he would soak again the next day before leaving. The feather bed felt good, and he slept deeply.

The smell of coffee awakened him before the slight sound in the hallway, and when his eyes opened, he realized he already had his Colt in his right hand. There was a knock on the door.

"Yes?"

"It is Lucky," came the reply.

"Come in," Joshua said, rubbing his eyes and setting his pistol back into its bedside holster.

Lucky entered the room with a grim look on his face. He carried two cups of coffee. He handed one to a nodding Joshua.

"*Bonjour*—I mean, good morning. I got in yesterday afternoon and knew you would be here. I have been down south at Fort Union," Joshua's boss said.

Joshua's head was swimming, and he splashed water from the basin on his face.

"Blackjack's death was very bad, Lucky," he said. "The killer was from my people, the Sioux nation," he added, using the term more familiar to the white man.

He went on while he dressed, "The killer is a monster, Lucky. He is seven feet tall and carried Blackjack quite a ways up the ridge without resting or setting his body down that I could see. The way he killed him, too . . ."

Joshua shook his head, and Lucky said, "Allan Pinkerton has gotten involved with thees case. He told me zat you are to use any resources and money you must to bring thees killer to justice. You know, een March, a deputy sheriff and one of our detectives were killed in a gunfight with thee Younger Brothers and keeled one of them. Mr. Pinkerton wants to geev killers of any Pinkertons a very powerful message."

Strongheart said, "I heard about it. Sad."

Lucky said, "We have another assignment for you, too. You can figure out how to work both cases, but finding and keeling this coward ees top priority. Let me buy you breakfast and I weel tell you about the other case."

Instead of eating there, they chose to ride to Annabelle's café, and her heart leapt a beat as it always did when Joshua walked in the door. She gave Lucky a hug, and remembering Joshua's cautions about her reputation, she grinned and gave him a hearty kiss. Several chuckles could be heard in the crowded eatery. She knew Lucky being there meant he wanted to discuss business, so she took their orders and left them alone to talk.

Lucky said, "Have you heard about zee Red River Wars going on?"

Strongheart took a sip of coffee, saying, "A little bit."

Lucky said, "Because of your stature weeth both zee Sioux and zee white world, Mr. Pinkerton wants you to get involved. Our client ees zee government."

"Tell me about it, Boss," Joshua said.

Lucky then spent the next half hour explaining about the Red River Wars, which had started earlier in the year, in July 1874, and it was now late autumn. So many people were traveling west and settling all over, plus then came buffalo hunters to supply them. Some felt that there was a secret "Indian Ring" in Washington who wanted all the buffalo killed to defeat the Plains Indians who relied on them. The army was assigned to protect all of these new settlers. To that end, they built a number of forts all over the frontier, as the West was called. However, many troops had left the West when the Civil War broke out, which emboldened the tribes to try to attack and get their lands back. The Comanche, Kiowa, Southern Cheyenne, and Arapaho (the brother tribes to Joshua's), and some Apaches, such as the Jicarilla, attacked and laid siege to the southern plains. But years had passed since the war ended, and after many complaints from all over, the government knew this situation was no longer acceptable at all.

Two reservations had been set up in Indian Territory in the Medicine Lodge Treaty of 1867. One was for the Cheyenne and Arapaho and the other for the Comanche and Kiowa. Joshua was to use his influence with Cheyenne and Arapaho to try to make inroads with the Comanche, who essentially were running or strongly influencing the battle plans of all these tribes. As usual, the ten chiefs who signed the treaty were promised housing, clothing, supplies, food, even weapons for hunting, and as usual the treaty was repeatedly broken. This was especially due to the giant influx of buffalo hunters

The great southern herd of buffalo, or bison, had started being hunted and killed by the tens of thousands earlier in the year. At the time, Lucky and Joshua did not know it, but these commercial buffalo slaughterers would kill them almost into extinction within just three more years. These jackals slaughtered the animals by the tens upon tens of thousands, and there was no retribution from Washington. Hides were sent back east daily, and the market demand was driving the need for more. This phenomenon would eventually force all the bison-dependent Plains tribes onto reservations, but for now it was forcing many to flee reservations to join a growing group of discontented warriors who wanted simply to rid their lands of this white menace. It made matters worse that the government promises made during the Medicine Lodge Treaty of 1867 and other treaties, as was becoming the norm, were not honored as they should have been. To slap the faces of the tribes even more, the restrictions and rules were suffocating the normally free people.

Lucky explained that many engagements had been occurring since earlier in the year, such as the second battle at Adobe Walls. At daybreak, on June 27, some months earlier,

Lucky explained, three hundred Comanches, led by a charismatic tribal leader, Isa-tai, and the already-famed Comanche chief Quanah Parker, attacked the Adobe Walls post. The warriors thought they would surprise the twenty-eight buffalo hunters at the post and would simply overwhelm them. However, what they forgot about was that these were men with high-powered, long-range rifles used for buffalo hunting, plus they carried a lot of ammunition. Needless to say, the white men at the post won decisively, and many Comanches and dispirited members of other tribes returned to reservations such as Fort Sill. Some, though, fought on, determined to rid the plains of the invaders.

There were a number of incidents and skirmishes in the Red River War Joshua's boss kept detailing as Joshua made mental notes. Lucky told about one incident where the John German family took years moving from Georgia, first to Kansas but destined for Colorado, and before arriving they were attacked by Comanches of Grey Beard's band. John German, his wife, teenaged son, and two daughters were killed. Four more daughters were captured. The older ones were turned over to Stone Calf's tribe and kept hostage and hidden on the reservation at Fort Sill.

Addie and Sophia, the two youngest daughters, were ignored by the Comanches and wandered about on the prairie for a while. But they were finally recaptured by the band.

In the fall, Company D, 5th Infantry, discovered the tribe, which numbered almost two hundred warriors and their families. The soldiers attacked and captured the village along McClellan Creek and repelled numerous counter charges by the Comanches by overwhelming them with their howitzer cannon. The great moment was when they found the two little German daughters—naked, emaciated, but alive in the village. The Comanches were sent on a rapid retreat and the cavalry eventually gave up pursuit.

After the attack on Adobe Walls, the U.S. government

had had enough with the attacks on settlers and decided to launch mutipronged attacks in the Red River, Palo Duro, and other areas, primarily in the Texas Panhandle region, to stop the attacks. The most clever and tactically tough leader of all the Plains tribe fighting was Comanche Chief Quanah Parker, whose mother was white. Therefore, he was very fluent in English and was very intelligent.

Lucky said, "General Phillip Sheridan spoke at length weeth Pinkerton about this, and Allan told him about you having a white mother and red father."

"So," Joshua said, "Mr. Pinkerton wants me to try to set up a parlay with Quanah Parker and see if I can convince him to stop fighting and try reservation living?"

"Exactly!" Lucky replied. "Zey feel that if he stops fighting, the rest will soon follow."

The door of the café opened, and a slender, wrinkled, bent-over old cowboy walked in with a short white beard. A rolled cigarette dangled from his mouth and his eyes swept the room. Annabelle rushed across the room, a big smile on her face, and gave him a big hug. He put his hand up with a wave and ambled over toward Joshua and Lucky. The three shook hands and he sat down.

"Zach Banta," Strongheart said. "What brings you to Cañon City? Long trip from Cotopaxi."

The old man signaled Annabelle over and patted the chair next to him. The three men rose as she sat down.

When they'd sat again, Banta looked at each of the others slowly and replied, "Wal, I looked at the shelves in my store and most items seemed lonesome. Had a couple mice come outta holes, put their front paws on their hips, and kinda stare at me. Seemed right angry, I reckon. I figgered it was time ta go ta town and git some supplies."

The other three chuckled.

Annabelle said, "Zachariah Banta, you devil you. You forgot to mention that you have spies all over Fremont

County and wanted to know whenever Joshua got out of the hospital and came here."

The oldster never missed a beat. "I reckon that's so. Look at me. I'm old. I wanted some young pup here ta load my supplies fer me. Other day, some old boy come inta Cotopaxi and compliments me on my fancy cowboy boots made outta alligator hide he reckoned. I told him, 'Mister. I ain't wearing boots. Ahm in mah bare feet.'"

The group laughed uproariously while Zach carefully built another cigarette.

The four spoke at some length, but Joshua Strongheart, though polite, was already formulating his plans. He and Lucky mounted up and followed Zach's buckboard to the mercantile building not far down Main Street. They loaded Joshua's supplies into the wagon.

Then they rode west on Main Street as Joshua returned his horse to a large brick building with a gable front and two large signs reading G MAKLEY AND CO BLACKSMITH and ELKHORN FEED STABLE. The building was joined by a large corral.

Lucky paid for the horses, and Joshua told the hostler he would escort Lucky to the stage depot and bring the mounts back. They rode south over toward the river and the depot.

Lucky briefed Joshua a little more and told him he could charge whatever he wanted or get reimbursed for anything by the Pinkerton Agency in regards to hunting down Blackjack's killer and effecting a rendezvous with Quanah Parker.

Lucky cautioned, "You must stay with the modern times. Take zee train with your horse as often as you can. Eet will be much faster, and you do not have to worry about money."

Joshua smiled, saying, "Yes, Ma."

Lucky laughed and said seriously, "And whatever you do, do not drink again."

Joshua smiled.

He replied, "Boss, I have not had a drink since that time you bailed me out of jail in Wyoming Territory. I will not drink again."

As he rode back toward the livery leading Lucky's horse, he thought back to the last time he drank. He could not remember the horrible beating he gave to three men or his arrest. He awakened in jail and found out he had tried to defend the honor of a dance hall chippy who was simply enticing prospective customers. Joshua knew then that he had become a mean drunk and was apparently affected by alcohol consumption the way many Indians were. Although he was not happy with Joshua at all, Lucky took care of it. And Joshua vowed he would never touch alcohol again no matter what.

He stopped at the café and went to the back door. Annabelle came out, and he pulled her into his arms. They kissed long and passionately.

Surprised a little, she stepped back and looked up into his eyes.

"I love you," he said.

Taken aback some, she smiled and said softly, "I love you, too, Joshua. This is so sudden it sounds like you are saying good-bye."

"No," he said, smiling softly, too, "I'm not, but on the train I started thinking. My work is so dangerous, and I do not want a wife who spends our whole marriage nursing me back to health. I have to leave today on a new mission and want us both to do a lot of thinking about us."

Annabelle said, "I don't need to, Joshua Strongheart. I love you and want to be your wife. Your biological father and you both have claw scars from grizzly bears. What are the odds of something like that happening? You survived the most horrendous bullet wounds I have ever seen after your gunfight in Florence, and that was after surviving your wounds in the stagecoach holdup. I have thought about what you said myself, but I decided you have been wounded enough for ten men, let alone one. I think the odds must be in your favor by now. I think it should be my decision if I want to spend my life nursing you back to health. In the meantime, I will be here waiting for you to make up your mind."

He reached up and touched her cheek softly, and kissed her lightly on the lips.

Joshua said, "You are an incredible woman, my darling."

She opened the back door, saying, "You wait right here, sir. I'm making you a pack of food for your saddlebags."

She disappeared, then emerged seconds later with a steaming cup of hot coffee, gave him a quick kiss, and went back inside, while he sat on a chopping block and sipped the coffee.

4

LAKOTA LAND

After a March special election earlier in the year, the citizens had agreed to funding a railroad spur from Pueblo into Cañon City. The long-anticipated Denver and Rio Grande Western Railroad spur was completed in July, and now just a few months later, Joshua Strongheart loaded Gabe onto a livestock freight car and found his seat on the train. He was first heading east thirty miles to Pueblo and then north through Denver.

Joshua thought about how much the West was transitioning into modern times as he trotted Gabe into his father's tribal circle just a few days later.

He was immediately greeted by several smiling faces, people he did not see often enough, who he knew as uncles, aunts, and cousins. He was taken to a teepee and fed, so he could rest from his trip and talking could begin tomorrow after a night's sleep.

The next day Strongheart shared a pipe with the tribal chief *Mato Conze*, "Angry Bear." They spoke in Lakota.

Angry Bear puffed on the pipe and, using his palm, tried to sweep the smoke over his face.

He passed the pipe to Joshua and said, "We heard about you counting coup and killing the mighty bear. Did he write on your flesh with his claws?"

Joshua grinned and stood, removing his shirt. He still had fresh claw scars and bite marks. Angry Bear took note of the many bullet scars, too.

Joshua replaced his shirt and sat again, cross-legged as was custom. They smoked some more and talked about many things.

Angry Bear said, "It is not polite to speak of the dead, but your father also bore scars of the mighty bear. This I think is a sign from the Great Mystery. The one who came before you was my friend. He was a great warrior and a member of the Strongheart society."

Joshua said, "It is good for me to hear these things. Nobody will speak of my father, so I have always wondered about him."

"What your heart has spoken to you about him," Angry Bear said, "is true."

Strongheart grinned. It was time to speak to Angry Bear about why he'd come.

"You are a wise elder," Strongheart said. "You have heard of Quanah Parker of the Comanche?"

Angry Bear puffed and nodded.

Joshua went on, "The Great Father in Washington wants me to parlay, to smoke the pipe with him."

Angry Bear grinned. "Quanah Parker, like you, is a man with two hearts, one red, one white. The Great Father is wise. He thinks you can talk with this Comanche because you and he will know each other's heart."

"Yes, this is true," the Pinkerton said. "Do you think he will meet with me?"

Angry Bear puffed thoughtfully and blew the smoke skyward. He passed the pipe to Joshua.

"You have a leg and arm which are broken. You have many scars right now," the chief said. "What if you must fight to get away?"

Strongheart said, "He is a red brother. I will not fight the Comanche."

"This is a good thing. We will tell our brothers, the Chy-ela," the elder said, referring to the Cheyenne. "They will tell Quanah Parker that your words have iron and your heart is quiet."

Strongheart smiled and nodded.

They smoked some more, and Joshua said, "Do you know of a Lakota who stands taller than all others? He is very strong like the mighty bear, and he kills—"

Angry Bear interrupted, "*We Wiyake*."

Strongheart said, "Blood Feather? Where is he from?"

The chief said, "We do not know. He kills our people, and he leaves, maybe one moon, two moons. He then comes back and kills again. He puts a feather with blood on the face of each."

"This man," Strongheart replied, "stands almost one head taller than me."

"Yes, he is the one," Angry Bear responded.

Strongheart said, "He comes to the south and kills the *wasicun*. Then he comes here and kills the Lakota."

One of Strongheart's cousins brought both men bowls of buffalo stew, and Joshua went to his saddlebags and brought out a tin of peaches, which he shared with the old man. While they ate, they compared dates and places of killings. Without using the term or even knowing what the term was, they figured out they were dealing with a serial killer, who killed once per month that they knew of, alternating between reds and whites. Joshua knew he had to pass this on to Lucky as soon as possible.

A small war party of Hunkpapa Lakota rode in. Joshua

saw that their ponies' tails were tied up in knots, and they wore war paint, indicating that they were looking for a fight, not game. They were fed and then met with Angry Bear while Joshua visited with relatives.

After they left, Angry Bear explained that one of the best warriors in that tribe had been killed by *We Wiyake*. They had been out tracking him, and he was spotted once from a distance. His size and musculature were incredible, and Angry Bear spoke about how the Hunkpapa described the killer in regards to his strength. The warrior had had his throat crushed, and of course his heart was cut out of his chest and a bloody feather left on his face.

We Wiyake had watched the war party following him. He was on a large ridgeline overlooking the prairie where he had purposely left tracks heading west. He would not kill these warriors unless he had to. They were not in his plans, but eluding them helped him feel something anyway.

Staying to the ridges, he followed them for five miles before deciding to move into the trees and go ahead of them. Normally, Blood Feather was on foot, but he had stolen a large draft horse from a Colorado ranch, and he was now riding it. He generally could not ride most horses, as they were too short for his over-seven-foot-tall muscular body. He knew where he and his mount would go, because he had laid this part of his trail down in case he was followed.

Sleeps in Light was the head of the war party and was an accomplished warrior, hunter, and tracker. The trail had been easy for him to follow, as the prey was so large. Now the trail was moving through woodlands, as it paralleled a flowing stream surrounded by cottonwoods and some hardwoods. From his pony's back, the party's leader easily tracked the large hoofprints on the ground. The party came to a large mud-walled cut bank and had to ride in single file.

Not knowing he was there, the first six riders in the party passed within two feet of *We Wiyake*. As the seventh member, a very enthusiastic sixteen-year-old warrior named Buffalo Hump, followed along the narrow trail, a giant pair of hands and arms reached out from the mud wall and grabbed his mouth and throat, yanking him from the pony's back. He was pulled into the mud wall, pushed face-first into the mud, before he felt the large blade plunge into his back over and over until he felt no more.

We Wiyake dived into the stream and immediately started washing the coating of mud off his body. A small drip of blood was all that leaked from the wall of mud concealing the brave's now lifeless upright body. *We Wiyake* returned to his horse and went on to the high ground.

The war party rode another half mile before seeing that their last man was missing. Sleeps in Light immediately returned them on their backtrail, all eyes scouring the ground for sign. It took a full hour before they could find where their fellow warrior's body had been shoved face-first into the muddy wall, standing up. They cleaned his body off in the stream and draped it across the back of his pony, which had followed along. Sleeps in Light decided they should get off of this trail and head to the far wooded ridgeline before making camp for the night. He felt that this trail must be being watched, and getting away from it might prevent further attack.

It was close to dark before they carefully selected a well-protected campsite, surrounded by large boulders and trees. They could make a fire and not worry about it or the smoke from it being seen in the thick branches overhead. They would keep the horses close that night.

Sleeps in Light took the first watch and had trouble sleeping throughout the night after his watch. The way his man had been killed totally unnerved him, and that was the goal of *We Wiyake*. The other members of the war party were restless, too.

Meadowlarks were chirping, and there was frost on the undergrowth as the sun slowly came up in the morning. Wounded Horse was the last man on watch when dawn broke. He was a man with an ever-present smile, except when he met with an enemy on the battlefield. Then, he was the enemy's worst nightmare. Sleeps in Light awakened to the sound of the birds and lay there, listening, not moving. He had to relieve his bladder and immediately stood and did so. Something was wrong. There was no figure seated by the fire, as would be the normal sight. Shivering up and down his spine, Sleeps in Light finished relieving himself and turned toward the fire. The sight caught his breath and then he smelled burning flesh. The body of Wounded Horse was before him, with the man's face in the campfire. His hair had already burned off. Sleeps in Light awakened the others, and the warrior's body was pulled from the fire. Each man grabbed his weapons and with his eyes scoured in every direction.

Now every man in this war party was totally intimidated and frightened. They could not even tell how Wounded Horse had been murdered, but he had been on watch. He should have seen or heard anybody before the killer got to the campsite, and Wounded Horse was a very responsible brave. He would never have fallen asleep while it was his turn to watch the campsite.

Sleeps in Light made the decision to leave his comrades' bodies on the battlefield. It was something that was not preferred but sometimes done out of necessity. They decided to head back to their own village and forget the search for this killer.

They began heading northwest at a fast trot, and the blank, distant eyes of *We Wiyake* watched them from the closest ridgeline. Having decided to intercept their route of travel, he mounted his draft horse and trotted along the reverse side of the ridgeline.

Joshua Strongheart chewed on some beef jerky as he looked at Blood Feather through a pair of binoculars. A slow whistle escaped his lips as he saw the size of the killer mounting up. The Pinkerton put his binoculars back in his saddlebags and climbed atop Gabriel, then trotted after Blood Feather while keeping his distance. He could occasionally see in the distance clumps of dust from the war party, but he did not have to keep the Hunkpapa in sight, only *We Wiyake*.

Two hours later, Joshua made a mistake. He lost sight of Blood Feather briefly and rushed forward to see if he could spot him after the giant had gone into a gulch. *We Wiyake* had stopped to watch just to insure he was not being followed, and he spotted Strongheart. He kept after the war party, but discreetly kept checking his backtrail to see if Joshua was still there. By watching, he could tell Strongheart was good, and he thought maybe he would finally have an adversary to match up against him.

It was the middle of the night when *We Wiyake* rose out of the undergrowth and slipped the rope war bridle over the nose and neck of Gabriel. He led the big sorrel-and-white paint off through the trees. Every one hundred yards, Blood Feather went back and carefully covered the horse's tracks as well as his, until he was far away from Joshua's night position. He was going to slit the horse's windpipe with his big knife, but then he saw the claw scars from the grizzly. This horse had powerful medicine, so he would let it live. He took it two miles away and tied it to a tree.

From there, Blood Feather moved toward the camp of the war party. He crawled up close to the camp and saw two warriors awake near the fire. He inched forward toward

Sleeps in Light asleep outside the circle of light from the campfire. The killer lay there covered with leaves for hours, just watching and waiting until almost dawn, waiting for Sleeps in Light to awaken and walk away from the campfire to relieve himself. The giant man crawled after the war party leader and then crouched as he got farther away from the fire. Sleeps in Light was standing by a tree relieving his bladder when he felt the giant hand clamp around his mouth and the sharp blade of the big knife against his throat.

Speaking in Lakota, *We Wiyake* whispered, "Walk quietly."

They moved far away from the camp, the blade still at Sleeps in Light's throat.

Blood Feather said quietly in a rumbling deep voice, "A man follows me who has two hearts. Who is he?"

Sleeps in Light said, "Joshua Strongheart must have followed us. His father was from that village where we were. His mother was white. He lives in what the *wasicun* call Colorado Territory, at Cañon City."

"Why did he come?" *We Wiyake* said.

"He seeks you," Sleeps in Light said, hoping the giant killer would spare his life.

"Uh," *We Wiyake* said and slit the warrior's throat, holding him up until the life drained out of his body. Then he dropped him and took off to return to his own camp without looking back.

He trotted through the woods and made it to his camp, but immediately he saw that something was wrong. His big draft horse was gone. The animal was not where he had picketed him. *We Wiyake* went to the place and got on his hands and knees searching the ground. The first rays of morning light were just streaking through the trees when he saw the tracks of Joshua Strongheart's moccasins, the ones Joshua always carried in his saddlebags. He had stolen the draft horse.

Blood Feather was not angry. As always, he was completely emotionless. He struck camp and started west toward the mountains. He was now on foot again and would utilize his mile-eating trot to get away from this new enemy and hide his trail in the high mountains. He knew he would now have to be more vigilant, and he would have to strike at this enemy's soul, then kill him and eat his heart, making his own medicine more powerful than ever. Maybe killing Strongheart and eating his heart would make him finally feel something, anything.

Joshua rode the big draft horse in ever-widening circles around his own campsite, looking for sign to show him where the massive killer had taken Gabriel. He was worried that the man might kill the horse, but so far there had been no sign of that, and he figured it would have been done right away.

As soon as he discovered Gabe had been stolen, Joshua had immediately gone on foot toward *We Wiyake*'s night position and stolen the big draft horse. He had read the war party's trail so far, found the two bodies, and knew the big man wanted to terrorize and frighten his victims. He figured he would simply turn the tables and steal his horse, too.

Actually, Joshua would have been better off to leave the horse, as the big draft horse with the distinctive oversized tracks would have left a much easier trail to follow. *We Wiyake* was now headed due west, toward the distant big range, but he was occasionally stopping to cover his tracks. He would also start false trails in several spots.

It took a while, but Joshua cut the trail a mile out and followed it the last mile to Gabriel. He was happy to saddle him up and thankful he had not been killed. Now he had to decide what to do with the big roan draft horse. He led the horse, which followed easily.

Strongheart got on the trail of the war party and caught up with them several hours later. They smoked a pipe, and the men told about the killing of their leader that morning. They said they'd found *We Wiyake*'s tracks heading west toward the Big Range and that he was running.

Joshua knew then the man's plans must have changed; he had decided to head into the big mountain range where it would be easier to hide his trail and route of travel. Strongheart also knew that the killer would cover his trail to such an extent that at some point Joshua would lose it. He decided to head south and try to attend to his challenge with Quanah Parker, as *We Wiyake* would show up somewhere in the southern Colorado area within the next month, to kill once again in the white community.

Joshua was going to head to the nearest location where he could send a long message to Lucky and tell him all he had learned and request that plenty of agents spread out around southern Colorado. Denver was the terminus for Western Union for the entire region and had a population of over thirteen thousand. Joshua decided he would head there to send his long telegram to Lucky.

He took the draft horse with him, deciding it was one a rancher might need. He assumed the horse had been stolen from a ranch by Blood Feather anyway. Strongheart was outside Laramie, Wyoming Territory and decided he would find a rancher who might want the horse, and he would simply give it to him. Laramie was a small, interesting town. It had rolling mills, a tie treatment plant, a brickyard, a slaughterhouse, a brewery, a glass-blowing plant, and a plaster mill. It also contained the Union Pacific railroad yards.

Six years earlier, three half-brothers—Town Marshal Steve Long, Con Moyer, and Ace Moyer—had opened a saloon in Laramie named the Bucket of Blood. The three would bully new townspeople and settlers, making them sign over deeds to their ranches and property. If any refused, they were challenged to gunfights by the three and killed. By October 1868, Steve Long had already killed thirteen men.

Many citizens tired of this very quickly, so the sheriff of Albany County, N. K. Boswell, who was also a rancher himself, formed a "Vigilance Committee." They went into the Bucket of Blood on October 28, 1868, heavily armed, and seized the three killers, marched them down the street to an empty building, and lynched them. Not long after that, the committee lynched more ne'er-do-wells and Laramie started calming down as a nasty town.

The town became a nicer place to live, but now that a group of vigilantes had enjoyed some success, many saw such men as the solution to other problems over the following years.

Strongheart was north of Laramie and rode over a rolling hill. Below him was a sprawling ranch, with a large house, a barn, outbuildings, several corrals, a squeeze chute, and a round training pen. He thought to himself that this would be a place that could use the large draft horse.

Hooves thundered behind him, and he turned in the saddle to see a group of riders approaching him at a gallop. Strongheart reined Gabe in and held his hand up in greeting. As they got closer, he saw that over their heads the riders all wore burlap bags with eyeholes cut in them. They brandished guns as they rode up.

Here was trouble Joshua had not expected. His mind started racing, and he immediately sized up the gang of riders to figure out who might shoot first, who might take the most bullets, and so on. This was the automatic response of any gunfighter: to immediately assess the threat response of any potential enemy.

Joshua said, "Hold on. If you are vigilantes, I am friendly. I am passing through here on my way to southern Colorado Territory. I am a Pinkerton agent. My name is Joshua Strongheart. If you boys are holdup men, then we are going to have a problem."

One of the masked men, on a handsome red dun, said, "Let's hang us a blanket nigger, boys!"

Another one said, "Aye. Let's do it, lads."

The one on the lead horse said in a deep voice, "Where did ya git that Percheron, boy?"

Joshua was not liking this at all, but he answered, "I stole it off a Lakota Indian in Montana Territory who probably stole it from a ranch."

"Damned right, you lying buck," the deep-voiced one said. "That horse was stolen by you from the Gillen Ranch. Killed old Casey when you done it, too. Joseph, what did the foreman say the Injun looked like?"

Another replied, "Like him here. He was tall, real tall, with lots of muscles."

Joshua said, "That man is named *We Wiyake*, which means 'Blood Feather.' He is a murderer, and he is over seven feet tall. I have been after him. He is Lakota. I am half-Lakota and half-white. Listen to me speak."

"Let's stretch his neck, boys," the one on the red dun said.

Joshua sized him up and figured him to be a cowhand who practiced shooting targets with his six-shooter all the time. He was not a gunfighter; Joshua could tell by the way he wore his gun and even how he held his hand readying to draw.

Strongheart knew he had to take some strong action and take it fast, or he would end up lynched without having a chance to prove he was an innocent man.

He said, "Talk awfully bold hiding behind a mask, mister."

"We all agreed to wear masks!" the red dun rider said defensively.

Now he was on the defensive, which was exactly what Joshua wanted. Now he thought he should put them all on the defensive.

"In fact, to me, you all are a bunch of cowards hiding behind masks to face one man."

The leader immediately removed his mask, and the others, seeing this, followed suit.

Joshua said, "Well, at least now we can talk to each other like men," and he stared at the man on the red dun. "Like you. You are awfully anxious to string someone up without checking out his credentials. Is it because you have this posse with you to give you some backbone?"

The man bristled and said through clenched teeth, "I don't need no posse backing me up! I ain't gonna be spoke to by no damned blanket nigger! Draw that smoke wagon, Injun, and go to work."

Joshua said, "No, I told you I am a Pinkerton. They wouldn't have hired me if I was not good with a gun. You draw first. I'll give you that, before you die, because you look to be a bigmouthed cowpuncher who's probably never shot a man before. Question is, if he grabs for his gun, are you men gonna jump in or keep out of this?"

The leader said, "We won't interfere, redskin. Ben started this dance."

Joshua said, "Well, Ben, like he said, you opened the ball, so you can ride away or you can reach for that hogleg and I will punch your dance ticket. What is your decision?"

Now Ben clearly had sweat on his upper lip and did not know how to get himself out of this predicament. Joshua knew he would draw. He had no choice and he had crazy eyes, jumping all over the place. Before his hand went to his holster, his face was like a giant sign telling Strongheart he was drawing.

The man's eyes opened wide, and he clawed for his gun.

It was just clearing the holster when he looked up at the business end of Joshua's Colt Peacemaker, and saw flame stab out from it twice in an instant and immediately felt two bullets slam into his chest and pass through his body. He could not breathe, and he felt his body roll backward over his horse's rump as he fell face-first onto the ground behind his dun. He was dead before he hit the dirt with a loud thud.

Joshua swung the gun toward the leader and held it on his chest. It was cocked.

"Now," Strongheart said, "if you boys decide to kill me, it will be with bullets and not a rope, but I am shooting, too, and it starts with you, partner. You die with me no matter what. Now, I have done nothing wrong and am not going to be strung up by a bunch of vigilantes just because you do not like half-breeds. So, mister, it's your turn to make a decision."

"Hold your water, boys," the leader said nervously.

Joshua said, "That is the first wise thing you have said. Now, have one of your men come over here, and I will show him my badge and a paper showing I am a Pinkerton agent."

One of the men climbed out of the saddle and walked over. Joshua handed him his badge and a note from Lucky on Pinkerton stationery. The man took it to the leader, who read it and had it taken back to Joshua.

The leader said, "Guess we made a mistake, Mr. Strongheart. I am glad we got things stopped. Ben there that you shot was always a big mouth and a hothead. We all saw that was a righteous shooting, and you even give him a chance to make his play first. What were you gonna do with the draft horse?"

Strongheart said, "I was going to give him to a ranch. In fact, I had decided to leave him at that ranch down there. You can take him and give him to the ranch where he was stolen if you want."

The leader said, "We will. Shore sorry how things worked out. We shouldn't have jumped the gun like we did."

"No, you shouldn't have," Strongheart said. "Now you have a man to bury, so you can think about it."

One of the men said, "With that long hair and gun skill, you sure you ain't really Wild Bill Hickok in disguise?"

The man nervously laughed at his own joke. In less than four years, James Butler Hickok would be murdered in Deadwood, Dakota Territory, by an assassin named Jack McCall hired by some gamblers to shoot Hickock, simply on the fear that he might decide to become a lawman in Deadwood and clean the town up.

The leader nodded at Joshua as he took the lead line to the draft horse, and the group rode away.

Strongheart gladly left them behind him, wanting as he did to get away from Laramie as quickly as he could. He went straightaway to the town and boarded a train to Denver.

It was dark already when he happily checked into a hotel there. In the morning, he went to the big Western Union terminus, made his report to Lucky, and waited there for the reply. Lucky sent a message back indicating that he would send as many agents as they could spare, and they would start sharing information about Blood Feather with lawmen, especially in the southern Colorado area.

Joshua was able to catch a train to Pueblo fairly quickly and would reach there late that afternoon. He then would take another train to Cañon City that afternoon or early evening, and that trip should only take about an hour. It was after dark when Strongheart reached Cañon City, and he immediately went to Annabelle's café.

She greeted him with a kiss near the door and showed him to a table.

"Hungry?"

"For your food, darling, always," he replied. "Been on

trains from Denver since this morning and haven't eaten much."

She prepared him a meal, and they talked over coffee. Joshua told her all about Blood Feather, and she shivered with the thought of the killer. He explained that he would leave the next morning for Fort Union in New Mexico Territory and would then head due east from there toward the lands of Quanah Parker in Texas.

5

QUANAH PARKER

Fort Union was built for the third time in 1868 and was the largest and most important fort, supply depot, and trading post in the entire area. The fort was built with native rocks, clay, and lumber. The adobe buildings were covered with red bricks brought in from Fort Leavenworth, Kansas. It was also well stocked with plenty of supplies brought in from Leavenworth by wagon trains on the Santa Fe Trail.

This was the final, post–Civil War version of the fort. It housed four companies of both cavalry and infantry. The Fort Union Quartermaster Depot supplied all forts in the entire New Mexico Territory.

When Joshua rode in from the north, the fort stood out of the trees on his right as a sentinel standing watch in front of the wooded foothills of the distant Sangre de Cristos. The Santa Fe Trail passed from east to west in several large tracts both north and south of the fort, a pathway to the west which had been used for centuries by Indians of many tribes and by white men, Mexicans, and Spaniards. Mountain men and Indians had been trading at Fort Union for years, and there were many trails coming and going from the busy fort. Now it was also occasionally getting attacks from those on the warpath, fighting for their very own preservation by trying to stop the recent onslaught of buffalo hunters.

The fort was abuzz with activity as Joshua rode up to it, and he soon found himself in the supply depot speaking with a burly, jovial man with a bushy shock of bright red hair and a body covered with freckles.

He shocked Joshua with the first words out of his mouth: "And you'll be Joshua Strongheart from southern Colorado. My name is Dutch O'Reilly."

He stuck out a beefy hand, which engulfed Strongheart's as they shook.

Joshua said, "You have a trace of an Irish or Scottish accent and your name is O'Reilly. Why do they call you Dutch?"

Dutch roared with laughter. "Beats me! I have always wondered that meself. Irish, by the way."

Joshua chuckled and replied, "You mean you really do not know why you're called Dutch?"

"Nope," the man replied. "No idea. Men started calling me that years ago, and it as stuck with me."

Joshua shook his head and said, "How did you know who I am?"

Dutch laughed again. "Zach Banta thinks the world of ya and described ya to a tee. Also heard from several all about yer gunfight up in Florence a year or so ago. Looks like ya had another shoot-out, the way you're favorin' yer leg and that cast on your arm."

Strongheart said, "Zach Banta knows everybody. That man is amazing! I suppose you probably know everybody, too, in your line of business?"

"Aye, it pays to know as many folks as ya can."

Strongheart asked, "How long have you been in supply?"

"Thirty-some odd years. Yeah, I know a few folk," Dutch answered.

"Do you know Quanah Parker by any chance?" Strongheart asked, and Dutch laughed.

Dutch replied, "Naw, and I sure don't want to now,
Strongheart. He is a fearsome enemy. The man has smarts.
Real smarts. I know some who have had dealings with him,
and each has told me he is one of the smartest men they
know, white or red. You gonna parlay with him?"

Joshua said, "Yes, they want me to have a talk with him."

"Aye, so you'll be headin' east outta here?"

"In the morning," Strongheart said.

Dutch said, "We'll fix you up some supplies and a nice
gift ya can take the ole bugger. Pick 'em up at daybreak."

Strongheart said, "Thanks."

They shook, and Strongheart went to find a place to stable Gabe and curl up for the night. He settled for curling up
in a pile of bedding straw next to Gabe's stall.

Joshua awakened to the smell of bacon, eggs, potatoes,
and coffee. He sat up and saw the steaming plate on a shelf
near him, a closed barrel sitting there for him as a seat. He
looked at the good-looking stranger who was about the same
height and build as him. His horse was saddled just beyond
and was a tall, beautiful line-backed buckskin with black
mane, tail, and four black stockings. The horse had four
black hooves. The stranger wore a pair of Colt Peacemakers.
He had a rugged and handsome face, and intelligent eyes
that seemed like he was on the verge of smiling.

Strongheart sat up and started eating.

"How do you like that Peacemaker?" the man said.

"It's a good gun," Joshua answered. "My stepfather died
and left it to me."

"I know," the handsome stranger replied. "I had it and
the holster made for Dan. He was a good friend. It was one
of the first Peacemakers ever made by my uncle."

Joshua stared at him.

Strongheart said, "Are you Chris Colt, nephew of Colonel Samuel Colt?"

Chris smiled, saying, "Guilty, Your Honor."

Joshua stood up and stuck out his hand. The two shook.

"I am so pleased to meet you," Strongheart said. "Dad could not say enough good things about you. It meant a lot for him to respect a man, and he respected you more than any man. He told me that you would live and die by your word and could be the best friend a man ever had and the worst enemy. I try to live my life the way Dad told me you live yours."

Colt said, "Dan was a very fine man, and your ma was all lady. I am sorry you lost them both so close together. I am working for the army as a chief of scouts right now out of Fort Union. I heard from Dutch that you were headed for a rendezvous with Quanah Parker. I need to head that way to scout the Staked Plains and the Red River area, so I wondered if you would like some company."

"Heck yes," Joshua answered enthusiastically. "I would be honored to ride any trail with you, Mr. Colt."

Chris laughed, saying, "Mister? I'm not that much older than you. Please call me Chris or Colt, either one."

They finished eating and both mounted up and headed toward the quartermaster depot. Dutch greeted them and gave Strongheart two oilskin bags full of food and goods to put in his saddlebags or roll up in his bedroll.

He said, "I put some rounds in there for your .45, too."

Strongheart pulled out some money and asked what he owed.

Dutch put his hand up, saying, "This one is a gift."

Joshua said, "Dutch, thank you, but I am on an expense account. The Pinkerton Agency can afford the bill."

"Aye, they can," Dutch laughed, adding, "but I'm old, and I can afford it, too. I don't give many gifts. Speaking of that, you'll find one there for Quanah Parker."

"Thank you very much, Dutch," Strongheart said as they shook hands.

"Colt, you'll be keepin' an eye on this young lad here," Dutch said.

Chris Colt said, "Who's gonna keep an eye on me?"

The two men set off from Fort Union headed east. It was going to be a long ride to the Texas Panhandle, and they would get plenty of chances to talk to and get to know each other.

The men were very much alike but now were just beginning their friendship. In a couple more years, Chris Colt would end up as chief of scouts for George Armstrong Custer, but he would be fired by Custer prior to the Battle of the Little Big Horn. He would also develop a friendship with Crazy Horse because of early introductions by Joshua Strongheart.

It was the third morning after they left Fort Union when they got the opportunity to cement their friendship. Nothing makes men closer than facing death together, and death would certainly visit them this day.

Laughing Dog was from the Quahadi tribe of Comanches, and so were the fifteen men in his raiding party. Two scouts had spotted Strongheart and Colt at a distance and ridden back to report to Laughing Dog. The war party closed in and kept the two men in sight until they made their night camp.

The men talked over cups of steaming hot cocoa, compliments of Dutch, as they lay by the fire. They had made their campsite in an arroyo.

Colt said, "Did you spot the Comanches following us?"

Strongheart said, "Yes, how many are there?"

Colt said, "I counted fifteen, but there may be as many as twenty."

Joshua said, "They'll attack us at first light."

Chris replied, "Yep, but we need to be in a better spot tactically when they do attack. Do you have a belly gun?"

Strongheart said, "Yep, I carry two in my saddlebags, plus my Winchester and plenty of rounds for that."

Colt said, "Good. We want to have the sun behind us so it's in their faces."

Strongheart said, "Why don't we ride or walk into their camp from the east and start the ball ourselves, right at or just before daybreak?"

Colt laughed. "That's a great idea! They don't like to fight in the dark."

Strongheart said, "Want me to take first watch?"

Colt laughed. "Why bother? Those boys are going to be restless and watching over us all night. Why don't we both get sleep? They aren't going to try putting the sneak on us."

Strongheart said, "Why don't we move our camp closer to them and leave some dummies by our fire?"

Colt chuckled. "That's another great idea. We can cover some bushes with spare shirts, leave our hats over the heads, and still wrap up in our blankets to sleep."

Strongheart said, "I'll get some logs that will burn a long time."

Chris got up and said, "I'll start making some brush dummies."

It was almost daylight when Chris Colt and Joshua Strongheart mounted up on their horses. Joshua had crawled in and memorized the layout of the Comanche camp and where each man was sleeping. He'd come back and drawn the layout on the ground with a stick so he could brief Chris. They started moving forward slowly on their horses.

Strongheart was nervous, as they were taking on so many. Fortunately, only a handful of the Comanches had guns. The rest had bows and arrows. The pair moved forward slowly on their horses, and now the Comanches'

location was in sight. The sun was just starting to peak over
the eastern horizon. Besides his prized Peacemaker, Strongheart had a Colt Army .45 single-action revolver in his left
hand and another tucked into his gunbelt at the small of his
back. Chris Colt had his own pair of matched, engraved
Colt .45 Peacemakers, and he also had a Colt Army tucked
into his belt in the front.

The two men continued to move forward slowly, Colt
from the southeast and Strongheart from the northeast. As
the Comanches tried to shoot, they would be getting direct
sunlight in their eyes from the breaking dawn behind the
duo. Two of the war party were already awake and preparing to leave, and the one on the right finally turned and
saw Joshua. He never got to yell his warning, as the bullet
slammed into his chest, and Strongheart saw the other one
fly backward from Colt's first shot. There was a cacophony
of explosions as the Colt six-shooters sent deadly round after
deadly round into the surprised Comanche warriors. A few
arrows were launched, and Chris Colt felt a tug under his left
arm, then a burn as a bullet tore a little of the flesh of his
trapezius muscle passing through his shirt.

Both horses seemed to sense what to do, as they moved
the riders forward while also moving side to side. As soon
as each man fired twelve rounds, he holstered his revolvers
and pulled out his carbine. Strongheart had a fancy, spe-
cially made Winchester, a gift from a Westcliffe bar owner,
and Colt shot a Henry repeating rifle in .44 caliber. Round
after round was levered and fired from both rifles, and by
the time they stopped firing, Comanche warriors lay all
over the area. Laughing Dog was one of those wounded.

Chris and Joshua both dismounted now, holding their
backup belly guns. They both reloaded their other pistols,
then, at an ungiven signal, both moved forward.

Without looking over, Strongheart said, "Are you hit?"

"Yeah, took one, but not bad," Colt answered. "I think. How about you?"

"Nope," Joshua said. "Didn't touch me."

There were three wounded, and Strongheart kicked away the weapons of one and handed him his canteen. The man nodded and smiled as he drank deeply, holding his hip, which was shattered. Colt knelt down by another who was bleeding from the side. Colt gave him some water and started to bandage the wound. Joshua walked over to Laughing Dog, who was bleeding from both legs and one arm.

He spoke to him in Lakota, but Laughing Dog did not understand. Joshua said, "You speak English?"

"Yes," the man said, "a little."

Strongheart said, "Who was the leader?"

Laughing Dog replied, "It is me."

Strongheart said, "What band of Comanches are you?"

"Quahadi" was the answer.

Joshua replied, "I'm going to patch you up. Then, I want you to take a message to Quanah Parker. Can you do that?"

As Chris walked up, Laughing Dog said, "I will do that."

Strongheart and Colt both worked on the man, cleaning and dressing his wounds. After they finished, Joshua retrieved ponies for the wounded men. Colt handed them their weapons.

Laughing Dog asked, "Why you not kill us?"

Colt replied, "We won. We don't have anything against you."

"What message?" Laughing Dog asked.

"Tell him I am Strongheart. I come to speak with him."

"That is all?" Laughing Dog replied.

"That is all," Joshua said.

They sent the three off on their ponies, then went over by the fire. Joshua cleaned and bandaged Colt's arm. They used the Comanches' fire and made a pot of coffee, then cleaned their weapons and rode off toward the rising sun.

Quanah Parker lived primarily in the Palo Duro Canyon area, and that was where the two were headed. He had been given the message from Joshua's father's tribe through the Cheyenne. To understand how he and Joshua might relate to each other, it helps to understand the background of Quanah Parker.

Quanah in Comanche means "fragrant." Quanah Parker was born the son of Chief Pete Nocona and Cynthia Ann Parker, a white woman who, when she was nine years old, had been abducted from the famous Texas Parker family. Cynthia Ann lived with the Comanche for twenty-four years.

She was recaptured when Quanah was around ten years old, but she was used to Comanche life and died after supposedly being rescued by the famous cattleman Charles Goodnight. She literally starved herself to death.

Quanah's father died shortly after that from a major infection, so Quanah became an orphan. Because he was a half-breed, Quanah was treated as an outcast among the Comanches, but this fueled his desire to be successful at everything.

Because of being an outcast, he left the other tribes and finally started his own band, the Quahadi, which means "the antelope eaters." Actually, most mountain men and true frontiersmen considered two types of meat as the most delicious of all game meat—antelope and mountain lion. Quanah was so successful as a chief that he attracted many warriors, and over time the Quahadis became the largest band in the entire Comanche nation. Although, because of being half-white, Quanah was always being tested by men of his tribe. This gave him even greater reason to be the best possible warrior and fighter.

Quanah's first wife was named Weakeah, but he mar-

ried several more women, too, and had many children.
Quanah started leading raiding parties allying his band of
Qahadis with his father's band and his father-in-law's band.
These were all victories.

Although a number of Comanche chiefs signed the 1867
Treaty at Medicine Lodge, Quanah Parker refused to sign
it and had been fighting since. At that point, with brilliant
tactics and hard fighting he, had been defeating the army
commanders that came against him.

Several more days of riding found Chris Colt and Joshua
Strongheart in Palo Duro Canyon. At several points each
had spotted distant coveys of quails flying, a sage grouse
taking off, and at one point when they stopped to look at
their backtrail two whitetail does and an older fawn came
running not far from them, the large white flags of their
tails swinging from side to side like a natural metronome
while they bounded off. These were signs normally unnoticed by white men, but which told them clearly they were
being watched and followed from the sides by Comanches.

So at lunchtime they rode up on a knoll along the trail
and built a small cooking fire and made coffee and something to eat. They sat there laughing and talking, waiting
for the Comanches to come to them. This plan worked,
because dozens of Comanches suddenly appeared and rode
toward them and up onto, and to surround, the knoll.

They looked around, and, smiling, Joshua said, "I wonder if one of them is Quanah Parker."

Colt said, "Yes, I saw him before at a distance. See the
good-looking one with the long braids wrapped in beaver
fur on the palomino?"

"Yep," Joshua replied, "I see him. He looks like a
leader."

Colt says, "Sure does."

Both men stood, and, again smiling, Strongheart held
his hand up to Quanah, saying, "Want some coffee?"

Quanah Parker rode forward and hand-signaled several braves back when they tried to join him. He rode up to the fire circle and dismounted to walk forward. Chris Colt handed him a steaming cup of coffee, and Joshua said, "You want sugar?" Quanah nodded, and he added some. The three sat cross-legged.

Strongheart said, "I am Joshua Strongheart. My friend is Chris Colt."

Quanah looked at Colt and grinned, saying, "I have looked at you before while you scouted for the Americans."

Colt grinned. "I saw you. It was in those rocks, and you were off to the side of them in the shadow overlooking the Red River right at the bend. Didn't know it was you though."

Quanah grinned again. He looked over at Strongheart.

"The Cheyenne," he said, "told me you are a great warrior. You want to speak with me."

"Yes, I do."

Quanah thought a moment and replied, "If I take you to our village circle, will you give me your word you will not tell others where it is?"

Joshua said, "My word."

Colt said, "I cannot. I work for the army, and if they ask me, I cannot lie, and I cannot say I gave you my word not to tell. I will be in big trouble." He stood up and said, "I will go back. I just rode with my friend here to keep him company."

Quanah said, "If they ask you, will you tell them you met me in Palo Duro?"

Colt said, "Yes."

Quanah grinned again and stuck out his hand and forearm to shake, saying, "They know I am here anyway."

Colt smiled and shook.

Then he shook hands with Strongheart, saying, "You go with Quanah, and I will take care of the fire. Have a good parlay." Looking at Parker, he said, "Hear his words. They have iron in them." Then he turned back to Strongheart. "It was good riding with you, Joshua. Looking forward to riding with you again."

Strongheart said, "I have a feeling you and I will cover some ground together, my friend. Thank you for coming with me and standing beside me."

Colt doffed his hat and started putting out the fire.

Strongheart and Quanah Parker mounted up, the chief still drinking his coffee, and rode off toward the east with the band.

They rode for another day and came to a circle of lodges in a grove that was totally surrounded by trees. A small stream ran through the center, and there were several rock outcroppings overlooking it and the surrounding country. Sentries could easily spot anybody coming from any direction.

Quanah Parker took Strongheart to a teepee and said, "You will stay here. Women will bring you food and water. We will smoke later."

Strongheart knew this meant they would talk. In the custom of his people, he did not say thank you, but smiled and nodded. He lay down on a buffalo robe and went to sleep immediately. He knew he would be safe here, as he had been welcomed as a guest by Quanah Parker.

He awakened an hour later, refreshed, and there was almost immediately a scratching on his teepee. A heavyset pock-faced woman came in with a broad smile and placed a large bowl of porridge before him. She left, and Joshua ate, then went to his saddlebags to retrieve the present for Quanah he'd gotten from Dutch. It was a small steel coffeepot and had a bag of coffee inside it, as well as a bag of sugar.

An hour later, he was in the lodge of Quanah Parker with Quanah and several elders. One, he learned, was Quanah's father-in-law. They passed a well-decorated pipe around the circle, smoking and waving the smoke over themselves. This was an important, spiritual tradition in Plains society.

Strongheart handed the gift to Quanah, who smiled and obviously appreciated it.

Quanah then handed Strongheart a Comanche bow and a quiver of arrows made from mountain lion hide. Both men nodded and set their presents off to the side.

"Why did you want to speak with me?" Quanah asked.

"I was told by my boss to speak with you. I am a Pinkerton agent. Are you familiar with that?" Joshua asked.

"Yes."

Strongheart continued, "They were asked by the Great White Father in Washington to find out if you will smoke the pipe of peace with them."

Quanah laughed, saying, "The Great White Father? Remember, you and I had mothers who were white. You do not have to say things like that to me. You can say 'President.'"

Joshua laughed.

Quanah went on. "I speak the poetic way of the red man, I live in the life of my red side."

Strongheart replied, "You and I do have that in common. We both have been treated differently in each world."

Chief Parker said, "No, you have, but I have only been in the red world. Do they treat you differently there?"

"I have learned that both the white and the red have good men and bad men. I have had whites call me 'halfbreed' like it is a bad word, but I have had Lakota call me *okisye-we* in the same way."

Quanah said, "I have had Comanche say I am of two peoples, so I have no true people. Instead, they should say I have the strength of the American and the strength of the Comanche."

Unlike many red men, Quanah Parker called the white man "American."

He continued, "The Comanche would not listen when I tell them the white man is brave and he is smart. Those are the ones who signed the Medicine Lodge Treaty and live on a reservation now, while we live free."

"I think men are pretty much the same all over. There are different languages, different clothing, looks, and habits," Joshua replied, "but all men want family, happiness, food, warmth, and friends."

Quanah smiled and said, "And women."

Joshua laughed and repeated, "And women."

"What are your thoughts about a peace treaty?" Quanah asked.

"I am not a chief," Strongheart responded. "I only have to think of me, not my people. If I was a chief, I would want to do what is best for my people. Is fighting the white man wise, or is making peace with him wise? I cannot answer these questions. Only you can.

"I can tell you this because you and I are almost like brothers in a way, because we have two hearts," Joshua added. "The red half of you has done very well. If you make peace someday, you should let the white half of you think. I bet you would do well in the white man's world, too."

Little did Strongheart know that Quanah Parker would smoke the pipe of peace a year later and would end up a few years after that becoming a millionaire businessman in the white man's world.

Quanah stood and said, "I will think about your words. We will speak again in the morning."

Strongheart went to his teepee.

The next morning at daybreak, Quanah Parker, armed with his hunting bow, and Joshua, armed with his, which he always carried rolled up in his bedroll, and his new quiver of Comanche arrows, went out together to look for a whitetail deer. Tall, rocky spires stood like chimneys throughout Palo Duro Canyon. This was considered low prairie, and there were plenty of grasses that whitetails enjoy.

A male whitetail deer has a route he traverses, usually a couple miles long, and he will stop under a tree and scrape the ground with his front hooves until he has made the whole area barren. Then he stands on his hind legs in the scraped-out spot and rubs his forehead to leave scent on small branches overhead. After this, the buck hunches his four legs together and urinates, with the liquid passing over heavily scented musk glands and running down on the inside of his back legs and into the scrape. These scrapes are signposts, and a good hunter can tell the size of a buck by how large or small the scrape is.

Quanah and Strongheart hunted for these scrapes and each found one, about a half mile apart. The two men separated and took hidden stands, each looking at one of the two scrapes. Within an hour of being in the stands, each man shot a small buck. After field dressing his deer, each carried his buck over his shoulders and they met up with each other. They rested when they met, sitting down on a cedar- and piñon-covered hillside to talk and smoke a pipe.

Quanah said, "It is good when men like us can hunt the buck; we can talk of many things and smoke a good pipe."

Strongheart said, "You have a good point, Chief."

The Comanche leader went on. "I have thought on your words. I think someday if I sit at the peace fire, then I will learn the ways of my mother's people." Smiling broadly, he added, "Maybe I can become a chief there, too."

Joshua said, "You said someday. Does that mean you will not surrender now?"

"I will fight for now." Quanah went on. "They send many bad men to kill all the buffalo. The Americans are smart, for this also kills the Comanche. I must fight against this."

Strongheart said, "I understand this, too. I am glad I do not have to make your decisions."

"Do I want my people to die like Comanche warriors with a lance or bow in their hand?" Quanah replied, "or do I want them to die of hunger with a wolf growling in their belly?"

He puffed thoughtfully on the pipe and waved the smoke over his handsome countenance. "It is hard to decide what to do, so I must also look in here for the answer," he said, pointing to his heart.

Strongheart said, "I think the heart always holds the best answers."

Quanah replied, "I think this is true."

Joshua thought again about his similarities with this man. He thought back to when he learned about his father's death and about the great love his father and mother had for each other. Prior to that he used to get upset because his mother would get tears when his father came up in conversation.

The day his father died, most of the men had left the tribal circle and gone out on a great hunt after the thousands of buffalo in the great herd spotted a half day south. A large band of Crow approached the circle of lodges, and the warning went up.

Claw Marks, Strongheart's father, a war chief, had been hobbled and was walking with a makeshift crutch, but this day he tossed the crutch aside. With two older warrior volunteers, he faced the charging band after sending the young warriors and children, including *Cate Waste*, Joshua's half brother, down the banks of the Little Big Horn, through the many trees there, until they got to what the warrior called the Badger Coulee and the remnants of the tribe could escape up the coulee, covering their tracks carefully.

Strongheart's pa and the two gray-haired warriors

knew they would die, and he was the young, vibrant, albeit wounded, warrior, so he knew it fell on him to keep the Crows at bay as long as possible, to cover the retreat of the family circle. They sang their death songs while firing shots and arrows at the charging Crows. Claw Marks looked up at a pair of red-tailed hawks swirling high overhead in the cloudless, endless Montana sky, and he smiled to the warriors, saying in Lakota, "This is a good day to die." They nodded and smiled.

Leaving them, he raised his hand to bid them stay back, and ignoring the leg pain, he leapt on his pinto mount and rode toward the reassembling Crows. They had lost several warriors already and were shocked at the ability of these three determined men. They had to admire their perennial enemies.

The Crows were planning a final charge, with the idea to count as many coups as possible, touching the enemy in battle. They were encouraging each other to "Brave up!"

Thirty yards off, Claw Marks dropped off his war pony and tied a long rawhide thong to his leg. He tied the other end of the twenty-foot leather thong to a stake, jammed it into the ground, and pounded it down with a nearby rock.

Claw Marks faced the Crow, a challenging grin on his face, and raising his rifle into the air with one hand and his war club with the other, he yelled, "*Hokahey!*"

They knew he was going nowhere and would fight to the death, taking as many as he could with him. They yelled back, more in admiration for his raw courage than to taunt a warrior. They agreed they would ride him down, and each warrior wanted to count coup on this mighty enemy, touching him without killing him with a coup stick, bow, or rifle. They charged, screaming and yelling, and he raised his rifle, taking careful aim—and bodies started falling. The group rode down upon him, and he swung his rifle one way and the other and broke the stock over the face of the largest Crow. Then he started swinging his war club, as he felt stab wounds and strikes hitting his body all over. His scalp was a great reward for the hardest fighting of the Crows, who finally struck the fatal blow against him. Near *Siostukala*'s, or Claw Marks's, body eight Crow bodies also lay on the grass by the shallow sand- and rock-bottomed Little Big Horn, and several more moaned and groaned with wounds.

The two elderly warriors wanted to help the courageous young man, but they knew they must lie back and wait, buying more time for their extended family members. They knew that they, too, would make the great walk this day. Inspired by his ferocious fighting and tremendous courage, they, too, held the Crows off for another hour, giving the tribal remnants plenty of time to hide in Badger Coulee.

After they had hidden far down the river valley, Joshua's young half brother crept through the tall waving buffalo grass high on a ridge that would be traveled years later by Custer and his men. He found a vantage point and actually watched the heroic death of his father. With no other warriors or tribal members around, he cried. But then he returned to the others. He was bursting with pride at the incredible courage of his father and vowed then to never tarnish such a family legacy.

When he had heard all this a year earlier, Joshua had felt like he could easily cry, wishing he would have known his father. After his stepfather died and his mother gave him the man's gun and knife, which he had gotten from the man who was now Joshua's new friend, Chris Colt—only then did she reveal to him about her relationship with Claw Marks. When his name was mentioned, she did not cry out of bad memory, as Joshua had always assumed, but out of pure love loss.

Strongheart thought about how much his own story reminded him of Quanah Parker's, and he really did not blame the chief for wanting to fight on to try to stop the slaughter of the buffalo, the life-giver of the Comanche, Lakota, Cheyenne, Arapaho, and other Plains tribes. He felt like he, too, probably would have kept fighting given the same situation and set of circumstances.

The two men retrieved their deer and returned to the lodges of the Quahadi. Once there, both of them went to some women tanning hides and lay the bucks down before them. The women seemed very grateful, and several made eyes at Strongheart.

As they walked away, Strongheart said, "You have been a good host, Chief. I will pass your words to my boss, and the Pinkertons will pass them back to Washington."

Quanah Parker grinned. "And those in Washington will then pass my words on to somebody who will send even more buffalo hunters."

Strongheart said, "I reckon they will."

Quanah grinned again, saying, "The Americans are like the weeds that grow in the prairie grass. They spoil the land but keep coming. But when they fight the Quahadi, it will be a remembered fight. Then, someday, if I smoke the pipe with the Americans, I will learn how to become a great chief among them."

Strongheart said, "Dan, my pa, the white man who married my ma and raised me, used to say that the best revenge in the world is success."

Quanah grinned again, saying, "That might be better than shooting the Americans. Instead of scalps I will collect their dollars."

Strongheart grinned also, saying, "Quanah Parker, I believe you will, if you decide to come to the white man's world someday."

He was serious, too. This chief really impressed Joshua.

He was wise, savvy, and very intelligent. He knew that, like himself, the man had something to prove. As Strongheart had said, the best revenge in the world is success. Joshua lived his life that way, because he had been sometimes called and oft-times simply treated or viewed as a half-breed, in the ugliest connotation of that word.

6

MEN OF TWO WORLDS

Within the hour, Joshua was packed up and headed back toward the mountains far to the west. Maybe it was because he grew up in central Montana. Maybe it was because of Cañon City and its environs, but although his people on the red side of his ancestry were called Plains Indians, Strongheart had become a man of the mountains, and he missed them when he was away. He liked the prairie and the desert, but he really loved the mountains. Joshua once told Annabelle that he preferred land that had personality, and the mountains gave land plenty of personality.

Although he was not pleased with Quanah Parker's answer, he'd left there with good feelings about his visit and about the Comanche leader. He had heard that Quanah Parker was aloof and hard to get to know, but Joshua had not felt that at all. The man did not seem guarded with him, probably because they were so much alike in so many ways.

We Wiyake was ready to make a kill again. It was time to take a *wasicun*. He had a new challenge too. Joshua Strongheart would be a tough adversary compared to all the others, but eating his heart would give Blood Feather more strength and stronger medicine than he had gotten from any other prey.

He had passed near Cañon City but was now in an area called High Park, north and west of the town and southwest of Pikes Peak. The terrain was rolling hills and valleys covered with large growth evergreens as well as piñons and cedars. The area had an abundance of grizzly bears, elk, mule deer, turkeys, and mountain lions, but very few people. The miners would come in droves, but not for a number of years. Now there were fur trappers, Ute Indians, and a few large ranches.

Blood Feather decided to get closer to civilization, as it was in his twisted mind to select only certain victims. There had to be something about them that would make him desire taking from their spirit. Usually, that trait was only the subconscious sense that he could intimidate them, but he also liked to challenge himself in some ways. Hence his desire to pit himself against Joshua Strongheart.

That is when the idea struck him. He would locate Strongheart's actual area, his place of living. He would find someone close to Strongheart and kill that person, or even better he would kidnap someone. He would make the halfbreed pursue him.

Joshua went to Fort Union first and found that General Phillip Sheridan was there, as well as several colonels. They wanted a briefing, Joshua was told. First, he would prepare his report for Lucky and then he would use that to brief the general.

There was a billiard hall at Fort Union, adobe but covered with red bricks. This was where the men congregated when they could manage a little time off. Joshua Strongheart, a year earlier, had gotten addicted to a new drink, iced tea. He could not drink alcohol because the Lakota blood he carried betrayed his system. He would become a monster if he drank.

Bellying up to the bar, he said, "Howdy, do you have a new drink called iced tea, by any chance?"

The bartender had a pleasant smile and a long handle-bar mustache, a white shirt and red sleeve garters.

"Right ya are, laddie," he said with a thick Scottish accent, "and a tasty drink it is. Ya want sugarrr with that, sirrr?"

"Plenty," Joshua responded with a smile.

The bartender chipped some ice with a pick, filled a frosted glass with tea, and added several spoonfuls of sugar.

Strongheart enjoyed the cold drink and spotted a large group of boisterous drinking soldiers around the several billiard tables. He noticed Chris Colt having words with several men. A black-skinned cowboy stood next to Chris. Strongheart sensed trouble brewing.

"I say that you cheated me, Scout!" Joshua heard a burly man saying with a strong Southern accent as he walked up.

Strongheart saw a man in an oversized, rumpled tunic with corporal stripes, and he had four men around him who seemed to be friends. They all looked like they were ready to jump on Colt if the leader started swinging at Chris. Joshua thought quickly, trying to figure out a way to defuse the situation so he and his new friend did not have a big fight on their hands.

The bruiser looked like he was ready to let go with a balled up ham-sized fist, and Joshua stepped forward holding his hands up.

"Wait a minute, boys!" Strongheart said. "Don't start fighting just yet. We need a strength test first."

The behemoth said, "Well I shore as hell aint havin' no durn blanket nigger tellin' me what ta do. Y'all heah him?"

Strongheart seethed inside but instead smiled and said, "Now, that's not the right attitude. Most men who want to toe the line around here do the strength test first, unless you are both too yellow to try it."

Chris Colt grinned, knowing Strongheart was trying to defuse things somehow, without having the slightest clue how he was doing it.

He said, "I'm not yellow, mister. I'll do it, I'll go first."

Joshua was glad Chris said that, as he needed him to go first.

The giant bully roared, "I ain't no lily-liver. Ef he is a doing it, ah'll do it, too. Ah'll do it better."

Joshua ran to the corner and got the bucket of wash water for the floor and carried it over to the crowd.

He said, "Back up, boys," and all the soldiers moved back.

Strongheart set a chair between two billiard tables, then looked at Chris and said, "Grab that cue stick there, mister, and stand on this chair."

Colt complied, and then Strongheart climbed up on one of the tables holding the wooden bucket of mop water.

He yelled, "Now, I need all of you except these two to go outside a few minutes."

Nobody could figure out what he was doing, but like sheep they filed out, holding beers mugs and cigars.

Strongheart raised the bucket overhead and pushed the rim against the ceiling.

He said to Colt, "Now, sir, push the end of that billiard cue up against the center of the bucket and hold the bucket tight against the ceiling."

Colt complied and Joshua counted slowly to ten. He then reached up and took hold of the bucket, carefully lowering it so it would not spill.

The bully thought to himself, *I can hold it a lot longer than that.*

Strongheart said, "Okay, mister, it's your turn. He passed. Let's see if you can."

"Hale yes, I kin," the big bruiser said, climbing up on the chair.

He sneered at Colt as the handsome scout handed the cue stick to him. Strongheart pushed the big bucket up against the ceiling and held it there until the big man pushed the stick up in the center and held the bucket hard against the ceiling himself. The hillbilly had not realized it would be that heavy to hold that way, but he knew he could certainly hold it a lot longer than the scout did.

Strongheart said, "Okay, are you ready?"

The heavy said, "Yeah, boy, ah'm ready."

Joshua hopped down off the table and grabbed Colt by the upper arm, leading him toward the door. The bully suddenly knew what was happening. He had to hold the bucket against the ceiling or be drenched with a bucket of dirty wash water.

"Hey, where the hell ya goin'? Come back here!" the monster yelled, while Colt and Strongheart went out the door laughing.

Outside, the assembled men looked at them coming out the door, and Strongheart said, "Your partner sure beat the scout here good. He is still winning and wants you to wait until he is done."

Several shrugged their shoulders, and Chris and Joshua walked away chuckling to themselves.

"Boy is he going to be angry now," Colt laughed.

Strongheart said, "But hopefully by the time we see him again, he will be sobered up."

Colt said, "I hope so. I really don't want to fight soldiers I am working with. That was quick thinking on your part. I'll have to use that trick again sometime."

The two men went to the quartermaster depot.

Dutch wore his ever-present smile and said, "Mr. Strongheart it is, and the Comanches have not lifted yer scalp, I see."

"Howdy, Dutch," Strongheart replied. "Some tried, but Chris Colt stopped them short. Do you happen to have a room where I can prepare a briefing? Have to brief the general in the morning and send a report to my boss."

"Aye," Dutch replied. "Go inta the office in the corner yonder. Ye'll find pen and ink, pencils, and paper. Help yourself, youngster, and old Colt and me will tell each other lies."

It took Strongheart two hours before he emerged with his report made out and briefing prepared.

"Come on. Let me buy you guys dinner," he said.

Chris said, "Sounds good. My belly is rubbing a blister on my backbone."

Dutch said, "Ah, you lads go eat. I have ta do inventory."

The pair left and headed toward a small saloon that served food. Five shadows appeared suddenly out of the darkness, and three were carrying what looked like axe handles. They waded into Chris Colt and Joshua Strongheart, and the two men instinctively dashed for the door, wanting to take the fight into the light, where they could see. Inside, Chris's right eye was swelling shut from a blow, and Joshua's left eye was swelling shut from the same.

Strongheart said, "Why don't we make this fight a little more even?"

He drew and fired, hitting one of the axe handles near the man's hand and shattering it. Almost immediately, Joshua heard Chris's gun boom next to him, and another axe handle splintered. Then both men fanned their Colt .45 Peacemakers and the third axe handle exploded.

The biggest man swung at Chris Colt, who ducked under it, and the big man was met by a thundering right hook from Strongheart, shattering his jaw. Colt hit the man closest to him with a head-butt tackle, sending him crashing over the bar. Joshua faced another tall man and suddenly pointed at the man's foot. The man looked down and Strongheart caught him with a vicious uppercut, lifting him off his feet and onto a table, which crashed over backward with him and several glasses and bottles. Colt and Joshua both hit the next man simultaneously, one with a thundering overhand right and the other with powerful left hook. The eyes of the last one looked like those of a small deer facing a family of mountain lions, as he gawked at Joshua Strongheart standing before him. He turned to run and was immediately tripped by Chris Colt, who hit him with a downward right as he fell forward. He was out cold when his face hit the floor.

Chris and Joshua looked at each other and the fallen men and started chuckling, both subconsciously touching their blackened eyes. They ordered steaks, and Colt had a beer, while Strongheart drank coffee. The defeated bullies each slowly left the room sheepishly as they awakened individually, while the two men spoke with each other and ignored them.

Strongheart said, "Tomorrow I have to brief General Sheridan. He is famous for the Civil War and his friendship with Grant, but I want to know from you what to expect."

Chris Colt started chuckling and Joshua said, "What's funny, Colt?"

Colt replied, "He will not like you from the get-go, for the same reason he does not like me."

His curiosity piqued, the Pinkerton asked, "What is that?"

Colt said, "You and I both stand about six-foot-four or so."

"So why won't he like that?" Joshua said.

Chris laughed and replied, "'Cause he's the very last guy to get snowed or rained on."

Strongheart laughed, saying, "Short?"

Colt said, "Five-foot-five. You ever hear the famous quote about Sheridan by old Honest Abe?"

"No," Strongheart said. "What did he say?"

Colt replied, "Abe Lincoln said of General Sheridan, 'A

brown, chunky little chap, with a long body, short legs, not enough neck to hang him, and such long arms that if his ankles itch he can scratch them without stooping.' I heard that several times from several soldiers and laughed every time."

Joshua was laughing hard himself at the late President's words.

Chris went on to reiterate that Sheridan was indeed just barely five-foot-five.

Another item, which he knew would anger Joshua as much as it angered him, was the fact that Sheridan was one of the prime backers of the program to slaughter the buffalo to defeat the red man. Colt was correct in his assumption. Joshua was very angry when he heard this.

Colt told Strongheart that Sheridan had had a mistress years before, when he was dealing with the Nez Perce, Modoc, and other tribes in the northwest. Her name was *Sidnayoh*, but he called her Frances. She was the daughter of the chief of the Klickitat tribe. Colt did not know it at the time, but she would never be mentioned in Sheridan's memoirs.

The two men went to bed, and Strongheart met the very short general the next morning. Sheridan had sharp creases and nary a spot or a thread showing on his uniform. He had a well-trimmed beard.

Colt showed up for the briefing, and there were a number of staff there as well. Coffee and fresh donuts were served, and a map of the tactical area was placed behind Strongheart.

The briefing did not start off well.

"Why do you and Mr. Colt have black eyes, Mr. Strongheart?" the flag officer asked derisively.

"We got in a fight, General," Joshua replied.

"With whom?"

Strongheart said, "Was about to tell you, General. You

know we tangled with some Comanches before we even got to Quanah Parker's area."

"Oh," the general said. "Proceed."

Strongheart briefed him on the fight with the Comanches. Then he told about meeting with Quanah Parker.

The general interrupted, "Mr. Colt, why didn't you escort him to Quanah Parker's stronghold?"

Colt grinned and said, "Well, sir, Parker did not like the fact that I would not give my word not to divulge his whereabouts."

The general grinned for the only time that morning.

But then he looked at Strongheart, saying, "So, Mr. Strongheart, did he take you to his stronghold?"

Joshua said, "Yes, he did."

"Good, good," General Sheridan replied. "I have been more concerned with that than his surrender."

Strongheart said, "He's not going to surrender, General."

"The pompous ass," the general hissed. "Do you know how to get to his stronghold?"

"Yes, I do," Joshua responded.

"Good, good," the general replied. "I will want you to lead us there. We will start out in two days."

Strongheart said, "Sorry, General. I can't do it."

"Don't worry. I will clear it with your superiors," Sheridan replied.

Strongheart said, "No, you don't understand. Quanah Parker took me to his stronghold because I gave my word that I would not divulge its whereabouts to anybody."

"Wait a minute, Strongheart. Do you have the temerity to tell me you will not lead us there because you gave your word to a Comanche?"

"No," Joshua replied, "because I gave my word, period. A man is only as good as his word. I do not break my word for anybody, for any reason."

The general, red-faced, stood up, saying, "I'll see you in irons!"

Strongheart said, "I am a civilian, General Sheridan, not one of your soldiers. I was going to brief you as a courtesy, but not when you speak to me like that. If you have a problem with that, take it up with Allan Pinkerton. I am leaving. Good day, General. Colt, you take care now."

Chris winked at him and said, "I live by the same code, Joshua. Have a safe trip."

The general glared at Chris Colt, who looked back at him with his firm jaw set on his chiseled face.

Strongheart strode toward the door and Sheridan jumped up.

He said, "Wait! Please!"

Joshua turned.

Sheridan said, "Very well, Mr. Strongheart. Army officers have a code of conduct, too. I clearly see you are half red, so I can understand your strong feelings about giving your word to a savage."

Very angry and insulted, Strongheart said, "If Quanah Parker makes peace, I would not be surprised to see him wearing an army general's uniform someday or whatever he sets his mind to, General Sheridan. He is a leader and a man I respect."

Sheridan was flustered.

He replied, "Was your mother an Indian or your father?"

"My father was Lakota, but I never met him, just his people, my people, but the whites are my people, too," Joshua replied. "All Americans are."

"Well, we started wrong here, and I would very much like you to proceed with the briefing, Mr. Strongheart. I understand your commitment to keep your word."

Joshua told the general about the trip and his conversations with Quanah Parker, his feelings about him, and his personal observations. He could not wait to leave Fort Union.

It was after noon before Strongheart could get away from the general and his other officers, many apparently wanting to impress the famous general with what they felt were intelligent questions.

It was late fall, and the sun went down much earlier, so Chris Colt said, "Joshua, why don't you stay here and pull out after first light?"

Strongheart grinned, saying, "I appreciate it, Chris, but I cannot wait to get away from that son of a buck. I'll hole up somewhere north of here in a few hours."

Colt grinned from ear to ear. "Can't say as I blame you. I made a commitment to scout for the army, and they tell me I'll be going up north to scout for the Seventh Cavalry and will be chief of scouts."

Little did Colt know he would end up having a major battle and test of wills with former brevet general Lieutenant Colonel George Armstrong Custer, which would keep him from being killed himself at the Battle of the Little Big Horn in little more than a year and a half.

The two men shook hands, giving each other that knowing look only two men like them could share, and Colt mounted up and rode away without looking back.

7

THE PREDATOR RETURNS

Annabelle lay nude on the bank of the tumbling, crashing, churning, angry white water of the Arkansas River. The sight of her near perfect body was something Joshua Strongheart dreamt about. The moonlight from the full moon overhead shining down on her beauty only made it more spectacular.

Joshua would surprise her with a soft, lingering kiss, he thought, as he grinned to himself, crawling forward on his belly on the soft sand where the river had receded away. She slept peacefully, and he wondered why she did not seem cold in her nudity. There was certainly a chill to the night air. He did notice he could see it on her skin, even if she was peacefully sleeping.

Closer and closer he silently moved, and suddenly something grabbed at his ankle. He looked down and both ankles were caught in a tangle of branches that had drifted downriver and accumulated like an oversized bird's nest. He tried to quietly pull his legs free and looked up to see if she was stirring. Joshua looked right into the eyes of the predator and his heart skipped a beat, and he panicked trying to jerk his legs free.

We Wiyake had deep, lifeless eyes that told nothing. They were blank and dark, but they bored right into Strongheart's own panicked stare. He struggled against the driftwood and tried to cry out to Annabelle, as he saw the moonlight flash on the blade of the giant knife. Blood Feather had slithered out of the river like a human serpent, and his long black hair hung down soaked with river water. He raised the knife and grinned at Strongheart. Joshua tried to scream, but nothing would come out, and he sat up suddenly, looking around. His mighty chest heaved and his heart pounded in his ears like the big bass drum he always enjoyed at parades. Strongheart's feet were tangled in his bedroll, and he kicked them free, stood, and walked away from his fire to relieve his bladder. He felt a shiver go down his spine as he did so. The nightmare had really unnerved him, but he was south of Raton, still in New Mexico Territory, and he still had several days' travel to Cañon City. He looked at the night sky and figured it was getting close to dawn. He went back to bed, after checking on Gabe, who was grazing peacefully nearby.

Strongheart lay there and kept thinking about the briefing and General Sheridan. He could not sleep, and he got up after about twenty minutes of trying. He built the fire back up and put on coffee and started breakfast.

In less than a half hour, Strongheart was in the saddle, astride the tall red-and-white overo pinto, moving north at a fast trot. The dream was too real to him, and he wanted to get to Annabelle as quickly as possible.

One-third of all cowboys on the frontier, the American West, were white, one-third were black, and one-third were American Indian or Mexican. Finally, on the fourth ranch he had been watching, Blood Feather had found what he wanted—a cowboy who was a Lakota. Now he was making his stalk.

The one place where the red cowboy would be segregated from the others would be when he went to the outhouse. Blood Feather did not want to eat this man's heart. There was nothing special about him. He had no special medicine.

Johnny Rabbit Legs was a full-blooded Lakota of the Hunkpapa tribe or clan. In his mid-twenties, he had been cowboying for close to ten years now and thoroughly enjoyed everything about the cattle business. His goal was to become so good at handling cows and men that someday he would be entrusted to be a foreman on a big spread. He already had cowboys ask him for advice, especially on trail drives, and it made him feel like he was making some kind of contribution.

He had also survived a gunfight, and that made him quite a celebrity with the other cowboys. They had been on a drive, and the whole crew had been paid and given some time off in El Dorado, Kansas, when he and some of his ranch hands were in a local saloon having a good time. Johnny was small in stature and slight of body, but he had practiced drawing and dry-shooting his .44 many times, just in case. Most cowboys did not actually practice shooting live rounds, because of the cost of ammunition, but they did practice fast draws a lot, and Johnny was pretty good. A cull who, being a typical bully, rode roughshod on many people because of his immense size, picked Johnny out of the crowd in the saloon. This character had practiced quick draw a lot, but as it usually was, neither he nor Johnny had practiced shooting and hitting small targets while their adrenaline was pumping. Johnny had met a shootist one time and listened carefully to his every word, which included the sage advice that it was much more important to accurately aim and hit someone than to outdraw someone.

The bully picked the fight, and both men emptied their six-shooters at each other, scrambling around two large poker tables in the bar and missing with almost every shot. With the eighth and twelfth bullet fired, Johnny hit the bully twice in the groin area, severing the femoral artery. He died a minute or so later. Johnny became a hero among the cowpunchers.

We Wiyake had already seen the pistol and his hand flashing for it several times, as if he was going to quick draw, which told him the Sioux at least had a good familiarity with getting the weapon into action fast. He knew that white men had to undo their gunbelts and holsters and set them aside, then drop their drawers to go to the bathroom.

It took Blood Feather a full day of patient crawling to position himself near the outhouse, watching the comings and goings of the various ranch hands. He waited until he thought Johnny would soon go to the small building, and then he slithered to the outhouse and into his hiding place in the darkness. The outhouse had a crescent moon on the front door, which Blood Feather felt was odd.

He hid in the darkness and waited for his newest prey.

Johnny Rabbit Legs entered the outhouse, removed his gunbelt and holster and set them aside, dropped his pants, and sat down. Something was wrong. He sensed it and a shiver ran up and down his spine. He looked down into the blackness in the hole below him and wondered if some creature could be down there in that stench. Instinctively and protectively, he grabbed a hold of his groin and held it while he performed his functions. His eyes strained as he peered intently down into the toilet opening, wondering why his warrior sense was warning him of danger. Johnny was very scared now but did not know why. He looked over at his gun and could not reach it. He pulled up his pants slowly, still looking down into that hole.

Suddenly, it was too late. He felt the impending attack coming and tried to turn upward as Blood Feather's seven-foot frame dropped silently out of the rafters and enveloped him with force. The red cowboy lay unconscious on the floor of the outhouse, while Blood Feather dropped the gunbelt and holster down the hole. Scooping Johnny up under his arm like a small sack of grain, the murderer looked through the crescent moon and saw no ranch hands, and he made it out and trotted away while keeping the outhouse between him and the bunkhouse.

Johnny Rabbit Legs awakened ten minutes later, as he trotted through trees on his own horse. It was being led by a giant Lakota, and Johnny's wrists were tied to the saddle horn, his ankles were tied, and the rope was joined under the horse's chest. If he got his hands free and tried to run off, or if he fell off, he would fall under the horse and perish to flailing hooves.

His head was swimming and he did not know what had happened. As mile after mile fell behind, his head started to clear, and he recalled the feelings of fear in the outhouse, something crashing onto him from above, and waking up on his trotting horse. This Indian before him had stolen Johnny's horse as well as his saddle and tack. He had never seen a man this large before, and the sight of his kidnapper's broad back frightened him. The man was on a draft horse.

At noon they stopped at a creek so the horses could water and rest. By this time, everybody at the ranch was talking about how strange it was that Johnny Rabbit Legs had pulled up stakes and left without talking to anybody.

In Lakota, Johnny said, "Why did you steal me away?"

Blood Feather said, "I need an interpreter. You will speak to the *wasicun* for me. I want to know about man named Strongheart."

Johnny said, "I have heard of him. He is a mighty warrior, half-white and half-Lakota."

We Wiyake said, "What else do you know of him?"

"He loves a woman in Cañon City, a *wasicun* woman. He fought many men in a gun battle in Florence and was shot many times, but he killed them all," Johnny replied. "He has very strong medicine."

Blood Feather said, "We will go there and find this woman and find where he stays."

"Will you let me go then?" Johnny asked.

We Wiyake said, "Maybe, or maybe I will kill you. I will decide."

He meant that, too. He killed when he felt like killing and did not kill when he didn't feel like it.

Blood Feather handed Johnny some beef jerky and hard-tack. He indicated that the cowboy should drink from the stream. Johnny did and filled his canteen with water. After the horses rested, they mounted up and *We Wiyake* tied Johnny to his horse again. They continued toward Cañon City.

It was two more days before they reached the outreaches of the city and made camp in the area called Garden Park. Strongheart could have made it in just one more day, but Blood Feather was close to four hundred pounds of muscle, and it was hard on any of the draft horses he stole to carry him very far.

He tied Johnny to a tree and went to sleep in the shadows away from the fire. *We Wiyake* lay on the ground thinking of eating the heart of Joshua Strongheart. It made him feel somewhat alive and was the only thing now that made him feel that way. In the early days, sometimes he would set fire to houses and watch them burn and that would make him feel alive somewhat, but now he only got that feeling by killing someone with special medicine and eating his heart. Very few things could make him not sleep, but this did make him keep his eyes open, staring into the darkness for some time.

The large killer got up and found a forked stick. He pulled out his knife and whittled the end of it into a point, then stuck it in the ground near his sleeping place. He

then removed his finger necklace and hanged it from
the forked stick so he could view it in the moonlight. The
necklace contained many little fingers, every other one red,
interspersed with white fingers in between. There was also
a bone hair pipe in between each finger. Besides eating the
victim's heart, *We Wiyake* also always amputated the little
finger on each victim's left hand. Two years earlier, he'd
passed up killing a Lakota warrior he had picked out with
"special medicine," because the man had lost the little finger and ring finger of his left hand in a trapper's beaver trap
when he was a boy.

Blood Feather lay in his spot looking at his finger necklace, recalling the events when each of the thirty-one fingers had been obtained. He fell asleep while staring at the
necklace.

The next night they camped in an apple orchard on the
south side of the Arkansas River, in an area called Lincoln
Park. Nobody would come around as the fruit was all gone
at this time of the year. They noticed how many large
branches were broken and both men wondered why. Actually, two big bears, at different times, had decimated the
trees in this orchard that spring, breaking the larger branches
as they pulled them down to get at the succulent fruit.

The following day they started moving around the Lincoln Park area, sticking to the trees and close to the river.
Blood Feather spotted a rider approaching on a strawberry
roan. The man had a slight build, and his eyes opened when
he saw the behemoth walk out of the trees and block the
trail. He clawed for his pistol tucked into his waistline, but
Blood Feather's giant hand reached out, grabbed the horse's
bridle, and jerked down, sending the horse sideways to the
ground. The man, Timothy LeDoux, was a ranch hand from
a small spread south of Florence, along Hardscrabble
Creek. Timothy sprawled on the ground, his pistol flying
out ten feet to his front.

We Wiyake jerked him up like he was a ragdoll and dragged him off into the orchard. He walked him back deep into the trees, and Johnny asked questions and translated.

Blood Feather spoke in Lakota and Johnny said to the man, "Do you know Joshua Strongheart?"

"Yes," he replied. "He's famous hereabouts, and I met him in Annabelle Ebert's café on Main Street. I jest wanted ta shake his hand."

"Where does he live?" Johnny translated.

"He don't live here. Jest comes a lot. He and thet widow woman Annabelle Ebert are sweet on each other," the nervous cowpoke replied. "I heerd thet he stays at the Hot Springs Hotel on the west end a town a lot, where Grape Creek come inta the Arkansas. Kin I go now?"

We Wiyake ignored his request and had Johnny ask, "Is he there now?"

Timothy answered, "Ah don't know. I heerd he was here a few weeks back and was comin' back, but Ah don't know when."

Johnny said, "What else can you tell us about him?"

"He is famous around heah," the man said, "real famous. He had him a gunfight in Florence and kept getting shot and jest kept on a-fightin'. He kilt I don't know how many men. I heard everything from nine ta twenty men in thet shoot-out. Almost died, but thet widow woman nursed him back ta health."

The cowboy went on. "He also is famous cuz he was in a stage holdup southwest a heah, on Copper Gulch Stage Road. He had a shoot-out then, too, but thet widow woman had her weddin' ring stole, and he give her his word he'd get it back, and he hunted down everyone a them banditos and done 'em in. He got her thet ring back, by golly. Now I been hearin' he got mauled by a big ole grizzly up near Lookout Mountain a few months back. Kilt it with his knife I heered."

"What else do you know?" Johnny asked, nervous himself.

"Nothin'," Timothy replied, his knees shaking and heart pounding. "I swear that is it. Kin I go now, please?"

Johnny translated, and in Lakota, Blood Feather asked Johnny if he knew the places mentioned. Johnny told him he did.

The killer stepped toward the hapless cowboy. Timothy saw the giant knife in his hand, and everything became a blur. He felt the excruciating pain in his abdomen, but by the fourth time the blade plunged into him, he felt nothing. His body was left where he fell. Then Blood Feather thought better of it and picked up the body while Johnny followed. He dumped it in the Arkansas River and watched it float rapidly downstream and sink as it filled with water. Next, they caught the man's horse, stripped his saddle and tack off, and tossed that into the river as well.

Blood Feather turned to Johnny, saying, "Now you will show me these places. We must move quietly through the trees."

Johnny Rabbit Legs was more frightened than at any time in his life. He knew that this monster would kill him as soon as he was finished.

He turned to Blood Feather, saying, "I can keep helping you. If I was to run off, I know you would catch me. If you stop tying me up, I will stay and do what you want and translate for you."

Blood Feather stared at him with those blank eyes and finally said, "If you run away, I will find you. I will cut your hamstrings, and you will run no more. Then I will build my cooking fire on your stomach."

Johnny smiled nervously and said in Lakota, "I will not run."

He wanted to stall as long as he could and help *We Wiyake* in any way that he could so he would be considered invaluable by the killer. That is until something happened, some mistake by *We Wiyake*, and then he could make his escape, maybe even kill Blood Feather somehow.

Joshua Strongheart rode into Cañon City on the dirt road paralleling the Arkansas River but running along the base of the foothills, which stood like a wavy five-mile-long row of sentries in a roughly east-west line between the two towns and protecting both towns from invading mountain goblins, storms, or other unpleasantries.

Gabriel knew where he was and knew this was one of his home areas, and he pranced proudly, tossing his mane and tail from side to side. For a short distance, he did a high-step trot sideways and acted like he had the energy of a young foal. Strongheart simply let him have his fun and enjoyed the ride.

He entered Annabelle's café through the back door. She came into the kitchen to prepare a plate, saw him, and ran into his arms. They kissed passionately.

Touching his eye, she said, "Nice shiner, Strongheart. You are supposed to duck."

He chuckled.

Handing him a key, she said, "I'm working. Why don't you go to my place, feed and hay Gabe, and rest up? I'll have someone cover for me and be home before the dinner rush."

Joshua winked and walked out the back door. He looked forward to some real sleep in a real feather bed.

Joshua opened his eyes and felt weight on the right side of his chest. The morning sun was streaking in the window. Where was he? he wondered. Then he realized he was lying on top of Annabelle's quilted bedspread, but she had apparently put another one over him. Annabelle, in fact, was asleep with her head on his right pectoral muscle and her right arm was draped across his body. There was a hint of a smile on her beautiful face. Now he remembered lying down across her bed before sunset. He must have slept through the night, and all the way until past dawn. He must have really missed a lot of sleep on his trip.

"Good morning, Mr. Strongheart," came the words that startled him.

He looked into the eyes of the woman he loved. He grinned at her but wondered how he was going to tell her that he had decided their love could not be. It would be just too dangerous for her, and he had already been through a mauling by a grizzly this year and had been very shot up in gunfights the year before. It would just not be fair to expect her to stick around while he lived a very dangerous life. Then again, he thought, maybe he could go into a business of some kind or act as a guide to hunters. He could scout like his new friend Chris Colt did. In fact, he felt sure he could go to Chris Colt and get a good scouting job.

Again, Joshua Strongheart was at odds with himself. He did not know the answer.

"I cannot believe I slept that long," he said.

Annabelle said, "You must have had no sleep at all on your trip. I got home and you were sleeping so soundly I just didn't want to wake you. I cleaned the house a little and I made you an apple pie. Then, I came in, lay down, and fell asleep, too."

They finished breakfast and drank coffee while Joshua told her about his trip and his new friend, Chris Colt. Throughout the conversation, he kept thinking about Blood Feather, wondering where he was, what he was planning, when he would strike again. He thought about the vulnerability of Annabelle Ebert being his woman. Little did Joshua Strongheart know that Blood Feather and Johnny

Rabbit Legs were in the rocks on the side of Razor Ridge, which ran along the western edge of Cañon City like a five-hundred-foot-wall, and they were looking down at Annabelle's house, clearly seeing Gabriel in the barn behind the house.

Johnny looked over at Blood Feather and spoke in Lakota, "That is the house of the woman he loves. Annabelle Ebert, and that building over there on Main Street with the yellow and black near the roof. That is her lodge, too."

We Wiyake looked at his translator with his usual blank stare and lifeless eyes.

He said, "You are not needed now."

The import of those words hit Johnny instantly, and before he could do anything else, his eyes opened wide and he saw the right arm of Blood Feather streaking toward his head, a brief flash of morning sunlight on the giant blade. Then, almost instantly, there was no more realization. The big knife came close to decapitating Johnny Rabbit Legs as it passed through his neck.

The killer paid no attention to the body next to him. Johnny had served his usefulness and was no longer needed. *We Wiyake* did not think like other men, white or red. The only time he ever felt any emotion was when he killed and struck terror in the hearts of others.

He would now watch and study. He would camp nearby and figure out a plan of action. Even planning such a killing and the stealing of Joshua Strongheart's medicine made him feel again.

He decided to carry Johnny's body away from the area so that buzzards and magpies would not be attracted to this spot, which would be one of his primary lookouts until he was ready to strike.

For the next few days or weeks, however long it took to formulate a plan, Blood Feather would lie or sit still in this perch among the rocks and watch the comings and goings of many *wasicun* men, women, and children in and around Cañon City. He would study Annabelle Ebert and watch her going to and from her house and café, and he would watch the movements of Joshua Strongheart, his prey, and when the time was just right in his mind, he would strike. Strongheart would die and his heart would be eaten and a bloody feather would be left on his lifeless face, a symbol of the power of Blood Feather.

8

THE PREDATOR STRIKES

Joshua and Annabelle talked for some time, and suddenly there was a knock on her door. She jumped up and looked out the window, a big smile spreading across her face. She opened the door, and a beautiful young lady with long flaming-red hair walked in with a little girl who also had long flaming-red hair.

Joshua stood grinning while Annabelle and the woman hugged and tears spilled down her cheeks.

Annabelle leaned down and shook hands with the little girl saying, "I read about you. You must be Melissa, but they call you Missy, don't they? You are so beautiful. I am your mommy's cousin Belle, and this big man here is my friend Joshua Strongheart."

Joshua knelt down and said, "Hi Missy. Are you home from college?"

The little girl started giggling and said, "I don't go to college. I'm too small to go to college."

Joshua said, "You could have fooled me. I thought you were a grown-up lady."

He shook hands with the mother, and Annabelle said, "Lucy, this is who I wrote you about, Joshua Strongheart.

Joshua, this is my first cousin and more like my sister, Lucille Vinnola."

"Well, I certainly see where Missy got her beautiful red hair from. Nice to meet you, Lucy. Did I hear Annabelle call herself Belle?"

She said, "Yes, everybody in the family called her that while she was growing up."

Annabelle said, "I picked up Annabelle when I became an officer's wife, but I actually prefer Belle."

Joshua said, "I think it's beautiful either way, Belle, but I will get used to it. Where did you come from, Lucy?"

"We came by train from Naperville, a village in Illinois, not far from Chicago," she replied.

She started coughing, and the hacking quickly became so violent that she had to sit down, so Joshua took her gently by the upper arm and sat her at the table. He poured her a glass of water.

Belle said, "Are you okay? Can I do anything?"

Lucy hung her head down and shook it slowly.

Belle grabbed Missy by the hand and, smiling, took her to the door. "Missy," she said, "would you like to go out front and play in my yard? There is a swing, and I think a neighbor boy left a stick horse out there."

Missy smiled and said, "Thank you, Belle."

Annabelle sat down, holding Lucy's hand, and said, "What's wrong, honey?"

Lucy said, "I came here to visit you but really to ask you to watch my daughter for a while." She explained to Joshua, "I am a widow, too. I lost my husband to consumption two years ago."

He said, "I am very sorry, Lucy."

Blood Feather had just returned from carrying Johnny's body a long ways off and hiding it among some rocks and brush. He had not been there watching when Lucy and Missy arrived.

Now he saw the flaming red hair on the little girl in the yard, and he was entranced. This little girl had powerful medicine from Father Sun. Her hair showed it. Blood Feather was transfixed watching her while she played, and he assumed she was Annabelle Ebert's daughter.

Lucy said, "The doctor does not know what is wrong with me, but this cough does not go away and has been getting worse. He said he wanted to send me to a sanatorium in Glenwood Springs, Colorado Territory. I am to stay at the Hotel Glenwood. That is the sanatorium and there is a mineral hot springs there that may do me some good."

Belle said, "There is a mineral hot springs here in Cañon City—several, in fact."

Lucy replied, "My doctor's brother is a doctor in Glenwood Springs, and they have cured several people with similar conditions. My doctor has already written him about me."

Belle said, "Of course, I will be happy to take care of Missy. Don't you worry. She will be fine and happy here."

Lucy hugged her and both women got tears in their eyes.

Joshua put his hand on the door and said, "I'm going to go groom the horses."

He walked outside and smiled at Missy playing on a stick horse.

He held out his hand, saying, "Come on, young lady, and help me groom the real horses."

She got excited and was starved for a father figure, so she jumped into his arms and he carried her back to the barn.

This was not missed by *We Wiyake*, who now assumed she must be the child of Annabelle and Strongheart. The killer was still amazed by the shiny red hair. While he watched, they went to the barn, and only then did Strongheart set her down gently. He handed her a brush and a curry comb and started to show her how to groom the horses, and she loved it.

After a while, Joshua set her up on Gabe's back while he groomed him. Both the horse and the little girl seemed to enjoy this immensely.

Blood Feather seemed to enjoy it even more so . . . if he was capable of enjoying anything. He decided he would sneak down into the town at night and find a telescope or binoculars like he had observed the *wasicun* using to see long distances. It might take several nights, but he would find what he wanted.

It was still daylight when Joshua went to the barn escorted by Missy, and he hooked up Belle's horse to the buggy. This time of year it got dark earlier, and Lucy had to board her train by 7 P.M., so he was going to take her, Belle, and Missy to the depot about six-thirty. It was a short distance to the new depot. In fact, Cañon City had just gotten railroad service that year. There was a long piece of leather hanging off one trace chain on the buggy, and Joshua started to grab his knife to cut it off.

Missy stopped him saying, "Here, use my knife."

She pulled out of her shoe a small pocketknife with a single two-inch blade. She handed it to Joshua. He looked at it, opened it, and tested the sharpness.

Strongheart said, "This knife is larger than you, Pumpkin. How did a pretty little girl like you get a pocketknife?"

"My mommy gave it to me. It was my daddy's," she replied. "Mommy taught me how to be really, really careful, and how to whittle and how to cut things with it. She said she always wanted me to have a tool like this to help me."

Strongheart was a little taken aback, but impressed nonetheless, and he could tell this little girl treated her knife with a lot of respect.

It was a long way from *We Wiyake*'s perch to Annabelle's house, and he watched this activity as best he could, still stealing glances at the little's girl's hair every chance he could. They were too far away for him to see she was showing a pocketknife.

She and Strongheart finished and went back into the house, and Blood Feather lay his head down on a tree limb arm and took a nap.

Lucy had already prepared Missy for her visit and stay with Belle, so the time was spent with Lucy and Belle catching up on old news and family stories. In the meantime, Joshua spent time with Missy and taught her how to play checkers. She was already very attached to him and secretly in love with him. She wished she was a grown-up so she could marry him.

It was after dark when the four emerged from the house and went to the street side of the barn, where the buggy was braked. Blood Feather was awake, but he could not see the other side of the barn, even in daylight. It was now after dark, and as far as he knew, Joshua, Belle, and their red-haired daughter had gotten into the buggy and ridden toward downtown through the trees. His eyes strained in the darkness to see where they rode, but they did not turn on Main Street. He would have to wait until they returned, but a plan was formulating in his mind. He would kidnap the little girl with the powerful medicine, but he would not eat her heart. She was too sacred. He would keep her and ensure her safety. He would also in that way get Joshua Strongheart to chase him and give him the challenge he sought. First, he needed to find one of those special glasses the *wasicun* use.

After the train left, Strongheart stopped at the Western Union office and sent a telegram to Lucky letting him know where he was and asking if anybody had had any sightings of *We Wiyake*. He told the clerk he would be at the Hot Springs Hotel at the west end of town and to deliver the reply message there. Then he, Belle, and Missy returned to Belle's house.

"Why don't you stay here tonight?" she said.

He replied, "I stayed here last night and felt bad about that, for you."

She said, "I didn't."

Joshua replied, "I did, and I need to get in the hot springs anyway. I cut the cast off the other day, and my other wounds are still healing now with no bandages. It will be good for me."

"I understand," she said, giving him a kiss, "I'll see you in the morning."

Missy ran up to him with her arms outstretched, and he swept her up so she could give him a big hug. Joshua winked at Belle and went out the door. In the barn, he saddled Gabriel not knowing that the seven-foot-tall figure of Blood Feather was at the base of Razor Ridge, moving silently toward him using trees for cover. Slowly, carefully, the killer moved forward in the shadows, the patches of darkness his ally.

Strongheart mounted up, and Gabe trotted out of the barn and headed south down the wooded street, toward the downtown section. He passed Main Street, then turned west on the river road, toward the Hot Springs Hotel, and put Gabe into an easy trot. Within a half an hour, Gabe was stabled and eating alfalfa and mountain grama grass hay, while Joshua was easing himself into the warm water.

In the meantime, the monster *We Wiyake* still moved through the shadows and actually bypassed the house. He did not know where Strongheart was going, but he knew he would be back. The predator was singled-minded in purpose right now and knew what he wanted to do.

He made his way down the alley running parallel to Main Street behind the numerous businesses. He came out at the end of the alley and turned south on Fifth Street and to the corner of Main Street. Staying in the shadows, he slowly made his way down Main Street to the first saloon, where four cavalry mounts were tied outside. Quickly, Blood Feather emerged from the shadows and went to each horse, checking it. Cavalry saddlebags were fashioned out of top-grain cowhide and had three straps with buckles holding the flap securely down. It took Blood Feather tense moments to figure out how to unbuckle the straps, but he did, and from the third saddlebag he pulled out a pair of binoculars.

A horse turned the corner into Main Street, and a man on a cremello mare trotted down to the second hitching rail in front of that saloon and then dismounted, tied his horse, and entered. He did not see the sevenfoot-giant lying in the shadows, large knife in his hand, next to the sidewalk by the cavalry horses. If he'd known who was there, all he'd have had to do was draw the Russian .44 he carried and blast into the giant mass of insanity several times, but he was unaware of the lurking danger.

The man went inside the noisy saloon, and *We Wiyake* moved quickly and quietly back to the corner of Fifth Street and turned north. He moved slowly, quietly through the shadows by all the houses, and in an hour was back at his perch on Razor Ridge, now armed with binoculars, which would help him to survey Annabelle Ebert's house more readily.

Joshua Strongheart really was starting to feel himself again. His broken arm had healed pretty well, as had many of the aches and pains from the grizzly attack. He could not believe how many scars he had for a man so relatively young, but he also felt it meant there was a good chance he had received his share of scars for a lifetime. He also was amazed by the fact that both he and his natural father bore the scars of a grizzly bear attack. He wondered if that had ever happened in history or ever would again. The hot springs really seemed to help him recuperate, and he was enjoying the time in the water.

A young man brought him a message from Western Union, and he had the youngster bring him his trousers and gave him a tip, which brought a smile from the boy.

He read the reply from Lucky, which read:

No sightings of killer STOP 2 draft horses stolen STOP 1 in Colorado Springs area STOP 1 in Auraria STOP Good report on Comanche STOP Investigate Colorado Springs theft STOP See local sheriff STOP Good luck STOP

Joshua dried off and headed to his room, deciding he had to leave in the morning, before daybreak. He would leave a note for Belle at her café. He would also be unseen by Blood Feather, but of course he did not know that. Joshua figured to be gone close to a week. It was a forty-six-mile ride to Colorado Springs, and he would also need to visit the location where the draft horse was stolen from, interview witnesses, and see if he could determine if it was stolen by *We Wiyake*. In the meantime, he knew that Lucky would assign another Pinkerton to check out the draft horse theft in Auraria.

It was well before daybreak when Strongheart took off toward Colorado Springs, first heading east toward Pueblo but soon turning north toward Colorado Springs on the well-worn stage coach road that would take him along the base of the foothills to Pikes Peak. He did not want to push Gabe too hard after all the traveling they had just done. He would go halfway or more to Colorado Springs and camp for the night, then go on the next day.

At daybreak Missy and Belle emerged from the house and walked toward downtown, holding hands and chatting. *We Wiykae* watched with his new binoculars and could not remove his eyes from "the little one touched by the Great Spirit." He kept watching and caught glimpses of them walking west on Main Street and then saw them opening the front of Belle's café and entering. He figured that Strongheart must be asleep inside the house. Blood Feather napped and waited all day, and then he noticed that Gabriel was no longer in the barn. Now he knew that Joshua had left sometime, maybe while he slept. That did not matter to the killer, though. He had his plan and would soon carry it out.

That night, when the café closed, looking through his glasses Blood Feather watched Annabelle lock the door and leave with Missy. Even at that distance the two were obviously happy. Belle had found the note on her back door from Joshua that morning, so she knew he would be back soon, and she was thankful for that. She was also grateful for her niece's company. Although Missy was not actually her niece, she seemed like one, and to Missy, Belle was the same as an aunt, not her mommy's cousin.

Over the past several days, the psychotic killer had been watching people going to other people's houses. They would knock on the front door of the house in every case. Someone usually answered, and they would enter the house. Although *We Wiyake* had not lived in a circle of lodges since he was a teenager and had been on his own in the wilds all that time, he remembered that this was similar to what the Lakota did. If you went to someone's teepee and wanted to visit, you would scratch your fingernails on the outside of the buffalo-hide housing next to the door.

He crept through the rocks to the hiding spot where he kept his big draft horse picketed. He placed the war bridle, the white man's saddle, and the blanket on it, and affixed the parfleche he carried his supplies in, as well as the rifle he had but seldom used, a Henry repeater, and a bow and quiver of arrows. Behind the saddle he had his giant buffalo coat tied.

He now started back down the mountainside toward

Annabelle's house. Being careful to stay among the shadows, the giant made it to her yard in just over an hour.

From the edge of the yard, he could see movement through the windows. Then, as he inched through the shadows, he could hear the faint sounds of laughter coming from Belle and Missy.

Creak! He froze as a streak of light shot from the front door of the neighbor's house across the street. A man walked out the door. He was wearing a six-shooter and walked directly at Blood Feather, who was only armed with his giant knife. His pace was fast, and Blood Feather stood still in the shadow of the several hardwood trees in the yard.

His hand squeezed the handle of the giant knife, but then the man simply reached down and picked up a stick horse sitting on the edge of Belle's front yard. He turned and walked back to his house.

Blood Feather's expression remained unchanged, as always. He moved slowly forward and finally looked through a window. Belle was seated near the front door, and Missy was on her lap smiling intently as the beauty read to her from a book.

We Wiyake moved around to the front door of the house, checking the dark street in both directions. There was no light in front of the house, just deep shadows of the trees, so he stood back a little in the darkness. His ham-sized fist reached out, and as he had seen the *wasicun* do, he rapped lightly and politely on the door. His other hand held his giant knife.

Belle was startled by the sound, and Missy jumped off her lap.

Bellle stood up and smiled at Missy. "I wonder who is visiting at this time?"

She looked through the small window but could not make out the figure in the shadows. Smiling, she flung the door open, and *We Wiyake*'s giant hand came out of the darkness and grabbed her by the throat, pushing her back into the room. Missy screamed as she looked up at the giant monster whose head was touching the ceiling. Annabelle tried to scream, but nothing would come out of her mouth because of Blood Feather's grip. She looked down at the giant knife blade and her heart beat in her ears; she felt weak in the knees and could not swallow or breathe.

The little girl started to run, and Blood Feather reached out with that gargantuan arm and snatched her up with one hand, pulling her up to his chest, where he held her tight. She screamed bloody murder, and he raised the knife to her throat. When she stopped screaming, he lowered it.

The sight of this behemoth would have been enough to make most women unable to speak at all. *We Wiyake* stared at Belle with those deep, dark, blank eyes. His head touched her ceiling, and he wore leather-fringed leggings, moccasins, a breechcloth, a few feathers in his long black braided hair, a buckskin war shirt, and that giant knife, which would almost have been a broadsword to a normal-sized man.

Missy silently sobbed in his massive arm, and as frightened as she was, Belle rose, jaw set.

She said, "Do you speak English?"

He just stared at her with that blank look. Summoning all her courage, she stepped forward, hands outstretched, to take Missy out of his grasp. The knife came straight up and cut away the front of her clothing, which fell off to both sides. She pulled it together covering herself, and her immediate thought was that she was now going to get raped, too. But she noticed that his eyes never dropped down to see the brief glimpse of her nakedness. He seemed to have no interest, and that she immediately sensed with a great deal of relief.

He stepped toward her and Belle's heart skipped a beat. She did not know what to say or what to do. She was almost paralyzed with fear, and all she could think of was not to make him angry or he might snap Missy's neck like a twig or even dash her against the fireplace. Belle wondered why he had stepped closer, and suddenly his arm swept up with blinding speed. She could not react, and the heel of his hand struck her on the point of the chin. She sailed backward through the air and felt her back hit the wall, and the room started spinning. Before she slid, unconscious, to the floor, she felt panic as she saw *Wi Wiyake* open her front door and step into the night with Missy in his arm.

9

TAKING FLIGHT

They moved through the shadows, and Missy knew she had to not yell. She could just sense it. She had stopped sobbing now. Now the little girl's mind was focused on survival.

He moved effortlessly and tirelessly through the rocks up the hillside and finally to his hiding place and his latest stolen draft horse. Missy had never seen a man so large in her life, and now she was seeing a horse that also was much bigger than any she had ever seen. He climbed up into the saddle and put her in front of him. They rode down the other side of Razor Ridge, to the road that wound its way out of town and up Eight Mile Hill. It would slowly climb up another thousand feet. However, *We Wiyake* was only going part of the way up that road, then back over the rocks to the area on the town's west end, where Strongheart usually stayed. The river was down there, and he forded the mighty Arkansas right after entering the steep-walled Grand Canyon of the Arkansas, which decades later would be renamed the Royal Gorge. He headed toward the egress of Grape Creek, where it poured into the big river, and he would follow the creek up to higher ground in the mountains.

Blood Feather had picked this route from his hideout up on Razor Ridge, simply because he saw that it was rocky, and he was on a gigantic draft horse, which would have been very easy to follow on normal soil.

Missy was so tired when they finally stopped, well after midnight, and camped briefly. She saw high rock walls all around them, and *We Wiyake* built a larger fire than normal to keep the little girl with the special medicine warm. He bound her wrists and ankles with leather thongs and placed her close to the fire, covering her with his winter robe. She slept very soundly despite her fear.

Although she did not know it, he named her *Wicicala Waka*, which is pronounced *Wee Chee Cha-La Wa-Kahn* and means "holy girl."

When Annabelle opened her eyes, she did not know where she was. Everything seemed foggy. She went out her back door and to the outhouse, then returned. Once inside again, she realized that she had been watching her cousin's daughter, Missy. Then the appearance of Blood Feather came back to her, his cutting of her dress, slamming her against the wall, and then, remembered with horror, the sight of him carrying Missy out the door.

Belle got weak in the knees then sick to her stomach. She ran out the front door and emptied her stomach in the front yard. Quickly, she ran across the street and banged on the front door of the neighbor who'd come out earlier.

He opened his door, gun in hand, and Belle was bawling and shaking. He holstered his pistol and set his night lamp down and held her upper arms.

"Annabelle!" the man said. "What is wrong? Come in! Come in!"

His wife walked in wearing a nightgown and robe and put coffee on the stove. She handed Belle a hankie.

Between sobs Annabelle said, "I musn't cry. We must hurry. My cousin's little girl, Missy, has been staying with me for two days now. Tonight a gigantic Indian knocked on my door and abducted her, and knocked me out! You have to help me, Clancy."

The man's wife let out a gasp of astonishment.

Clancy said, "How long ago did this happen, Annabelle?"

She thought and shook her head, saying, "I don't know. I was knocked out. When I came to, they were gone. His head touched my ceiling, Clancy. My ceiling is seven feet tall."

Clancy whistled and said, "Martha, you stay with Annabelle and take care of her. I will get help! The sheriff must raise a posse quickly!"

Belle started sobbing again and said, "It is obviously the brutal assassin named Blood Feather who Joshua has been after. He is the same killer who murdered Joshua's friend, the Pinkerton agent, up on Road Gulch Stage Road. When Joshua was mauled by the grizzly, he was looking for his friend's body. I must get ahold of Joshua."

Martha said, "If anybody can find them and save her, Mr. Strongheart can."

While she comforted Belle, and they spoke about what had happened, Clancy was out rounding up two sheriff's deputies, and they got a dozen men together. One was a Ute Indian who was an expert tracker. These men were loaded for bear and anxious to go after this renegade who stole a little girl.

Sheriff Frank H. Bengley, who was helpful when Joshua had his big shoot-out in Florence, showed up and immediately swept Annabelle into his arms and tried to comfort her.

She said, "Thank you so much for coming this late at night, Sheriff. Can you try to get word to Joshua? He is in Colorado Springs."

He said, "I will send a telegram immediately to the El Paso County sheriff. Don't worry."

Men stood in the yard with torches while the Ute tracker began searching for Blood Feather's tracks and sorting out the trail. An hour later the entire posse followed the tracker up the side of Razor Ridge.

Belle spent the rest of the night at the neighbors' with no sleep. Strongheart arrived the next day before noon. Gabe looked well lathered. Clancy summoned him to his house and told Joshua he would get a stable boy to come and take care of Gabriel. Joshua handed him the money to pay the young man and went into the house.

Belle saw Strongheart walk in the door, and she leapt up from the Victorian couch and threw her arms around his neck crying. They kissed fervently and then he set her back down gently. Martha brought him a cup of coffee, and Belle told him all she knew.

This hit home hard with Strongheart. Although Belle had not been kidnapped, she could have been, and her innocent little charge, Missy, had been. This was his fear. The reason why he should not marry her. Now it had come home to roost.

Within an hour, Gabe was saddled and Joshua was downtown looking for a deputy.

He found one and spoke to him, learning that the posse had tracked *We Wiyake* to the mouth of Grape Creek and had headed up that gulch. Strongheart took off at a trot.

The Grape Creek drainage ran northeast from the Sangre de Cristo mountains near Westcliffe to Cañon City, pouring out into the Arkansas River right at the finish of the treacherous stretch of white water at the end of the Grand Canyon of the Arkansas. The drainage consisted of very scenic wild terrain, and the area had brook trout–filled pools and riffles in the high, forested ridges south of Cañon City, with elevations varying from 6,400 to 9,600 feet.

There was much colorful vegetation, including sagebrush, rabbitbrush, cholla cactus, and yucca in the canyon, as well as piñon-juniper woodland, ponderosa pine, and Engelmann spruce forest, along with typical forest meadows at higher elevations.

There were many predators in the Grape Creek area, from grizzly bears to a high concentration of mountain lions, black bears, bobcats, coyotes, and many eagles, hawks, and falcons. Attracting the predation were high densities of mule deer, elk, and many types of smaller mammals.

The drainage was very rugged, with high rock walls in many places, lots of overhangs, caves, and a few unforgiving narrows along the creek, making it a rough ride for horseback riders, a very rough ride of thirty miles or better. What concerned Joshua was the fact that Grape Creek had many excellent ambush spots where the killer could hide and pick off posse members easily.

He pushed Gabe up the drainage quickly, at a mile-eating trot most of the time, figuring that being on the easy trail of the posse would be reasonably safe, as Blood Feather would be more likely to ambush the posse or individual members than someone trailing them.

Strongheart rode into their night campsite a couple hours after dark.

Blood Feather went high up into the rocks to make a campsite, where he built a smokeless fire in a large jumble of rocks with a flat caprock overhead. The fire reflected off the three rock walls and gave a lot of comforting heat. Missy was very hungry and ate heartily of the bowl of food Blood Feather handed her. She knew there was meat in it and wild vegetables but didn't really want to know what it was. She ate a second bowl.

Strongheart sat across the campfire from the sheriff, while both men drank coffee.

Joshua said, "Well, Sheriff, I wanted to give Gabe some time to rest, drink water, and eat some grain and graze. I need to saddle up and get going though. I will be riding well ahead of you and the posse."

The sheriff said, "Well, Joshua, I know there would be nothing I could say that would stop you. If we can hear shooting, we will come running. Best of luck. We have a lot of grub. Why don't you take some extra with you?"

Strongheart said, "Thanks, but I am okay. I will drop sign for you along the trail so you can move faster."

They shook hands, and Joshua whistled for Gabe while grabbing his gear.

It seemed that every man in the posse came over and shook hands with him, wishing him luck before he left. Strongheart headed up Grape Creek toward a date with destiny, another dangerous journey into the unknown, possibly against his toughest opponent ever.

Missy was so frightened of this crazy man, but she was praying that Joshua Strongheart might well be on their trail now. *We Wiyake* now had her sitting on a rock cross-legged, with the firelight playing on her long curls. He had painted his face with war paint and was smoking a pipe and, it seemed, singing a song to her. He would use his hands to brush the smoke over his head as it came out. He sang a deep, guttural song, and Missy could instinctively tell that he essentially was worshipping her.

Strongheart rode for miles, rightfully figuring that Blood Feather would stay in this gulch. Knowing the killer would camp up high, he finally spotted what he had been looking for. There was a faint glow high up on a ridge to his right front. Most people would not have noticed it, but Strongheart was looking for just such a thing. The reddish tinge reflected off the high part of several large rocks and showed him where *We Wiyake* had his small campfire.

Joshua rode Gabe up into the rocks and ground-reined him. He took his soft-soled Lakota moccasins out of his bedroll and stored his boots and jingle bob spurs in his saddlebags. The Pinkerton took a long swig of water from his canteen, checked his pistol, tucked his extra Peacemaker into the belt at the small of his back, and moved silently into the shadows.

He headed up the ridgeline and disappeared quickly, his movements a whisper gliding silently in and out of the rocks and piñons. The landscape here was very rocky on both sides, with Grape Creek cutting through the middle of the gulch. Iron Mountain towered over the area to Joshua's right, and the gulch spread out just ahead into a flatter area with more trees, an area called by the locals McClure Gulch. Just beyond that it came out of the Wet Mountain Valley, passing just north of Westcliffe, and into the Sangre de Cristo range near the base of fourteen-thousand-foot Hermit Peak.

The glow on the rocks grew brighter as Strongheart drew closer, and now he could hear the deep, guttural sounds of *We Wiyake* singing his chant to Missy.

Joshua now slithered on his belly, moving in and around boulders. He had gotten to the outside of the red and brown rocks surrounding Blood Feather and Missy, when suddenly there was a loud rattle from the rock directly in front of his face. It was a rattlesnake, a large one, and it was two feet in front of Strongheart. He froze. The chanting stopped, and now he heard a loud thud to his right. The snake rattled even more, and Strongheart felt drips of sweat rolling off his cheeks. Silence! His hand moved up slowly, ever so slowly, and finally reached his hat brim. He moved his hat down in front of his face and felt the snake's head hit the hat as he backed away from the rock.

He looked over and saw the large rock that had made the thud near him. *We Wiyake* knew the snake was rattling because it was alarmed, so he'd tossed the rock in hopes of exposing or startling whoever was stalking him.

Avoiding the buzztail, Strongheart slowly crept up over the rocks, a pistol in each hand, and peered into the camping spot Blood Feather had made. The fire was going strong but no Missy, no *We Wiyake*. Joshua did not want to walk into a trap, so he slowly circled the rocks and in the moonlight saw where the draft horse had been tied. It was gone, which is what he'd anticipated. As soon as Blood Feather heard the rattlesnake, he would have tossed the rock and gotten out of there quietly and quickly.

Strongheart decided to simply use the same site, same fire, and get some rest for himself and his horse. Knowing that *We Wiyake* would not be stupid enough to simply continue straight up Grape Creek, Joshua would divert to another route. The Pinkerton turned Gabe loose in a small park nearby and then on hands and knees studied the inside of the circle of rocks for any clue no matter how slight. He found nothing.

Knowing Blood Feather would be working hard to distance himself and not leave a trail, Strongheart slept the sleep of the dead that night, counting on Gabe to warn him of any danger. When they left shortly after daybreak, Joshua noticed that the posse had not even caught up to them yet. They were probably still getting organized, he figured.

Now Joshua would have to track carefully but as rapidly as possible. It was obvious that *We Wiyake* was insane, but he was, at the same time, very cunning and intelligent. The murderer would wait until daylight before setting off on a new side trail, because he would need daylight to securely cover his tracks. So he would push on at a fast clip, and at some point when it felt right he would slow down and start watching for the new cutoff trail.

Strongheart moved rapidly up the creek bed and soon left Iron Mountain far behind him. The trees finally thinned out, and he was blessed with the sight he never tired of. Across the valley floor, less than ten miles away, the majestic Sangre de Cristo range rose up before him, and there were snowcapped peaks as far as he could see to both the right and left. He emerged from McClure Gulch, turned northwest, crossed a small strip of prairie, and headed toward Reed Gulch. Strongheart just could never tire of this view, of what had been aptly described by many explorers and geographers as "the most beautiful mountain range in the world." Starting to Joshua's right, it extended from Poncha Pass south 242 miles through southern Colorado, all the way to a spot north of Santa Fe in New Mexico Territory. There were ten peaks over fourteen thousand feet in height and twenty-five peaks over thirteen thousand feet tall. In some places the Sangre de Cristo mountain range was up to 120 miles wide as well. It was a wild, rugged area, which had enthralled all who'd cast their eyes upon it, but also had taken the lives of many who did not respect the sheer power of nature that traversed the entire range. The area was teeming with grizzly bears, black bears, usually colored in a cinnamon or blond phase, mule deer, bison, pronghorns, mountain lions, elk, big horn sheep, Rocky Mountain goats, wolves, wolverines, golden and bald eagles, hawks, falcons, wild mustangs, donkeys, bobcats, coyotes, foxes, martins, badgers, beaver, mink, and many small game animals.

It also had landlocked lakes filled with cutthroat and rainbow trout, and also many glacial streams filled with brook trout. The views from above the timberline were some of the most pristine in the world, and the dramatic oft-times red hues on the snow at dawn and dusk gave the mountains their name, *Sangre de Cristo,* "blood of Christ."

But, like a beautiful cobra, gila monster, or Bengal tiger, the mountains could also kill a person quickly and violently if they were not always treated with the utmost respect. Many times, prospectors, mountain men, hunters, trappers, travelers, and explorers would find themselves at eleven thousand or twelve thousand feet and above the timberline on a balmy summery day, with sweat soaking their hatbands, and suddenly, they would look at the nearby peaks and see angry storm clouds breaking over them, having maybe been on the San Luis Valley side pushing against the burly granite sentries for several days or hours. Then the hapless person would find himself with hurricane-type winds and rain whipping his face, lightning crashing around him, or a freezing cold, vicious blizzard encompassing him and quickly blanketing the whole area with a deadly quilt of frozen dispatch. Flash floods, avalanches, and landslides frequently would send house-sized boulders, giant hardwood trees, ice, snow, mud, or silt crashing down the side of a mountain as quickly as a falling object, taking life and many things in the path of destruction.

Joshua thought of the giant hiding place looming before him as he continued onward, knowing that Blood Feather seemed headed toward the Big Range. What challenges lay before him? he wondered. It was late fall, and the weather anywhere in southern Colorado Territory could turn from a nice sunny day to pure terror and murderous conditions in less than an hour. He had guessed correctly about *We Wiyake* leaving Grape Creek. Shortly after entering the evergreens of Reed Gulch, he found tracks of the big draft horse going through the trees within sight of the hard-packed wagon road. The killer figured the posse would follow Grape Creek towards Westcliffe, but Reed Gulch, a few miles north, would still wind its way westward toward the Big Range, his intended destination.

Joshua knew he was getting close and had to be very careful. Just then, there was an explosive movement to his left. He drew his Colt and spun in the saddle, and heart pounding, he saw a majestic, sable-colored, six-by-six bull elk which had been bedded down under the fir tree immediately to his left. The bull disappeared into the trees, and then Strongheart saw the rumps, heads, and sides of cows and younger satellite bulls headed farther into the dark morass of green.

Then, as if his thoughts had brought it on, Strongheart looked above Spread Eagle Peak directly before him. It had been enveloped in a swirling, angry storm cloud, and it was clear a blizzard was blanketing its fourteen-thousand-foot crest, but now, as if by Satanic signal, the blizzard headed straight at Strongheart. He knew he was in trouble, but more importantly Missy was in trouble.

He could not save her if he did not find immediate cover himself. Gabe sensed that they were in trouble, and he headed into the trees with his nostrils flaring in and out.

Missy was so scared and tired, and now she was frightened more than before. Even she could see the blizzard sweeping across the valley floor toward them. *We Wiyake* spotted a ranch ahead of them and rode up to the barn. He dismounted and set Missy down, pulling his Henry repeater out of his blanket roll, something he rarely did. They walked toward the ranch house front door.

Ed and Myrtle Hazleton were from Manchester, England, and had come to America with one express purpose. They wanted to see and help conquer the American frontier, the Wild West. They spent one year in Denver City, but it was way too urban for their tastes, so they came to the Wet Mountain Valley in a Conestoga wagon and purchased the ranch from another couple. They saw the giant killer Indian and little girl coming across their yard. Ed stepped out the front door; he was used to friendly Utes stopping by from time to time. A smile spread across his face as he looked at Missy, but then Blood Feather lifted the Henry and fired, then levered and fired two more rounds into the man's chest. A curious Myrtle was looking out the window and started screaming from inside. *We Wiyake* ignored the screams as he stopped, pulled out his knife, and cut the man's left little finger off for his necklace. Tucking it in his waistband, he went inside and saw the woman in the corner holding a rolling pin up, tears streaming down her cheeks. He walked across the room, set the rifle across the table, and strode over to her while she kept screaming. His hand came up with the knife, and he grabbed her right wrist as she swung the rolling pin at him. He then plunged the knife deep into her abdomen and, one-handed, lifted her up, still impaled, off the floor as she screamed in pain and terror. He just stared into her eyes up close until they became lifeless and her body went limp.

He dropped her and then picked her body up, carried it outside, and dumped it across her husband's. Missy just watched all this in shock. *We Wiyake* started carrying in many pieces of firewood and added some to the fire already going in the fireplace. A large pot had stew in it cooking.

Next, he quickly explored the property and found a stone-walled underground fruit cellar with many canned goods there in Mason jars sealed with paraffin. Blood Feather could tell by looking what they were, and he quickly figured out how they probably would open. These were actually screw-top Mason jars, which had existed for almost twenty years at that time.

Strongheart kept in the same direction of travel, but a little to the north he spotted a large dense outcropping of rocks rising up around five hundred feet. He cantered to it and galloped around the circumference. Near the base was a large grove of trees, mainly pines and cedars. He found a

spot where there was a jumble of boulders on the lee side of
the outcropping. They were large enough to provide some
shelter for both Gabe and Joshua.

The blizzard had already enveloped the ranch where
Blood Feather had taken over. Josh took Gabe into the trees
and started finding large, dead branches, which he tied to
his saddle horn and dragged to the rock outcropping. He
cut down several long pine boughs and dragged them to the
rocks, and with the storm almost on him, he got more firewood branches. He raced the horse back to the rocks dragging branches, then dropped the lasso, took off his bedroll,
got out his Hudson Bay coat, and covered that with his rain
slicker. Strongheart pulled a scarf out of his saddlebags,
which he wrapped around his face, and slid on his leather
gloves to go back out.

Then the cold, windy, wet white blanket enveloped him,
and he had to make sure he kept his bearings, because he
and Gabe would have to make it back to the campsite blind.
After getting more wood, he forgot the precise route back
and almost slammed Gabe into the rocks they appeared so
fast. Quickly dismounting there, Strongheart grabbed the
live pine branches and placed them as a roof over the rocks.
Gabe stood comfortably inside the confines of the man-
made cave watching as Joshua put together a fire.

He left Gabe there and walked to the closest trees, blinking his eyes against the driving wet snow. Normally, in this
part of Colorado, almost all snows were very powdery, but
once every year or two a very wet snow like this would fall,
the kind they normally got in the eastern half of the country.
It produced a bone-chilling cold. On top of this, there were
hurricane-strength winds, so snow was covering the area
faster than Joshua Strongheart had ever seen, even having
grown up in the Montana area.

Now bundled up, he made one more trip into the trees
for firewood and a few smaller green pine branches to make

a bed. Adding more wood to the fire, he put on a pot of coffee and began preparing his camp for warmth. The blizzard was now an absolute whiteout, and the few branches he could see were bending down low from the wet snow. Already, he could hear loud cracks every fifteen to thirty minutes, from tree branches breaking and that was with a howling, treacherous wind to blow the snow away.

Inside, Joshua was anxious to saddle up and just plunge blindly through the storm in a desperate attempt to find and rescue Missy. However, his good sense told him he must stay put and that Blood Feather would indeed be staying put, too. Assuming that Blood Feather was raised in the Dakota or Montana territory, Joshua knew that the killer would have a similar set of survival skills to Joshua's and would know how to cope with such an unexpected winter storm.

Indeed, at that time, using guttural sounds and gestures, Blood Feather had directed Missy, as small as she was, to pour them each bowls of stew from the pot in the fireplace. Having helped her mommy many times, she even got them spoons and napkins. He did not know what the napkin was for, so he ignored it. She found a coffeepot on the stove, and although her mother would never let her near such a hot utensil, she poured *We Wiyake* a cup, and he added a great deal of sugar to it. She hoped this might help appease him, and it appeared to. The ranch house was well insulated and very warm.

In the meantime, Strongheart bundled up once more, attached his lasso to a rock, and held it as he walked out and leaned into the howling white morass. He went the thirty-foot length of the lasso and moved right to left until he came to a large pine. He attached the end of the lasso to it and found a long branch. He followed it with his hands to the end and found one at another tree and followed it to its trunk. Using his knife, he marked a blaze on the trunk at the end of that branch. He then cut off many more branches, with as many needles on them as possible. Carrying these, he held the branches and then the lasso and retraced his steps, now totally covered over by blowing snow, already several feet deep.

Weaving them like a giant green basketwork, Joshua worked the evergreen branches into his roof, trying his best to block out every spot where snow was coming through. He built the fire up more and was thankful the branch ceiling was high enough he did not have to worry about it catching fire. Although he had been freezing cold out in the sudden blizzard, he was glad he'd taken the extra effort, as the expedient stone room he had created was now warm and toasty. Using rocks, he fashioned a small trough and lined it with birch bark that had already been lying in the circle of rocks, having blown there in a previous windstorm. He then placed snow in the trough and decided to continue doing so, so that it would melt and provide Gabe with a supply of water to drink. The heat in the large rock room would keep melting the snow as he added it.

Joshua knew he could not help Missy by worrying himself about whether or not she was safe or warm. He was relieved that she had at least been abducted by a man of the wilderness like himself. He knew that *We Wiyake* had been through many sudden blizzards just like Strongheart had. Searching the last hideout, Joshua saw that Missy did not seem to have been molested or harmed. He saw this by many signs, such as that she had been allowed to make and find her own toilet area, which was private. He knew right now the best way to help her was to concentrate on surviving himself and taking care of Gabe. In one more day, he would have to worry about finding Gabe some graze somehow, but he would worry about it then. For now he had a little bit of corn in his saddlebags he could give the gelding, and the horse would have water and be warm. He still had plenty of food, water was plentiful from melting snow, and the shelter he had created was keeping both of them dry.

Joshua slept soundly all night and awakened to see the entire area blanketed with a deep, wet snow. The blizzard was past and the sun was now shining. Strongheart wondered how Annabelle was doing back in Cañon City, and if she might be very worried.

10

WORRY AND MOURNING

Fremont County sheriff Frank H. Bengley came back with the posse as they fled the oncoming blizzard, escaping its frozen clutches somewhat unscathed but unnerved by the enormity of the storm. It was the talk of Cañon City. The next day, as always in the area, snow started melting quickly in the morning sun. Branches were down everywhere, breaking off the trunks all over town, their frozen tentacles still hanging their lengths. This southern Colorado territory, unlike the mountains to the north and northwest, did not get that much snow, less than a foot per year in Cañon City and Florence. Throughout most of Colorado, unlike in the east, the snow was always powdery, not like the wet snow brought on by this blizzard. Residents were used to walking outside in light clothing on sunny winter days, as it was usually so mild. Children in Cañon City and Florence could seldom make snowmen as the snow was so devoid of true moisture.

However, one thing that could happen in this whole area was high winds. Away from the Front Range and even occasionally in the Wet Mountain Valley, where Strongheart was marooned, there were sometimes tornados.

Sheriff Bengley and the posse told many tales about the speed, severity, cold, and blinding horror of the storm, and it seemed to Belle that everybody was talking about it, and many posse members were certain that Strongheart as well as the kidnapper and ther little girl had either perished or would soon. Tracks were gone, buried under several feet of snow and ten-foot and deeper drifts in the Wet Mountain Valley.

Annabelle had been to Westcliffe and that area a number of times, and it was well known that there was a lot more snow and colder temperatures in the almost eight-thousand-foot-high mountain valley. She was very worried about Missy but knew that Strongheart would find shelter and survive the storm.

Two days later, she really began to worry though, as reports from that area were that it was all snowed in. She pictured the poor little girl with that beast of a man in the bitter cold and deep snows. She wondered if she should try to get word to Lucky in Chicago but also did not want to interfere with Strongheart's job. She decided the best she could do was to keep herself very busy, and she started this by baking a number of pies for a couple of the local churches that were having bake sales. Next, she invited the sheriff, his deputies, and the members of the posse to her café for a free lunch.

It had now been five days since the blizzard hit and all the posse members were thoroughly enjoying her free spread for them. Most of the snow in Cañon City was gone, but many knew how treacherous the mountains could be.

Belle and her assistants were busy serving when the café door opened and a white-haired, white-bearded man with a very familiar face walked in and sat down at a corner table. Belle almost ran over to him and kissed him on the cheek.

Zach Banta said, "Wal shucks, I reckon if I's a-gonna

get me a peck on the cheek like thet, I woulda come ta town long ago. Last summer mebbe."

She chuckled.

He ordered food and she asked, "Did you have trouble getting here?"

"Nope," Zach said, "I come down the river on a boat with some crazy fur trapper comin' from the Poncha Springs area."

The enormity of his statement floored her as she looked at this old, weathered, white-haired man.

Over 1,450 miles long, the Arkansas River was the sixth longest river in the United States and was the lifeblood of Cañon City, Florence, and Pueblo. It began near Leadville, a ten-thousand-foot-elevation gold mining town since 1859, with its water feeding it from the glacial runoff of the Collegiate Mountain Range.

From Cotopaxi, where Zachariah Banta lived, to Cañon City, thirty-four miles to the east, were some of the roughest white-water rapids in the world, where the mighty Arkansas dropped over 4,600 feet in elevation, at 250 cubic feet per second. Every year a number of people would die in those rapids and icy water.

"How, why did you traverse such a treacherous river, in the wintertime, no less?" Belle asked.

Zach chuckled and rubbed his beard, saying, "Wal, I reckon I jest wanted to. Ain't never traveled like thet before. The rapids ain't nothin' in the wintertime, and this old feller had a big old canoe with these little side canoes on it. He called it an outrigger. Said he was a Christian missionary for bout ten year out in the middle a the Pacific Ocean. Bunch a islands called the Kingdom of Hawaii. Interestin' character, and he said these little canoes on the side would keep it from flippin' over."

Belle shook her head and laughed, saying, "Mr. Banta,

you are one of the most interesting characters I have ever known. Let me get your meal."

She left him and returned with his food, leaving him to eat, but she returned with coffee and sat down.

"Have you heard about Joshua and my niece?" she asked.

"Reckon thet's why I'm here," he said.

"How so?" she asked.

He smiled, "Wal, I reckon you would be a mite upset and worried. That was a nasty blizzard an' it come in like a stampede or flash flood. Ya know, jest like thet." He snapped his fingers.

Tears welled up in her eyes, and Belle said, "I am so glad you are here, Zach. It is truly a comfort. I have been keeping myself busy, because I would be beside myself if I did not."

"Wal," he said, "I reckon ya already know thet there ain't no man, nowhere, who could do any better at finding yer niece than him. Only other man I know of, Joshua made friends with down ta Fort Union, Chris Colt. He could track an earthworm over a flat rock on a hot day, but he is gone up north now. Gonna scout fer General Custer."

Sheriff Bengley, who had left an hour earlier at the lunch, came back and walked up to Belle. He doffed his cap and shook hands with Zach.

"Annabelle," he said, "I'm afraid I do not have good news. I had two men try to head up there and see if they could get through, and there are still snowdrifts over ten feet deep. That area gets a lot more snow than we do down here."

She said, "Sheriff, you know Mr. Banta?"

"Oh sure," Bengley said. "Get much your way during the storm?"

Zach said, "Naw, Sheriff. Up the road we done, but it

seemed to go past Cotopaxi. We got some, but not like ya even got here."

The sheriff said, "I sure hope Joshua holed up somewhere and found some firewood, water, and shelter real quick. Your niece? Well, young lady, she is in the hands of the Good Lord to protect. I really wish I could take the posse back up there, but my deputies could not even move in that snow hardly. I got a telegram, and that boss of Strongheart's, the Frenchman, is coming in today on the late afternoon train."

Lucky was upset and was now riding toward Cañon City on the Denver and Rio Grande Western narrow-gauge railroad. Only three feet wide to save cost on construction and cars, the line from Pueblo had just been completed and in just a few years would go through the Grand Canyon of the Arkansas, which was now being called the Royal Gorge by locals. It would pass by Cotopaxi and go farther west along the river for miles.

Lucky had received several reports about the storm, the kidnapping, and Strongheart's pursuit, and he was quite frankly very concerned.

Riding along and looking out at the Greenhorn Mountains a dozen miles to his southwest, Lucky thought back to the day when he hired Joshua Strongheart. Lucky had been dining with a female companion in Rector's, a very popular upscale restaurant in downtown Chicago, a city already becoming known for great eating places. He noticed his date eyeballing a man who had walked in and was escorted to his table by the maître d'. Tall, broad-shouldered, and very handsome, he was obviously half-Indian and half-white, and Lucky could not help but notice the way all the women looked at him.

At the table next to Lucky was a very large, boisterous, drunken police lieutenant. It was clear that was his profession because he made it clear in a loud voice that that was what he did. The man obviously was a mean drunk and wanted to intimidate all who were within earshot. Worse yet, he intimidated and embarrassed his wife, who was seated at his table. The man was complaining about anything and everything. His cursing of the wine steward and his waiter both finally brought the maître d', who tried to politely ask the man to leave.

The large police lieutenant stood and shoved the maître d', who fell over a chair, and several people in the room murmured. The waiter helped the man up.

The bully bellowed, "Do you know who I am? I am Lieutenant Daniel Alexander of the Chicago Police Department! If you think you can bamboozle me, you . . ."

His slurring was stopped by Joshua Strongheart standing up, and Alexander gave him a mean look, saying, "What do you want, you blanket nigger? What are you even doing in this place?"

Joshua kept smiling and said, "Sir, didn't you say you were Lieutenant Daniel Alexander?"

"Yea, sho what?" the man snarled.

Joshua extended his hand, saying, "I have heard all about you and your heroism, sir. I just wanted to shake your hand."

The drunk was taken aback, and he extended his hand, but when they shook Lucky noticed the big man grimace in pain. That was when Lucky saw that Strongheart, while shaking, had stuck a pencil between the policeman's ring finger and middle finger and then squeezed his hand. He then grabbed the man's elbow and, appearing to be friendly, strong-armed him toward the door, all the way talking nicely to him. The wife sat in her chair and buried her face in her hands and cried.

Lucky excused himself and walked over to the window, where he watched outside as Strongheart first stuck his foot out and tripped the big man and then slammed his head into a gas lamp post. The lieutenant slumped to the ground

unconscious. Joshua then summoned two other police officers over and spoke to them, and they began to laugh and
shake their heads. They both shook hands with Joshua and
grabbed the downed officer by his upper arms. Lucky sat
down with his date.

Strongheart came back in and went right to the wife's
side and handed her a handkerchief. She dabbed at her eyes,
and he held her chair as she stood and then gave her his arm
and walked her out of the restaurant, snatching her presented
check from the waiter on the way. Apparently having seen
that she had transportation and sending her off, he reentered
and sat down at his table as if nothing had happened.

Lucky excused himself again and walked over to
Strongheart's table, extending his hand and offering Joshua
a card. Strongheart motioned for him to sit.

Lucky said, "Sir, my name is Frank Champ of the
Pinkerton Detective Agency."

Joshua said, "Pleased to meet you, sir. Name is Joshua
Strongheart. With an accent like that your name is Frank
Champ?"

Lucky laughed, saying, "My name was François Luc
DesChamps, and I was born in Paris, but came to the U.S.
as a young boy and changed my name to Frank Champ.
But everybody who knows me calls me Lucky."

Joshua said, "Well, pleased to meet you, Mr. Champ. I
certainly have high regard for the Pinkerton Detective
Agency, a fine organization."

Lucky said, "Please call me Lucky. I came over here to
introduce myself because we are looking for a good man
who can think on his feet and handle situations like you
just did admirably. I saw the pencil."

Strongheart said, "You saw the pencil?"

Lucky replied, "I am a detective. We must always
observe."

Joshua laughed.

Lucky said, "You're speaking. You seem to be an educated man."

Joshua laughed again, saying, "Why do I look like an Indian but can actually talk?"

"Oh no, monsieur," Lucky protested.

Joshua put up his hand and said, "It's okay. I get that a lot. I could cut my hair short, not wear beadwork, and so on. I am proud of my background. My father was a mighty warrior of the Lakota. The French call them the Sioux tribe. I never knew him. My mother was white and raised me to appreciate him and his people, as well as my father who raised me. I guess he would be called my stepfather, and he was a lawman, a good one. My mother made sure I got education, lots of it. I have even studied the works of Shakespeare and find myself quoting him on occasion."

Lucky said, "I have a date and should not ignore her. Please join us at our table."

Joshua and Lucky walked to the table, and the young lady rose.

Lucky said, "Miss Charlotte Smith, this is my new friend, Mr. Joshua Strongheart."

She tried to shake hands, but Joshua lifted her hand and gently kissed the back of it, saying, "*Enchanté*, mademoiselle."

She shivered, and he held her chair while she sat down.

"Thank you, sir," she said.

The two men sat down, and Lucky said, "By any chance, Mr. Strongheart, might you be looking for work, or would you have an interest in leaving what you are doing to pursue a career of excitement, very good pay, lots of travel, and challenge?"

Strongheart grinned, saying, "Sir, I have my letters of reference in my hotel room down the street. I was going to the Pinkerton Agency office tomorrow to see if I could get a job. That is why I came to Chicago. Plus, I wanted to see the town."

Lucky jumped up saying, "*Sacre bleu!* Marvelous. You come to my office tomorrow! You have got the job. Tomorrow we will speak about compensation and answer all your questions. You showed me tonight more about yourself than I could learn in a dozen interviews."

The narrow-gauge train started down an incline toward Beaver Creek, and Lucky grinned to himself, looking out the window, thinking about his initial meeting with and impression of Joshua Strongheart.

Since that time, Allan Pinkerton himself had become a fan of the man of two worlds. He was also bound and determined that the man who killed Blackjack Colvin pay for his murder, and both managers felt that the one man who could accomplish such a task was Joshua Strongheart.

Before going to see Belle, Lucky met with the sheriff. Most of the people he spoke with at the sheriff's office believed that the kidnapper, Missy, and Strongheart had all perished in the storm and were probably dead from hypothermia and buried under ten feet of snow.

At the restaurant an hour later, he sat down with Belle and Zach Banta.

"Annabelle," he said, "not only do we all want to get Missy back safely, but Mr. Pinkerton wants Joshua to get thees Blood Feather killer very badly. We weel spend whatever money we need to, to help Joshua. I weel send a paid posse out tomorrow to look for him."

Zach said, "Wal I reckon thet is a right good idea, and yer better to hire three really good men, instead of ten outta the saloon. I'll help ya find some good ones thet know the area and how to git around in the mountains."

11

FROZEN HELL

The sun was out and snow was melting but still very deep in many places. Joshua could not wait any longer. Gabriel had to have some graze. He also knew that Blood Feather would not stay holed up for very long. He broke camp, saddled up Gabe, and left his cocoon of warmth and safety for several days.

Strongheart looked at the snow in all directions and saw that it got considerably deeper as he rode back into the shade of the trees. He rode west for miles and crossed a high mountain meadow, the snowcapped peaks of the Sangre de Cristos jutting up into the sunlit sky to his front, with virgin snow all around and tall evergreens poking up here and there. The snow was deep here, coming up over his stirrups and boots in some spots. He and Gabe were trotting through the deep snow, piled in some places to where his movement was almost like bucking as he plunged through the deep stuff. He was moving at a very brisk pace, which was always his way, when suddenly it happened. Gabe's front legs went down into the snow and kept going down, down, down. He went forward in a roll, and Strongheart flew over his head, kicking his feet out of the stirrups.

He went headfirst into snow with no bottom, but somehow still held the reins in one hand. Looking back, he saw the red-and-white horse lying on his side, kicking all four legs, hoping to regain his footing. Struggling to his own feet, Joshua tried not to panic because he kept sinking in the deep snow. They apparently were in a bowl, drifted over and filled with snow much higher than their heads.

One second Gabe was trotting, and the next they were both in icy claustrophobia. Strongheart could not see which way to go, but he knew one thing immediately. Gabe was panicked, and Strongheart didn't blame him. Joshua half swam and half tried to run in the deep morass of white. Gabe was behind him bucking and rearing, trying to lunge forward through the frozen quagmire, while Joshua wondered if he was going to die under those thrashing hooves. His normally trail-wise horse's eyes opened wide in sheer terror. He tried hard to stay calm and keep moving, but the white demons of snow and exertion were pulling on Joshua's joints, arm, and leg muscles. His right arm was outstretched behind him holding his horse, lest a flailing hoof strike one of Joshua's vertebrae, a kneecap, or his Achilles tendon and snap it like a twig. He could only see the overhead branches of the closest tree, so he kept that as his goal. There had to be a lee side of the tree with less snow, he figured.

He really started to get scared and truly wondered if he was going to die, up high on a frozen wilderness, trying to find a kidnapped girl and a psychotic killer.

Strongheart made the tree trunk and literally crawled around it to find he was out of the bowl. Still panicked and wide-eyed, Gabe followed in his wake, and both man and horse stood on the lee side of the tree, their sides heaving from exertion.

They trotted for several more miles and came in sight of the ranch yard and ranch house. Strongheart stayed out in the trees and circled around, checking the place carefully.

He found fairly fresh tracks going west, and they were those of the draft horse and another horse. That gave him more hope that Missy was still alive. He decided to go in and check the ranch house and see what clues were there, and he simply had to find hay for Gabriel, or they would not be able to go much farther.

In the barn, he found hay, a grass and alfalfa mix. This entire Wet Mountain Valley was known for some of the best hay around, so Joshua felt very relieved to learn this rancher had indeed put up some good horse hay. Cows could eat anything, old, stale hay with mold, but horses had very sensitive digestive systems and had to be very carefully fed. This was especially true with alfalfa. There was another horse in the corral, so Joshua figured he would take it along as a pack animal. For now he had to limit the amount of alfalfa that Gabe ate, and he found some oats as well. He unsaddled the horse, knowing he simply would have to take the time to take care of his mount or lose him.

He would go inside, but only after checking around the outside first.

Joshua found where Blood Feather had dug through the snow to the two bodies. Joshua looked at the frozen bodies of husband and wife and shook his head. Then, he saw that Blood Feather had apparently dug through the snow to find them simply to cut the little fingers off both. Belle had told him about seeing the necklace of fingers around the killer's neck.

He went inside, but only after he happily saw where Missy had made tracks to and from the outhouse. The killer apparently knew that with the high snows she could not and would not even try running and hiding. He was also relieved to see by the rumpled blankets that Blood Feather had slept by the fire and that Missy had slept in the large feather bed.

Then a piece of firewood came crashing down on the back of Strongheart's head and everything went black.

The seven-foot-tall figure stood above his prostrate figure and simply stared. He pulled out the giant knife and rolled Joshua over with his foot. He knelt down, opened Strongheart's coat, tore open his shirt, and moved the knife down above his chest. He started to cut into the chest, and suddenly the scream stopped him.

Missy stood there, tears streaming down her cheeks, and she put her hand out in a halting gesture and shook her head while yelling, "No! No!"

Blood Feather stopped. He had been waiting for this opportunity and had hidden out in the trees watching, knowing Strongheart's heart would provide him with the strong medicine he needed to feel emotions without killing. However, this was the first time the little girl had uttered a word. She had special medicine from the Great Spirit, and Blood Feather did not want to do anything to upset that. His mind did not work like a normal person's, red or white. He thought maybe he would keep her longer and be careful. But at some point, when the Great Spirit gave him a sign, he would kill her and eat her heart, too. He would then become the mightiest warrior ever, with the strongest medicine. Although his blank expression belied it, he felt good inside, because he was not eating Strongheart's heart now. He felt good inside because he knew that this would truly terrorize the mighty warrior Strongheart, letting him know that Blood Feather could let him go and simply plan on killing him later. In the meantime, he would enjoy the challenge of being tracked and trailed by Joshua Strongheart. It would continue to help him feel alive, like he had ever since he took the girl with the powerful medicine.

She ran over and threw herself on Strongheart's chest, but *We Wiyake* lifted her up and carried her out the door. He closed the door behind him, but then turned around and reentered. He grabbed some firewood and put logs in the fireplace to build a fire. Blood Feather pointed at Strong-heart and the fire, showing Missy that he had done this so she would approve, and they left. His feeling was that this brazen act would frighten Strongheart even more.

Strongheart lay on the floor in front of the fire, unmoving, dried blood on his massive chest where *We Wiyake* had just begun to cut.

The warrior moved so slowly through the dense forest, he was barely noticeable. Up close though, he was a marvelous specimen. He could look down and see the top of the head of almost any fellow Lakota Sioux he was ever with. In fact, he had to look down at most people.

Most items that he would grab ahold of would move. They had no choice if he wanted to move them. His long black hair was braided this day, and beneath the red and black war paint, which obscured most of his face, his cheekbones were high, his jaw firm and strong, and his lips thin. His eyes were special—deep, dark brown, they looked very intelligent and, at the same time, like he was always ready to smile.

They scoured the ground in front of him now, sweeping left to right, right to left in ten-foot arcs, and every few seconds he would look up in the trees. About once a minute, he would slowly turn his head and look behind at his back-trail, as the way you walk into an area does not necessarily look the same when you walk out.

At the top of each bicep and at the base of each bulging deltoid, he wore a tight leather band which made the cantaloupe-sized biceps look even larger.

The bow looked tiny in his left hand, and he knelt down to look closely at some tracks. Each track looked like an upside-down letter V, and he looked at the crispness of their edges, then a slight movement caught his eye. A grain of sand had fallen from the edge of one V and down into the track. This deer was less than a minute ahead of him. There was a small pile of round pellets. He picked up one piece of manure in his fingers and examined it closely. It was round like a tiny brown marble, but on one side there was a tiny groove. Although most people could not tell the difference between a buck or a doe by looking at their sign, he could because bucks have a tiny anal protrusion in their bowel which makes a faint groove in each piece of feces. He knew this was a very large, heavy deer just by the size and depth of the tracks, but now he also knew it was a buck, which is what he wanted.

The warrior turned and looked back into the deep green morass to his rear. Finally, she was noticeable. The young Lakota woman had been shadowing him at a distance and was very well camouflaged herself. Even at that distance, her great beauty was obvious—the long, shiny black hair, olive complexion, and dark eyes. He held his hands up to the side of his head, extended fingers sticking up in the air, the sign for buck deer or bull elk. She smiled and remained motionless. This warrior was helping her and her mother so much; he was tall and handsome, and he truly cared, unlike so many braves.

He moved forward slowly on hands and knees, his bow in his left hand. Every few seconds now he paused and looked. He spotted movement, as a large twelve-point buck grazed on buckbrush and tufts of grass a short distance to his front. It took the warrior five minutes, but he rose to his feet and inched forward, the bottom of his bow now almost touching his hip. He moved with his left side forward, his right hand on the bowstring. The nock of the arrow rested between his index and middle finger, and his ring finger curled around the string. He would not look directly at the grazing deer, as he knew that deer and most prey animals,

as well as some learned and experienced warriors had a
sixth sense, a sense of knowing when a predator was staring
at them. This was kind of like the feeling you got, the chill
down the spine, when someone stared at your back through
a window and you sensed it. The warrior watched a spot a
few feet behind the deer, but his dark eyes were looking for
one movement. There is a nerve in deer that makes a slight
twitch in their tail an instant before they raise their head up.
Just by experience alone, this brave knew that deer had a
different type of vision than humans, which only allowed
for them to see the graze beneath their head when their
head was down grazing. He knew from experience and his
childhood teachings that the deer, no matter how close,
could not see him as a person when its head was up, as long
as he did not move at all. Each time, the warrior saw the little flick in the buck's tail, he froze, even if one foot was
raised.

A half hour passed and now he was so close, he also
squinted when he froze, so the shine off his eyeballs would
not spook the deer. His bow came up slowly, inch-by-inch,
and while the head was down, he drew the arrow back.

The tail twitched, and he froze. Most men could not
hold the powerful bow at full draw for very long without
their arms shaking from total exertion, but this man was
conditioned and very disciplined. The deer's head went
down, the string slipped off the warrior's fingers, and he saw
the arrow's almost instantaneous impact as it tore through
the buck's left flank just behind the lower part of the left
shoulder. It passed through the heart and then through the
right lung, exiting the far side, as the buck leapt with the
shock. He ran less than fifty feet, then struggled as the life
drained from him, and lay still.

The warrior prayed to the deer's spirit and wished it well
on its journey. Then the young woman, who was closer to the
age of a girl, came forward and watched his dexterity with the

knife. He first removed the heavy musk glands on the inside of
the buck's back knees. Then he carefully cleaned the razor-
sharp Bowie knife, knowing the smelly gland could taint the
meat. She marveled at the heavily beaded and fringed sheath
on his left hip, the giant shiny blade, the elk antler handle. He
removed the testes and anus and again cleaned the blade thoroughly. He then cut through the pelvic bone and slit the belly
all the way up well into the chest cavity. Next, he slit the throat,
reached in and cut the esophagus, and then pulled the entrails
out along with the lungs and other organs.

Walking to her village, the young woman was amazed
at how small the mighty buck looked across this brave's
shoulders. Soon, they were at the lodge, and the carcass
was hung outside to be skinned and butchered.

Lila *Wiya Waste*, which meant "beautiful woman," was
the warrior's cousin, and her husband had been killed by
the great bear. She and her mother had nobody to bring
meat to their lodges, but Joshua Strongheart would come to
her village and help her to get meat for the lodge because he
was her closest relative. She accompanied him so she could
learn. Joshua told her not to just marry again but to wait on
a warrior who was worthy of her. She wanted to know how
to be self-sufficient, for her cousin was not around the village circle very often, just a few times per year.

The tall warrior grabbed his bag and headed to the
nearby stream to bathe, clean off his war paint, and change
clothes. The Lakota and their allies the Cheyenne and the
Arapaho were meticulous about bathing and keeping clean,
and he was amused how so many racist *wasicun* used
expressions such as "filthy redksins." The Lakota actually
viewed many whites as being very dirty and unkempt.

Thirty minutes later, he returned from the stream to the
circle of lodges. Lila *Wiya Waste* looked with a great long-
ing at him approaching. She wished he was not her first

cousin, but wished more that he would look at her the way the other braves did. He now was dressed in his normal manner and looked like a totally different person, a white man, with Lakota features.

His long, shiny black hair was no longer braided but hung down his back in a single ponytail, and it was covered by a black cowboy hat with a wide, very flat brim and rounded crown. A very wide, fancy, colorful beaded hatband went around the base of the crown.

He wore a bone hair pipe choker necklace around his sinewy neck, and a piece of beaded leather thong hung down a little from the front with a large grizzly bear claw attached to it.

His soft antelope-skin shirt did little to hide his bulging muscles, and the small rows of fringe that slanted in from his broad shoulders in a V shape above the large pectoral muscles, stopping at mid-chest, actually served to accentuate his muscular build and the narrow waist that looked like a flesh-covered version of the washboard the *wasicun* women used.

Levi-Strauss had recently patented and started making a brand-new type of trousers out of blue denim with brass rivets, which whites were calling "Levi's." Joshua had bought a couple pairs from a merchandiser, who bought them himself for $13.50 for each dozen pairs. They were tight, and they did little to hide the bulging muscles of his long legs.

Around his hips, Joshua wore his prized possessions, one a gift from his late stepfather and the other a gift from his late father. On the right hip of the engraved brown gunbelt was the fancy holster with his stepfather's Colt .45 Peacemaker in it. It had miniature marshal's badges, like his stepfather's own, attached to both of the mother-of-pearl grips, and there was fancy engraving along the barrel. It was a brand-new single-action model made especially for the army in this year, 1873, and this one had been a special order by his stepfather's friend Chris Colt, who was a nephew of inventor Colonel Samuel Colt.

On his left hip was the long, beaded, porcupine-quilled, and fringed leather knife sheath holding the Bowie-like knife with the elk antler handle and brass inlays that had been left to him by his father.

He wore long cowboy boots with large-roweled Mexican spurs that had two little bell-shaped pieces of steel hanging down on the outside of each that clinked on the spur rowels as they spun or while he walked.

Because he had always been trained to keep his weapons clean and knife-sharp, Joshua pulled the large knife from the sheath and examined the blade. As usual, it was scalpel-sharp.

Lila *Wiya Waste*, his cousin, handed him a cup of hot coffee from the large pot he had given her months earlier. He sipped the steaming brew and thought about his childhood quest to learn about his biological father and search for blood relatives.

Then he stared at her longingly and tossed the coffee aside, sweeping her into his arms. Their lips came together and meshed as they pushed against each other passionately. She released the leather straps on her buckskin dress, and it fell away, revealing her immaculate body.

She breathed into his ear, "Oh, Joshua! Oh, Joshua! I have always wanted you so!"

He stopped kissing her and looked into her eyes, but she was no longer his cousin. She was Belle Ebert, but they were still in the buffalo-hide lodge.

She said, "Oh, Joshua!"

He shook his head and thought, *I must be dreaming. She is pushing my head against something that hurts.*

He opened his eyes and saw the ceiling of the ranch house and felt the warmth of the fire. He looked around the room and then down at his chest. Something was amiss. Then, he thought, *Who started the fire?*

Joshua jumped up suddenly, and his hand whipped out his Colt Peacemaker. He looked around, startled, and jumped to his feet. It was night, and his head felt like Gabe was prancing on it with new shoes.

Joshua looked on the floor and picked up the piece of paper that had fallen off his chest. He lit an oil lamp and sat down to read it. It was a little child's writing. Missy's. It read:

Mr. Stronghart,

Pleese save me. I am being brave.

Love, Missy

He reached back and felt his head. There was a lump and a cut on it. He looked over and saw on the floor the piece of firewood that *We Wiyake* had struck him with; then he looked down at his shirt opened up, and the small, sharp cut where Blood Feather's knifepoint had penetrated his skin. The man had lain in wait for him, followed him into the house to knock him unconscious, and apparently had planned to cut his heart out. What stopped him? Did Missy have some kind of influence? Did she cry and *We Wiyake* felt sorry for her?

That did not make sense. Strongheart knew he had to get some food into his body and get a night's sleep while his horse fed and rested. He was not terrorized or frightened. He was angry, very angry, especially at himself for being so foolish. He had let his guard down and probably was only alive by God's blessing. It would not happen again.

He knew for sure that Blood Feather was now putting distance between himself and the ranch. Gun drawn, the

Pinkerton almost ran to the barn and corral to make sure Gabe was still there and unharmed. He was relieved to see that the big gelding was fine.

Returning inside, Joshua made some food and checked for items he might need. He saw where *We Wiyake* and Missy apparently had gone through clothes to get some cold weather gear, so he was relieved at that. He lit a few more lamps and sat down to write a letter to the posse he knew would eventually show up. He also left the letter from Missy and told the posse she must have dropped it on his chest while the killer was not looking. He itemized the things he was taking from the ranch, vowing to replace or return them, including the gelding in the barn and a pack saddle and panniers.

He would take no more chances with *We Wiyake*, although he was certain he was safe that night. He took a spoon and wedged the handle above the door. If anybody opened it, the spoon would fall to the floor and he would awaken immediately. He rigged the tops of the windows the same way, although he was positive that Blood Feather was now miles away.

Strongheart went to bed and slept the sleep of the dead. The next morning, his headache was not quite as bad. He put together a pack, even carrying some grain for the pack horse and Gabe, and headed west on the trail of the little girl he was determined to save and the brutal murderer he was determined to kill.

Strongheart just shook his head as he saw Blood Feather's trail going higher up, directly toward the Big Range and Spread Eagle Peak above him. He entered the big trees and saw that the killer was using a large harem of elk to pave his way through the forest. In a way, Strongheart was glad, because they would also lead him toward areas where the horse could get graze in the deep snow. The sky was sunny this day, and even on the mountainside temperatures were warmer. However, Strongheart also knew that some harems of elk would cross all the way over the Sangre de Cristo range to the San Luis Valley side.

He did feel good about one thing. He had been all through this area before and up above at Lakes of the Clouds. He was worried, as it was late fall, and now much of the snow from the blizzard was melting, and another blizzard could appear anytime. Some of the towering cliffs above the timberline, and even before he got there, were definite candidates for killing avalanches. At Lakes of the Clouds, right at timberline, there were rocky ridges that went almost straight up and came right down to the water. He remembered there were several avalanche chutes there on each ridge.

As Strongheart followed the killer's trail, he heard a stream of water running down the side of the mountain beside him, but he could not see it. It was rushing down the mountain under the blanket of snow, tunneling its way to the valley floor, creating its own white frozen pipeline. He liked it being there as it covered the sound of him going up the ridge. He came up over the ridge where it flattened out, and there he found Blood Feather's camp. It was a short distance off the trail in a a grove of evergreens that was part of a small park. He searched it thoroughly and could tell again that Missy apparently had not been touched. He was relieved about that but very upset that she had apparently witnessed the murder of both the rancher and his wife. He could tell by the tracks that *We Wiyake* also needed sleep and had set out from there late that morning. Strongheart was closing in. The tracks showed that Blood Feather had the other ranch horse as a pack horse and apparently had Missy riding on the pack while he led it.

Suddenly, the killer's tracks showed that he'd turned left and started heading south across the face of the range.

There was a well-used trail there, which decades later would become part of a 110-mile-long north-to-south trail across the eastern face of the Big Range, called the Rainbow Trail. Apparently miners had already established this well-worn trail, and even snow could not hide the traces of it.

The other thing Joshua started seeing, in less than an hour, was that the snow was not as deep. The edge of the snowstorm must have gone through this area, and much of it was melting away already. He had been down this trail before, too, and it would lead to two different passes over the range, the Medano Pass and the Music Pass. They were fairly close to each other. Strongheart wondered if *We Wiyake* knew about them, too and if that was where he was heading.

Joshua stopped suddenly right on a curve in the trail. He slowly backed the horse up several steps and dismounted. He moved forward slowly, with Gabe following. The gelding was trained to walk behind if his reins were tied over his neck or saddle horn. If Strongheart dropped them straight down, Gabe would not move and would ground-rein. This was easily trained. In the first month he could spend time with Gabe, Strongheart buried several sections of logs in different spots. Gabe would follow him when he walked with the reins up on his neck and would be rewarded. Then sometimes Strongheart would stop over one of the buried logs and drop the reins, then dismount and pet Gabe while lifting with his foot the leather thong attached to the underground log. He would carefully, with no fanfare, hook the thong to the bottom of Gabe's bridle and walk away. When the big paint would try to follow, the hidden line would stop him dead in his tracks. After a few stops over hidden lines, the big horse knew to ground-rein whenever the reins were dropped straight down.

Strongheart had stopped on the trail because his eyes,

like any experienced tracker's, were always searching for something out of the ordinary. Up ahead, his eyes had noticed a spot in the snow where the two horses of Blood Feather had stopped, turned, and moved around a little by the trail. Looking more closely, Joshua could make out Blood Feather's giant moccasins tracks overtop the horse tracks in the trail, walking back toward him and then away.

Strongheart got on his belly and crawled forward to where the tracks had stopped and then walked away, near some trees by the trail. He looked carefully and then saw what he wanted. Two or three feet above the trail, a piece of white thread went across it between trees. He crawled back and found a long stick and tossed it forward so it would hit the thread. There was a loud cracking sound and Gabe jumped. A young sapling about fifteen feet tall had been bent backward and tied to a figure-four trip lever behind the tree. It swung forward across the trail three to four feet above the ground, with several sharpened sticks lashed to it and facing toward Strongheart. Had Gabe hit the trip wire himself, at least two of the sticks would have stuck in the horse's legs or chest and probably more. Joshua shook his head.

The idea again was just to inconvenience Strongheart and terrorize him, but the terrorizing effect would not happen. It only made Joshua more determined to be careful and catch up with this madman.

Joshua pulled his knife out and started chopping away the booby trap so no innocent animal or passerby would get cut by the sharp stakes.

When he was finished, he mounted up and continued forward. His eyes swept the trail in front of him in arcs from left to right, right to left. The trail was now getting muddy because of quickly melting snow.

Out on the valley floor thousands of feet below, he could see the buildings of Westcliffe and beyond that Silver Cliff,

as well as various valley ranches. These fell behind as they
traveled farther south.

As Joshua had guessed, Blood Feather's trail turned
west at Music Pass, which would bring the killer and Missy
out by the Great Sand Dunes in the San Luis Valley.

The San Luis Valley was a very extensive alpine valley
in both Colorado and New Mexico territories, with an area
of 8,000 square miles. In fact, it was the highest large
mountain valley in the world, with an average elevation of
7,500 feet above sea level. The valley was over 120 miles in
length and about 74 miles wide. With the Sangre de Cristo
range to the east, it had the San Juan Mountains to its west
and ran from the Continental Divide on the northwest rim
into New Mexico on the south. Semi-arid, the San Luis Valley received very little precipitation, and in fact, the snow
from the blizzard that had hit the other side of the Sangre de
Cristo range did not drop much snow on the San Luis Valley
side, and it was dry now.

The Great Sand Dunes lay directly to the west of the
Sangre de Cristo Mountains, right up against their base.
Some of the sand dunes reached over 750 feet above the
valley floor and were the tallest sand dunes in North America, and they covered about 19,000 acres.

The dunes were formed of sand and soil deposits from
the Rio Grande and its tributaries, flowing through the San
Luis Valley, then blowing across the valley and nestling
against the Big Range. As the valley winds lost power before
crossing the Sangre de Cristo range, the sand was deposited
on the east edge of the valley.

Night was coming on when *We Wiyake* rode into the
stand of quaking aspen trees overlooking the Great Sand
Dunes. He was on the San Luis Valley side of the Big Range
and now guided both horses through the aspens, looking for
a good hidden campsite. He saw deep dark fir trees ahead
and headed into the thicket, winding his way between trees

until he found himself in tightly woven, very thick blanket of green. He could make a good fire there and not worry about the smoke being visible in the moonlight. When he dismounted, he saw the little girl on her back fast asleep, lying on the pack lashed over both sides of the packhorse. A normal person would have been moved by seeing this, as it was cute. Blood Feather, however, had no such feelings.

Strongheart decided that, although it was colder, he would camp up higher on the western slope, where he might spot fires or even catch a glimpse of Blood Feather after daybreak. He rode into a group of boulders that would offer plenty of protection. First, he glassed for any signs of a campfire down below. Seeing none, he built his own fire and made a camp. He was back in the saddle at daybreak, but Blood Feather, who was camped several miles west of him, had been on his horse an hour before daybreak. By the time Joshua discovered *We Wiyake*'s night camp and started to investigate it, the killer had turned right at the bottom and was now flanking the Great Sand Dunes rising up seven hundred feet on his left. The Sangre de Cristos, however, rose way up on his right, as he headed north along the eastern edge of the massive valley.

Joshua did not arrive there until mid-morning, and he could tell by the age of the tracks that they were several hours old. He got well north of the dunes and decided to pull off the trail and fix breakfast, which he had not had earlier. He figured that for getting bushwhacked he would be sticking out like a sore thumb now, so he would have to be very careful.

He built a fire and put on coffee and fixed some food, trying to figure out how to trail the killer without exposing himself too much. Out in the valley, Strongheart saw a group of what looked like cavalry soldiers. They were riding north, too, but suddenly turned right and headed straight at him. This really bothered Joshua.

He ran to the fire and started to kick the fresh dirt pile over it, but then decided that would be a waste of time, as the riders were certainly coming to this place anyway. Besides, he didn't have time to go anywhere unseen.

He checked his guns—his regular Colt Peacemaker and his belly gun—and grabbed his rifle, making sure all were cleaned and loaded. Then he lay down among the rocks and waited, watching the dots grow larger and larger. It was a cavalry troop, but again Joshua sensed something wrong. He listened to his intuition, always. In this case it told him to play it easy but careful; to keep his cards close to the vest.

Strongheart sat up, put more coffee in the pot, and set it on the fire. He now leaned against a large rock as he sat on another one. He moved and seated himself on a log, laid his rifle across his lap, and lit another smoke.

The patrol rode up and ground-reined their horses below the cottonwoods at the base of the rocks. They walked up with a friendly enough demeanor. It was a squad-sized patrol, with one corporal and five privates.

It dawned on Joshua suddenly why he was troubled; the patrol was not riding in any type of formation. They had no point, flankers, or rear guard out. He understood that it was just a six-man patrol, and they didn't necessarily have to be in a formation, but it was enough to make him suspicious.

Strongheart got more concerned when he noticed the men walking toward him without the squad leader issuing any kind of orders to anyone to water horses, watch for bad guys, straighten their gig lines, or anything of the sort. He might just be an inefficient squad leader, but it was one more thing to make Joshua wary. All the men walked toward the spring he cooked next to, emptying the remainders of their canteens.

"Howdy," the squad leader said. "Looks like you had yerself a bit a lunch, stranger."

Suddenly it dawned on Strongheart that these men had been in the saloon where he and his new friend Chris Colt and had gotten into the fight at Fort Union.

He sensed they recognized him, too.

Joshua said, "I am looking for a very large Sioux riding a big draft horse and leading a packhorse with a little white girl with flaming red hair. Seen 'em?"

One of the privates said, "Nay, laddie, we ain't seen the likes a anybody for all the days we been out an' about."

The corporal gave the man a dirty look and said, "We're with Troop K, Seventh Cavalry. Been out on patrol for a long time."

"I guess," Joshua said, fishing, "it's way over one hundred miles to Fort Union."

"Recognized us, huh?" the corporal said. "We seen yer red-and-white paint from that far off and knew it was you."

Strongheart noticed one of the privates off to his left start to reach for his pistol, but another grabbed his wrist and stopped him.

The corporal smiled. "Yeah, that horse is a looker."

"Who's your CO?" Joshua asked.

"Captain Goodwyn," the squad leader replied.

At the same time, one of the privates started to say something else, but a stare from the squad leader shut him up.

Joshua smiled and took a swallow of coffee, waiting to see what they would say or do next.

He heard a gun cocking off to his right and turned to see a blond-haired, red-faced trooper pointing a pistol at him. "This is bull squat, Reg! He's gonna spill his guts when he gits to Fort Union and tells 'em where he seen us! We gotta kill 'im, so quit pussyfootin' around. Now, get shut a that rifle, Injun."

Joshua felt anger begin to burn in his ears. His face flushed. "You're making a big mistake, mister," he said.

"Sure, it's obvious to me you're all deserters, but by the time I get to Fort Union again, you'll be long gone from here."

The man said, "But it's less than fifty miles to a telegraph key. Sorry, but you gotta die."

Joshua started to stand and said, "Now, look."

With that, he swung the Winchester up and fired from the hip while diving to his left. He saw flame blossom from the man's gun and heard the crack of the bullet as it passed him by. A big red patch appeared on the man's dusty blue tunic, over his heart, as he flew backward, quite dead. Strongheart cocked the rifle, and as he hit the ground he drew his belly gun with his left hand.

Another private felt lucky and went for his gun, but he was clumsily fumbling with the big leather flap over the butt when the Pinkerton's left-hand gun spoke loudly. The bullet took the man right through the left cheek, tearing the side of his head off. The man fell to the ground and clawed frantically at the bloody mass where his face had been. He twitched a few times spasmodically and died, after having run away from the cavalry to avoid just such a horrible death in battle.

This scene had a very sobering effect on the other troopers, who all raised their hands. Strongheart kept them covered with both guns and signaled that they should all drop their gunbelts and step away, which each man did quickly and efficiently.

Joshua said, "Now, you lily-livered cowards, you unsaddle those mounts and shoo them off."

"Mr. Strongheart," the corporal said pleadingly. "You ain't gonna leave us out here without horses, are you?"

Joshua said, "Your friend was going to leave me out here dead, and I didn't see you stopping him. You're playing a rough game, mister, and you shouldn't have picked up the cards if you weren't willing to call or raise."

One of the privates stepped forward and said, "You talk

big with a gun in each hand, and we're unarmed. You ain't leaving me without a horse, you red blanket nigger."

Joshua smiled and said, "Dad burn it. I was going to have a big poker game next week and invite you, but it seems like you don't like me very much."

He pointed his right-hand gun and fired.

The trooper's hat flew off his head, and Strongheart said sarcastically, "Please?"

"Set those guns down, and we'll see how tough you are," the private went on.

Joshua laughed. "I'm tough, but I'm not stupid. Speak one more word, and you'll find out how tough I am."

The man, shamed by Strongheart's talk, looked at his cohorts, all of whom were looking to see if he would do anything.

He said, "I told you that . . ."

Boom! The fancy Peacemaker roared, and the man went down onto his face with a scream, both hands grabbing at the bloody hole through his right thigh. All the men looked at Joshua, as he cocked the gun again.

The Pinkerton agent grinned broadly and said, "A man is only as good as his word. If I say something, I mean it. Now, anybody else want to argue?"

The men just stood transfixed, then as one they started to shake their heads no.

"Good," Joshua went on. "Get those horses ready. I'll be on my way."

Joshua had hated to shoot an unarmed man, but on the other hand he'd had to take bold action against superior numbers, guns off or not. Besides that, cowardly men who could leave their friends before an upcoming battle sickened him. He himself had felt fear many times. He was afraid every time he confronted danger, but Strongheart had learned that by conquering that fear and doing what was right you improved and strengthened yourself.

He left the bewildered deserters behind him at the rock tank, their guns lashed to the saddle of the last horse behind Strongheart. When he was two hundred yards up the road he unlashed the guns, and they fell to the ground with a clatter. He knew that the ex-soldiers would be watching him intently, as they would most certainly be lost without guns to protect themselves. He checked all the horses and ensured that the lead line of each was tied in a knot to the tail of the horse in front of it.

He was headed north now, toward Poncha Pass. He would turn the mounts loose.

He felt sore. His head pounded like it was on the receiving end of a miner's doubletree. His back was sore from slamming into the ground when he was hit at the ranch house, and the side of his head would probably continue to hurt for several more days anyway. He also would get irritable, because he felt confused. Strongheart had seen enough of head wounds to know that that was a fairly normal occurrence. He had seen others lose part of their memory and also have trouble adding and subtracting things for months afterward. It was natural to get frustrated over those small details.

Strongheart had gone far enough that he wouldn't have to fear the deserters following him on foot, although he didn't believe they wanted a part of him again. Joshua was puzzled by men like that. They felt the same fear he and every other man felt, but they succumbed to it. He wondered how they would be able to go the rest of their days knowing that they had sneaked away from their duties like a thief in the night.

Strongheart watched the ground around him for signs of potential ambush by *We Wiyake*. He grinned to himself as he remembered a conversation with his stepfather years earlier.

Joshua was the love child of his white mother and the Lakota warrior Claw Marks. The young half-breed longed for a father and was excited as a young boy when Dan Cooper, the town marshal of the new blossoming community of Flower Valley, got serious about his ma. He was tall and slender, maybe six-foot-two and 190 pounds, but that was all muscle and sinew from years of hard work.

Marshal Cooper had high cheekbones, a prominent nose, and honest, intelligent hazel eyes that would bore daggers through anybody. Much older than Joshua's ma, he had a little gray in his mustache, which was always well trimmed and full, running down in a point just past the corners of each thin lip. Like his hair, it was primarily dark brown. He was not given to talking, just doing. Dan was a very harsh taskmaster on Joshua when he was growing up, but he was all man and was bound and determined to make his stepson a man. He said the country was too unforgiving.

The one thing Joshua remembered most about the only father that he ever knew was how good the man could fight even though he was much smaller than some of the giant buffalo hunters and mountain men he had to arrest. Dan had actually taken a section of log weighing over two hundred pounds, shaved the bark off of it, and the two thick branches that extended out for two feet, and sanded them, rounding the ends so they would resemble thick arms. Joshua would watch the man for hours on end tossing the log backward, sideways, and in various combinations of those directions, working on numerous grappling moves.

Dan was also an incredible shot with pistol or rifle. He started Joshua when he was small and taught him first how to shoot a long gun. He learned to shoot with an 1860 Henry .44 repeater, and his stepdad gave it to him when he turned twelve years old.

The lawman and young Joshua Strongheart were having

a conversation about courage one day when Dan Cooper said, "Joshua, the difference between a coward and a hero is about one minute in time."

Strongheart was perplexed by that statement, and it bothered him for a long time afterward, but he had finally gotten a handle on it. He got into a fight with two brothers whose family owned a small ranch farther up the valley. Their family and his had attended the same church, but the two brothers were about the farthest thing you could get from walking the Christian walk of life. They were troublemakers from the get-go.

The two bullies simply beat up everybody, and finally Strongheart's turn came up, along with the numerous half-breed remarks and taunts. Everyone had backed down from the bullies because they were so tough and brutal—they would chase a person down and beat him senseless. When one of them started to pick on Joshua, he tried everything he could think of to avoid getting into a fight. When one of the two, however, made some disparaging remarks about a girl in Joshua's church whose father had been arrested for public drunkenness, Strongheart finally had had it. He was scared—their brutality had become legendary locally—but he was beyond caring at that point.

He had stopped at the blacksmith's before school to pick up four horseshoes for his stepfather. His mom owned a general merchandise store, but Marshal Cooper rode a seventeen-hands-tall Thoroughbred with very large feet and had to get his shoes from the blacksmith. These were conveniently tucked into the back waistband of Joshua's trousers.

They knocked his schoolbook from his hand and started laughing. Joshua managed to seem so ferocious in his demeanor alone that the two bullies looked a little unsettled. He had heard from his stepdad that a man using his head has a much better chance in a fight than one who just uses his muscle, so he tried to think his way out of trouble. When the first punch was thrown, it landed square on Strongheart's temple and sent him reeling to the ground. His right hand closed around one of the horseshoes, and he grabbed it without his adversaries noticing. Then he grabbed another with his left hand, figuring if they were going to gang up on him, he would even out the odds.

The two brothers ran up and both kicked him in the rib cage, knocking the wind out of him and severely bruising the ribs. Most boys would have folded over and cried, but their kicks simply made Joshua furious. He came off the ground with a fury and tore into both brothers. His fists were swinging so wildly and so quickly, nobody noticed the horseshoes sticking out of both ends of his right and left fists. The faces of the bullies, however, showed signs of the horseshoes. Within a minute, both brothers were lying on the ground unconscious, each sporting two black eyes and a broken nose. Strongheart tucked the horseshoes back in his waistband, and nobody ever saw them.

He became the hero of the young girl he had defended, and of the whole community. His reputation grew, as it did with each telling the story of the fight. As he grew and gained confidence, Joshua realized how smart he had really been. One thing he never forgot was the butterflies he'd felt in his stomach when he'd had to face the two bullies, and the great fear that had clutched at him. It would have been so easy to start his life out as a coward back then; instead, Joshua Strongheart had chosen to act like a man. That decision started him on a pathway of being a hero whenever danger reared its ugly head.

He saw that the tracks of the big draft horse suddenly turned toward the southwest, far to his left. *We Wiyake* had gotten to a small brush-clogged arroyo running through the valley east to west and entered it, probably hoping the brush would obscure his tracks and slow Strongheart somewhat.

Joshua followed along the arroyo and kept his eyes moving along the ridges in front of him. Many of the ridges to the west, where he headed, were devoid of vegetation, which would offer much cover, but directly behind them were taller ridges covered with large growths of dark timber. Joshua Strongheart was positive that was where Blood Feather was right now watching and waiting in those trees, maybe preparing an ambush.

Missy watched the large back of *We Wiyake* while he looked through the stolen telescope he had resting and steady in the fork of a small tree. She was so frightened of this man, as he had started paying closer attention to her the past few days and was acting differently. Something about it made her even more nervous and much more uncomfortable. The little girl knew now was the time to do what she had been planning. Her hands were bound as usual by leather thongs, but she reached into her shoe and pulled out the little knife that Strongheart had heard about in the stable. She quickly cut through the bonds, replaced the knife, and slowly, quietly made her way back into the trees where the horses were. She knew every few minutes the killer would turn around and quickly look for her, and he would soon be after her with a fury. She was very, very frightened, but knew she must act now. Missy had been waiting for an opportunity like this.

She got the packhorse she had been riding, put the bridle on him, and tried to mount up bareback, but he was too tall. The little girl kept looking back toward the area of the trees she had just passed through, knowing the seven-foot monster would come charging through any moment. She thought of something new and quickly ran to his big draft horse, untied his lead line, and pulled him behind her. Reaching a small tree, Missy climbed up the branches sticking out each side, and jumped on her horse's back. She was so scared now she was whimpering in fear, tears streaming down her cheeks, but she had her mind made up.

She kicked her horse with both heels as hard as she could and held the lead line of the other horse in her right hand. The packhorse took off at a trot, with the big draft horse following. A few hundred yards away, Missy let go of the lead line and the draft horse quickly slowed and started grazing. The giant had already seen that she was missing and was running to catch up now.

Knowing he would soon be following, Missy kept kicking the horse's ribs, and finally got him into a canter. All she could see was trees, but she knew that Strongheart was in the valley toward the big peaks of the Sangre de Cristos, so all she had to do was ride toward them, seeing them easily in breaks between the trees. In minutes, Missy heard the hoofbeats of the large draft horse cantering far behind her and branches breaking as the seven-footer pursued. Tears streaked down her face.

Panicked, she cried and kicked the horse harder over and over, trying to get him into a full gallop. She looked back, and suddenly the giant killer on the big draft horse burst out of the trees, charging after her. Fortunately, the draft horse was no match for her mustang mount, especially with her not weighing more than a passing thought. The little mount sensed her desperation, and the gelding turned on his steam engine full throttle.

The killer raised his rifle and fired. She heard the bullet crack as it went past her left ear, and she actually felt pressure from the bullet as it whizzed by. Missy was almost paralyzed with fear. She was begging the little horse in a whisper to go faster. She did not know it, but Blood Feather was trying to shoot her horse in the head; he was still not ready to kill her. He never considered the fact that shooting her galloping horse in the head could very well kill her, because his mind did not work like any normal person's, red or white.

It now seemed to Missy that the harder she tried to make her gelding go faster, the more it slowed down, and she felt the monster was gaining on her. She wondered if she should give up and just stop and let him take her hostage again. The little girl had never been so scared, helpless, and lonely in her life.

Then she saw him. It was Joshua Strongheart, atop Gabriel, riding toward her at full gallop. Now tears streamed out of her eyes with hope. She saw his hand streak down and come up with his Colt Peacemaker, and she saw him carefully aim and fire. She heard the bullet crack as it passed over her, and she turned her head.

Blood Feather spun slightly on the horse's back as a bright spot of crimson appeared on his left shoulder. He turned the big horse and headed back toward the trees, bending down low over the horse's back. Joshua sent more bullets after him, pulled up, holstered his gun, and turned Gabe.

As Missy approached, Joshua yelled, "Keep going!"

She rode right by him, and he put the spurs to Gabe, quickly overtook her, reached over, pulled her from the saddle, and swung her behind him. She wrapped her little arms around his muscular body, and he headed east across the valley toward the towering Sangre de Cristo range. She held him as tightly as she could, closed her eyes, and laid her cheek up against his back.

Strongheart let Gabe stretch his legs in a fast lope, as they streaked across the wide valley floor toward the Sangre de Cristos. They were at the north end of the San Luis Valley, which was like the bottleneck of a giant water or milk jug. Here the valley was miles across instead of dozens of miles. Strongheart was about a mile or two south of the small town of Villa Grove. Hayden Pass was used by the Utes to cross from the Arkansas River to the San Luis Valley, and a small road came almost straight across the valley to the town of Villa Grove. Joshua hit that road in minutes and set out for Hayden Pass. It was named for an early Wet Mountain Valley settler on the other side of the range named Lewis Hayden, but just that year, 1875, another man, completely unrelated but named Ferdinand Hayden had crossed over and started telling people the pass was named after him.

Right now, Joshua did not know or care who the pass was named for. He was headed for it at a full gallop. First, he would head into the trees in the foothills, and then he would turn north to head to the trail going over the pass. The trail was steeper on the San Luis Valley side; then at the top there was a long ridge which slowly ran up through evergreens to timberline, to 12,500-foot Galena Peak and, to the south of the pass, Nipple Mountain, a breast-shaped mountain that had earned its name from obvious features. Then there was a long trail that switchbacked from the top of the 10,000-foot pass, and would lead Joshua to come out less than ten miles west of his good friend Zach Banta in Cotopaxi.

Joshua got inside the tree line so he was out of sight by anybody out in the valley. He stopped and dismounted. He pulled Missy down and wrapped his big, safe arms around her. She held on and just started sobbing.

He stroked her hair, saying softly, "I have you now, and I will not let him get near you again. I promise. You are safe, Missy, and I am so proud of you for surviving. We still have to move fast, because he will chase us. You might get tired and hungry. Will you keep being brave for me?"

"I want my mommy," she said, but then added, "I'll be very brave, Mr. Strongheart. That man is mean and his head is crazy. He scared me so much."

"How did you get away from him?"

She smiled. "Remember the little knife Momma gave me? I hid it all the time in my shoe. Then today, I cut the rawhide when he wasn't looking. He was in those trees," she said, pointing toward them, "watching you with a spyglass. What about my horse?" she asked.

He said, "You do not weigh that much, so I decided to keep you with me so I can protect you better. Gabe doesn't mind. He likes pretty little girls."

She grinned and put her head up against his broad chest and held tight to his shirt.

He mounted up, holding her, and set her up on top of his saddlebags, saying, "Okay, young lady, let's get you back to Cañon City. It will take us a couple days, but we will get there as fast as I can."

They took off up the narrow weather-beaten road winding up the not-often-traveled Hayden Pass.

We Wiyake quickly built himself a fire and stuck the end of his giant knife in it. He had to remove the bullet from his arm and get the bleeding stopped before anything. He was insane, but he was not stupid. In fact, he was extremely intelligent, but there had been a sickness in his brain from childhood.

While the knife heated, Blood Feather thought back to his childhood. He had witnessed his uncle murdering his aunt with a skinning knife. The uncle, an enormous warrior, saw him and gave chase. *We Wiyake* was a youngster and his uncle was monstrous, but fat, too. The boy made it to a war pony and jumped on its back, taking off at a gallop as two arrows whistled by his head. The uncle mounted up and gave chase, and the young *We Wiyake*, who was then called *Agleska*, which means "lizard," pushed the little war pony as fast as he could go. Figuring his uncle, who was far back, was out to kill him and would not give up, he headed toward the closest trees. Since the uncle was so tall and fat,

Agleska reasoned that the big man would get held up by thick branches. He was correct. The uncle gave up shortly after entering the trees, but the young man slammed his head on a thick branch. It snapped his neck back, and he somersaulted backward off the rump of the galloping pony and fell unmoving on the ground.

Fortunately, the blow did not kill him, but it did crack his skull and gave him what would now be a grade-three concussion. He lay there unconscious for hours with a subdural hematoma. In short, his brain bled and was severely bruised. He awakened after darkness and had no idea where he was or how he got there. *Agleska* wandered aimlessly and in an hour got dizzy, fell, and hit his head on a rock, causing a second concussion within hours. In about three weeks, some of the headaches started to subside, but his personality had changed dramatically, and he suffered from permanent depression. He had amnesia and did not remember what had happened that day for about a half a year. He became essentially emotionless, and over the years that he lived on his own in the wilderness, his mind created his own spirit world, and these spirits, so to speak, became his mentors and the closest things to friends he would ever have.

That day was the last time he ever saw any of his family members, except one time in his twentieth summer when he came upon his village. A female cousin had married, and he sneaked into the village circle of lodges on the wedding night and crept into the wedding lodge to murder his cousin's new husband in his sleep. Then, lying next to his body, he tore off his cousin's buffalo robe and attempted to rape her, but he was unable to perform. He instead acted like he was prolonging the rape ritual just to see her frightened. Then, he started cutting her just to watch the sheer terror in her eyes. This was when he first learned this was the only thing that would bring him some feeling of being alive. Fascinated, he covered himself with her blood. As time went on, his killings became more ritualistic, and each part of the murder held some special meaning to him.

When he left his cousin's lodge, a red-tailed hawk feather came out of his hair and was soaked in her blood. The tribal elders then started calling him *We Wiyake*, "Blood Feather." He learned of this later and kept the name, because he felt too old to be called "Lizard" anyway.

His eyes remained emotionless as he dug the knife blade into his bicep to cut out the Colt .45 bullet from Joshua Strongheart. It was mushroomed and half-buried in his humerus bone, which was cracked down the middle. *We Wiyake* knew he must first fix his arm and stop the bleeding or he would never get the girl back or eat the heart of his enemy.

Joshua made it over the rugged pass and was heading down on the Arkansas River side of the Sangre de Cristos. They rode into a narrow gulch that ran crosswise of their path toward the mountains. One quarter mile down, the gulch widened out and deepened. Missy could now see the thin ribbon of a stream far down below them, and figured that was where they were headed. Numerous slashes in the ground cut down into the sides of this gulch, and the possibility of hiding places lay everywhere. About halfway down to the stream there was a very long dead cottonwood log, which stretched out from the east.

As they approached it, Joshua said, "See that log down there?"

"Yes, sir," Missy replied.

"When we ride by it, I'm not going to stop," Joshua said. "I'm going to swing you down with my left arm, and you need to walk to the end of the log and wait for me."

Missy whimpered, "I'm scared. I don't want to leave you. If he gets me again . . ."

"I know you're scared," he said firmly. "So am I, but

there's no other way. I'll come and get you, but I have to throw him off our trail."

"Maybe he won't follow us," she said hopefully.

"Maybe, young lady, cows will fly," he replied. "Get ready."

They came to the log, and Missy held on to Joshua's axe handle–like forearm while he swung her off the saddle onto the log. He turned his head and nodded at her, as she looked after him with a frightened faraway look in her eyes.

He kicked his heels to the horse as the trail narrowed down and steepened. The big paint's rear end almost slid on the ground as he plunged down the path. Strongheart figured that, with the deep sand in the gulch's bottom, the killer would have trouble telling that the horse's load had been lightened. He knew Blood Feather would assume he was heading into the thick areas to hide, so he would make it look that way. He figured this might buy him more time.

The big horse seemed to sense Joshua's desperation and stepped out with more urgency now. They plunged down as quickly as possible and within fifteen minutes were in the knee-deep stream. Strongheart knew that whoever it was who'd said you can lose someone by walking down a stream was either full of bull or a dude. Footprints in a clear stream bottom hold for a while. Besides that, many rocks get turned over and scarred by the horse's hooves. Joshua counted on that.

He went west up the stream, toward the thick undergrowth, but finally climbed out on a grassy area, passing up more obvious spots where tracks could be hidden easier. Again, that was what Joshua counted on. Blood Feather would look more carefully at the most obvious places to leave the stream and would probably pay very little attention to this one.

Leaving his horse ground-reined in a little grove just beyond the grassy area, an apparent tributary course when the stream overflowed its banks during the rainy season, Joshua climbed from the saddle and pulled his extra cotton shirt out of his bedroll. Crawling forward on his hands and knees, he carefully dried the wet grass with his shirt, checking to be sure he had left no threads. He then carefully covered each hoofprint in the soft ground with dirt he brought from the depression beyond the grass, before he manipulated the grass back into place. This took the Pinkerton a long time to accomplish, but he knew being thorough would save his life and, more importantly, the little girl's. If it hadn't been for her, he might have just set up an ambush and taken on Blood Feather, but he could not let his ego get in the way of her safety. Satisfied that he had done a thorough job, he moved his horse beyond the depression and covered up those tracks as well.

He kept looking back up the giant slice in the earth they had come through, but he saw no sign of the psychotic warrior. He knew that he would be coming.

He mounted up and rode slowly along a long, flat rock outcropping. He went from this to each new outcropping with as few steps as possible in sand or soft dirt. In each instance where he had to, however, he dropped down off the horse and cleared away the tracks again. Strongheart passed the area where he had originally entered the stream and kept going up the watercourse. He then had Missy walk along the log and from rock to rock, until she reached him and jumped onto Gabe's rump, where he caught her.

One quarter mile along, he found a flat spot, turned the horse around, and spurred him toward the far bank. Reaching a ten-foot-high cut in the banks on both sides, he leaned out over the horse's neck and let Gabe fly.

He turned his head to Missy and said, "Hang on tight!"

The big horse cleared the cut with inches to spare and Joshua reined him up on the far bank and dismounted, patting the steed on his muscular neck.

"Good boy, Gabriel," Strongheart said.

Blood Feather had a couple potatoes in his parfleche. He took one out and chopped it repeatedly with his big knife, then mashed it. He then mixed it into a poultice and applied it to the bullet hole, pushing it into his arm. He covered this with moss and wrapped it all tight with leather and tied it down with several leather thongs.

He mounted up and headed west at a fast trot. The *wasicun* had a big head start on him, but he planned to catch up, kill him, eat his heart, kill the little girl, and eat her entirely. Blood Feather reasoned that consuming her whole body would bring him the greatest medicine. He would decorate his war shirt with strands of her bright red hair and make a separate necklace of her fingers.

Now that he thought about this, he felt a new twisted sense of hope. Blood Feather simply never felt anything, except an occasional minor thrill when he took a life. He lived for those moments when he at least had some emotion in his life, and he was always after those elusive moments when he could really feel alive. Strongheart was such a powerful enemy, and the little girl was touched by the Great Spirit, he felt. Stealing her medicine would make him truly alive and mighty, he was sure.

It was well after dark when Zach Banta heard the knock on his door. He saw Strongheart through the crack and opened it with a big smile.

"Wal, I reckon," he said. "We got a sleepy little princess here. Reckon you two could use a bit a grub."

Joshua stuck out his hand and shook with the old man, grinning simply from the contagious effect of the old man's twinkling blue eyes. Zach handed Strongheart a cup of coffee and stoked the fire up in his big stone fireplace. He opened the lid on the big cast iron pot hanging over the fire and stuck a large soup ladle in.

"Bet ya would like some nice soup and bread with a

glass a milk," Zach said. "If yer gonna be the queen a England someday, ya gotta eat good vittles so you'll stay purty and grow up big and strong."

Missy giggled and said, "I'm not a princess. I'm just a little girl."

Zach winked at her, saying, "Yer a little girl awright, but yer certainly a princess, too. Even if ya ain't from England."

Missy climbed into Strongheart's lap and said, "He is funny."

She lay her head against his chest and was asleep in less than a minute.

Zach said, "Wal, reckon ya don't need no war paint with them dark circles under yore eyes. You two outta git sleep whilst I stand watch."

Strongheart took a sip of coffee, saying, "No time to rest, Zach. I need to get her back to Cañon City and then locate her ma and get them out of the area. I guess because of her red hair, he was worshipping her in a way. They need to get on a train and head back east where he has no chance of finding her."

"Look how exhausted she is," Zach said seriously. "You both are. Rest heah. He comes, I'll blow him outta the saddle with mah Sharps."

"I know you can, old partner," Joshua said, "but I have to get her out of the area completely. I was hoping to get a bite of food from you and we are off."

Strongheart, as much as he hated doing it, awakened Missy and set her at the table. Zach handed each of them large bowls of stew, and the girl woke right up, eating like she had never been fed. Banta kept the stew, coffee, milk, and bread coming, and the two stuffed themselves.

When he first arrived, Joshua had grained Gabriel, after stripping off his saddle and bridle. The horse sensed his urgency though and was ready to go. Gabe knew he was near home, and the closer he got, the more excited he would get. This was a familiar comfortable place, but Cañon City was home to the big horse. Missy slept while Joshua took the time to give Gabe a good brushing and rubdown, then saddled up. The horse pranced in the stall, anxious to get his legs moving again.

Instead of taking the stage road, Strongheart decided to go directly along the river trail, straight ahead to Cañon City. Actually, at Parkdale they would leave the river and head up Eight Mile Hill, cross the plateau, and drop back down one thousand feet, coming out at the west end of Cañon City, just below Razor Ridge, which decades later would be called Skyline Drive and would be a major tourist attraction. He would make camp along the river at some point, get a few hours' sleep, then finish the ride into Cañon City, but first he wanted the big pinto to eat up some miles and put more distance between him and the monster.

The sun was still fairly high in the western sky the next afternoon when Joshua Strongheart pranced into Cañon City with Missy holding his waistline. The first person that noticed it set off the alarm to others, and by the time they reached Annabelle's restaurant, a small cheering crowd had gathered out in Main Street.

A broadly smiling, crying Belle stood in the front of the townspeople, and it looked to Strongheart like every woman in the crowd was dabbing at tears. Strongheart stopped in front of them all and handed the little girl to Belle, who hugged her like someone might try to steal her away. The two just cried happy tears while the townspeople applauded to beat the band. The news was quickly spreading and the crowd was quickly growing larger.

Joshua dismounted, and a cowpuncher grabbed his reins with a smile and a nod, and a dozen other men slapped him on the back. He went forward, engulfing Annabelle and the

little girl in his big grasp, and he and Belle kissed softly and
for a full minute. As their faces pulled apart, they gave each
other knowing looks that told each other volumes.

The man from the livery stable two doors away took the
horse, saying, "Joshua, ole Gabe heah is plumb wore out.
Ah'l take care a him fer ya and give him some rest and
food."

Strongheart nodded and smiled, saying, "Thank you
very much, my friend."

They went inside the café, and Annabelle locked the door
behind them, opening it only when the sheriff came in. He
shook hands with Strongheart, giving him a wink and a nod.

The monstrous killer was atop one of the steep ridges
overlooking Cotopaxi, watching the activity there for any
signs of Strongheart or the flaming red hair of the little girl.
He watched through his binoculars as Zach Banta tilled the
road into Cotopaxi over and over, making small furrows in
the ground on the road surface. The serial killer only knew
it was a *wasicun* activity, not realizing that Zach was
destroying all traces of Strongheart's tracks coming and
going. Blood Feather would pick up the trail, however, by
simply riding around the small settlement from the western
part of the Arkansas River to the eastern end of it and finding Strongheart's tracks again.

Sheriff Bengley took a sip of coffee, saying, "Annabelle,
you did not tell him about Mrs. Vinnola yet."

Joshua looked at Belle, and she said, "Oh yes, my cousin
Lucy is back and staying with me. She is going to be so
excited to see Missy. Missy, your momma is back from the
hospital!"

They all looked again and sighed, as they saw that the
little girl was sitting up at the table but had fallen fast asleep.

Joshua said, "What happened with Lucy?"

"They believe," Annabelle said, "that she has an allergy
to a flowering plant which grows all over her yard. Once

she got away from the plant, she started breathing better. By the time she got to Glenwood Springs, she was almost completely back to normal. She simply must remain away from that plant and she will be fine."

"Do they know which plant causes this?" Strongheart asked.

"Yes, they think it is a flower, goldenrod," Belle replied. "The doctor told her not many flowers ever cause allergies, but that is one of the worst when it does occur, and she has goldenrod all around her house."

Strongheart said, "Does she have friends or relatives she can stay with back east? We have to get this little girl out of here right away. They must go back east on the train. That is the only way Missy will be safe."

Belle said, "Yes, she does. How soon must she leave?"

"Today! Now!" Joshua said. "This killer is touched in the head. When he held Missy hostage, he treated her like she was an idol or a deity. She could not understand his words, but he was worshipping her. I would guess her bright red hair has a lot to do with it, but lately she felt more and more in danger. Our senses tell us a lot, and she got more scared in the last few days with him."

The sheriff said, "Why don't we let your horse rest. I will have a buggy brought up and two deputies. They can take you to the house, then to the depot."

"That is good, Frank," Joshua said. "Thank you. I will accompany them to Pueblo and then see they get on the train for Denver. Then I will feel a whole lot better."

Belle said, "If the deputies will be around, why don't you two get some sleep first, then leave?"

Strongheart said, "No, I guarantee you he is coming hell-bent for leather. In fact, I would prefer you ride with me to Pueblo and back."

He added, "I shot him in the arm and know I got him good, but he will not let that stop him."

She said, "Well, you are going to get some food in you."

It was not stated as a question or suggestion, so Joshua shut his mouth and waited while she fixed a plate each for him and the little girl.

The sheriff headed for the door and said, "I have one deputy outside now, but will have two come shortly with a buggy."

Joshua got up and walked over to him, extending a handshake. "Thanks so much, Frank."

Frank smiled and walked out.

Strongheart walked to her and swept Belle into his big arms. They kissed long and passionately, then stepped back.

She said, "I missed you."

Joshua said, "I love you, Belle. I have held back because I kept worrying about marrying you and having you vulnerable because of my work. I had decided we could never marry, but while I was gone I thought about you all the time."

Her heart leapt at the prospect of thinking he might propose. A tear crept into the corner of one eye.

Strongheart said, "Belle, we live in a tough country and you are a tough woman. I could not think of ever living my life without you by my side. I love you with all my heart, darling. Will you marry me?"

"Oh yes, yes, yes, a thousand time yes!" she said, kissing him deeply again.

Joshua said, "Not the most romantic setting, but it was something I needed to say or burst."

"Oh, Joshua," she said, "I don't care. I have prayed for this moment for so long!"

Her eyes glistened.

Strongheart said, "Honey, I hate to get out of the moment, but we better move fast. I am really worried about getting Missy and her mom out of here. When they are gone, we can shop for an engagement ring in Pueblo."

She went back to preparing food, saying, "No, you are going to sleep for a day at least before we do anything."

The buggy arrived and took them to the house a half hour later. Missy was wide awake after being told her mommy was there. They pulled up, and she jumped down, running to the door of Belle's house. The door opened, and Lucille came out to sweep her little girl up in her arms. She hugged her and kissed her over and over.

She then set Missy down and ran forward to hug Joshua and say, "Oh, God bless you, Joshua! Thank you so much! Thank you so much! I can never thank you enough! You saved my baby."

She started crying and threw her face against his chest, hugging him tightly while she sobbed. The two deputies just grinned, and Belle got choked up.

Lucy pulled away and grabbed Missy again, picking her up and mouthing the words to Joshua "Thank you. God bless you."

They went inside.

Grabbing Lucille's suitcase and throwing it on the bed, Belle explained, "You have to move back east immediately and get Missy out of here."

Lucille said, "I don't understand. Didn't you kill that beast of a human, Joshua?"

"No," he said, "and he is following us. I wounded him, but I know he is headed this way. He is obsessed with Missy, and we must get her out of the area, far away. We are going to ride on the train with you to Pueblo and stay with you until you are on your way to Denver."

Lucille started crying again and said, "Joshua Strongheart, you will be in my prayers every day the rest of my life. We heard stories of this killer and I was certain she was lost forever, but you returned my Missy to me. God bless you!"

Strongheart said, "You gave her a little pocketknife she showed me when she was here before. She kept it hidden in her shoe and used it to cut through the leather straps she was bound with. She jumped on a packhorse and ran away with him chasing her. Your little girl is the hero, not me. You have taught her to be a survivor, Lucy, which will always serve her well."

Both Belle and Lucy listened with mouths open, shaking their heads in amazement. They looked at Missy, who was fast asleep on Belle's davenport.

Lucy was soon packed, and Strongheart carried the still-sleeping little girl to the buggy. They left for the train depot. Within an hour, they were on their way to Pueblo. In Pueblo, they got lucky again, and quickly put Lucy and Missy on the train for Denver, where they would make a connection in a few hours and head back east. Once Strongheart got them on the Denver train, he was much more comfortable.

It would not be that many years before Pueblo would start being called "the Pittsburgh of the West." However, Joshua Strongheart was not interested in industry or the railroad yards. He wanted to take Belle shopping.

Holding hands, they walked along the street in downtown Pueblo, a town that had started out as a place Indians liked coming to winter at the confluence of the Arkansas River and the large Fountain Creek. Joshua and Annabelle found a mercantile that had a collection of jewelry and fine china. Two very large bearded men who looked to be teamsters walked in. Both smelled like a brewery.

They stared at Belle and Strongheart, who were now acting very romantic, snuggling and kissing. The men at first whispered and snickered, and Joshua knew trouble was coming. They finally approached the couple.

The larger one said, "This makes me sick to my stomach. I cain't stand seeing no red nigger hand-holding a white woman."

Here it was, Strongheart thought, and he stood ready for battle, sizing up both potential opponents. He stared at them but spoke to Annabelle, saying, "Darling, if we are to be married, I warn you we will occasionally hear remarks like this from ignorant people."

Both men spread apart a little to give each other swinging and kicking room. One pulled an axe handle from a basket and was ready to use it. Belle stepped forward, putting her hand on Joshua's forearm.

"It's okay, darling," she said, smiling at the two behemoths. "I just read an article the other day in *Harper's Weekly*, and it stated that they did a study and discovered that men who make such statements do so because of immense feelings of inadequacy. Usually the problem stems from such men having very tiny penises."

Joshua could not believe what he had just heard from his fiancée. He turned his head and stared at her, but he also could not help but notice how red the faces of both men were. They stared at Belle, then each other, with startled looks and then, as if on a silent signal, simply turned and quickly left the store.

Belle's face was red, but she looked at Joshua and started laughing, and he just bellowed with laughter.

"Where did that come from?" he said, still laughing.

She said, "I just made it up. I didn't want any fighting today."

"I never heard anything like that in my life," said the storeowner who was behind them, tears of laughter spilling down his cheeks. "I could not believe how quickly those two varmints egressed the store. That was some slice of pumpkin pie, young lady," he added. He turned his head slightly and said, "Did you hear what the young lady said, Henrietta?"

Joshua and Belle, still laughing, turned their heads to see a roly-poly, gray-haired woman in a gingham dress literally lying across a table of linens, laughing so hysterically she could barely breathe.

It seemed almost providential that they would find the engagement and wedding rings they wanted in that store. Belle told Joshua she could simply wear her former wedding ring, since he had gone through so much to get it back for her when they first met. He was insistent though that her rings would be picked out by them together. She found several that were less expensive, but he could tell there was one set she was drawn to. He told the storekeeper that was what they wanted. Her eyes glistened as he paid for the rings. He then stuck them in his pocket and led her outside.

"Where are we going?" she asked.

He led her outside town to the banks of Fountain Creek, which had Russian olive and manzanita trees along them. There now were no people around, and there was still daylight in the sky. He knelt down in front of the fast-flowing creek and said, "Annabelle, I have loved you since the first moment I saw you. Anything and everything I do is simply to make you proud of me. Please say yes, you will marry me and spend the rest of our lives together."

Tears filled her eyes and she could hardly breathe she loved this man so much.

"Yes, Joshua," she said. "Oh, my word, yes. I love you with all my heart, darling, and will forever."

He placed the engagement ring on her finger, stood, and they kissed long and slowly.

Their ride home to Cañon City did not begin until right after dark, and the whole way they talked about the future and their plans. At the depot, they found a neighbor with a wagon who offered them a ride to the house. Belle kept looking at her new ring, then she would look at this brave hero of hers.

They went into her house and soon had a fire going and started kissing on the couch. Strongheart wanted this woman so badly, and she would soon be his wife. He got up and took a deep breath.

She stood, and he said, "I am going to head to the Hot Springs Hotel, honey, and will see you for breakfast in the morning."

He took one step and her hand grabbed his. She pulled him close.

Belle said, "Joshua Strongheart, you are my fiancé now, officially. You will soon be my husband, and as far as I am concerned, you already are. You are not leaving me tonight."

She turned and led him by the hand toward her bedroom.

In the morning, they walked to the café right after daybreak. After the very long day and longer night, Joshua felt strangely very refreshed. He was in love, deeply in love. He felt this had to be a love like his biological father, Claw Marks, had had with his mother, but he would not ride off like his father. He planned to be with Belle until death came for one of them, hopefully many decades into the future. They got to the café, and he carried firewood in for her.

The sheriff came in for breakfast, and grabbing a cup of coffee, Joshua sat down with him.

"Sheriff, until I can track down this killer," Strongheart asked, "can you spare a deputy to keep an eye on Belle when I am not around?"

"I sure can, Strongheart," the lawman replied. "I have a good deputy, Stephen Vaughn. Big man himself, maybe three hundred pounds. I will put him at your disposal starting this morning."

Joshua stayed at the restaurant until Deputy Vaughan arrived riding a big bay Morgan-Thoroughbred cross. He had a deep, booming voice and low-key relaxed manner. He wore a Russian .44 in a cross-draw holster, and by the wear and tear of the leather Strongheart could tell he had practiced that draw many hours.

Joshua walked out of the back door of the restaurant and looked at the new McClure House hotel just a block away. Mrs. Maria M. Sheetz was the first manager of the hotel, and it had sixty rooms, three suites, and even ten indoor bathrooms in it. Little did Joshua know that the McClure House, which was one of the most popular hotels in the area, would be sold to British investors in twenty-six years, at the turn of the century, and renamed the Strathmore Hotel. It would have shocked him to know that it would still be standing in 2012 completely renovated. The redbrick building was solid. Right then, it was brand-new and had just officially opened, although it had been built two years earlier, in 1872, and William McClure had used red bricks made right there in Fremont County.

He wondered if he should take a room there or at the Hot Springs Hotel at the edge of town, and he decided on the McClure House. He would make sure he got a room where he could keep an eye on Belle's restaurant, too, or at least the back of it. He had spent the night with Belle and knew she would want him to stay, but he did not want any gossips wagging their tongues about her any more than they already were because he was a half-breed.

Strongheart knew how cruel people could be. He had grown up with it. First, he was the bastard love child of an Indian and a white woman, so even while very small he could sense rejection from some. Then, when his mother married Dan Cooper, his stepfather, who became a real dad to him, things got much better. People had no choice. Dan was a tall, quiet man who was quite serious, but crossing him, by any man, was as wise as trying to lasso a cyclone.

He fondly recalled the time that the town blacksmith's son started teasing him at school, calling him "half-breed" and "red mongrel." Dan came home for lunch and found Joshua hiding in the barn, and streaks on his face showed he had been crying,

"You been playing hooky, son?" the lawman asked.

Joshua Strongheart simply would not lie, so he shyly said, "Yes, sir."

Dan said, "Get me a stout switch."

Joshua hung his head and walked out the barn door, hearing the shout after him, "Never drop your head down, boy. Hold it high, even when you're in trouble. Especially when you're in trouble."

He came back five minutes later with a stick he'd cut and shaved with his pocketknife and handed it to Dan, who sat on an upended barrel. Dan held the switch in his right hand.

He said, "You know you do not miss school, period. And you know you are getting a whipping, but first you get to have your say. What do you have to say about this, Joshua?"

"Nothing, sir," young Joshua said. "I don't have an excuse. I am sorry, Pa. I'm ready to take my whipping."

"Well, boy, you said the right thing," the graying marshal said, "but it is just you and me here. You were crying before I came in. Why?"

"I'm sorry I cried, Pa," Joshua exclaimed, panicked thinking that he would get a worse spanking now.

Dan grinned, saying, "Never apologize for crying, son. I cry myself sometimes."

"You cry?" Joshua said, totally surprised.

"Sure, sometimes a man needs to cry," his stepdad explained. "Just don't do it that often. Womenfolk want and need a *man* around, not some dandy, so always be a man of parts. Now, what happened?"

"Well," young Joshua said, "you know the blacksmith's son Billy?"

Dan nodded.

Joshua said, "He started calling me 'half-breed' and 'red mongrel' and 'blanket nigger.' I ignored him, Pa, but he kept it up and got some of the other kids to do it, too."

"Then what?"

"He shoved me, Pa, so I hit him the way you taught me and gave him a bloody nose and knocked him down," the boy stated, "then the teacher just saw me hitting him and told me I was getting a paddling today."

"Did you tell her that he shoved you?"

"Yes, sir," Joshua replied. "And she said that he only shoved me, but I hit him, so I was in trouble. I didn't think it was fair and didn't know what I should do, so I acted like a yellow belly and played hooky."

"Okay," Dan said. "Yer not getting a spanking today or tomorrow. I'm taking you to school tomorrow and am sending a message to the blacksmith to meet us there with his boy, and we will have a meeting with the schoolmarm. Get out of here and do your chores."

"Yes, sir!" Joshua said, running toward the barn, a big smile of relief on his face and a ton of worry sliding off his shoulders while he ran.

He could not wait until the next morning.

The next day as they walked to the school Joshua was excited, as there was no red hue in the sky.

He remembered his father had told him before many times, "Red sky in the morning, cowboys take warning, but a red sky at night is a cowboy's delight."

It would be sunny this day, and his pa was defending him. He simply couldn't feel any better and had a definite spring in his step. They walked at a brisk pace, and young Joshua had to take two steps for each one his stepdad took. He wondered if he would ever be that tall when he grew up.

They walked into the schoolyard and up the steps to the wooden schoolhouse. The teacher had the other kids playing outside, who were genuinely curious about what was going on. As the meeting started, every few minutes some child would try to peek in the windows but be shooed away by Miss Vendetti, the schoolmarm.

Dan presented the case in a matter-of-fact way, and the very large blacksmith seemed to be frustrated. He was not used to speaking in such a meeting, only to customers talking about shoeing horses in his stable, where the surroundings were familiar. As the meeting wore on, he seemed to get more frustrated and was soon on his feet pacing. Dan stood up, too, being cautious.

Dan stared at the blacksmith, saying, "You know, Whitney, what really bothered me about the story?"

"What, Marshal?" the blacksmith growled.

"The fact that your boy here referred to Joshua as a red mongrel," the lawman replied. "Does your son at his age have a big enough vocabulary to even know what a mongrel is or to use the term 'blanket nigger'?"

Whitney's large face grew beet red, and then before he could speak, Dan turned his attention to the man's son, Billy.

"Boy," Dan said, "can you tell me what a mongrel is?"

"A person?" the boy obviously guessed.

Dan said, "So that was a term he heard at home."

Whitney tried to step forward, being used to intimidating people with his bulk, height, and brawn. Then it dawned on him that he would never intimidate this marshal ever. He relaxed his stance a little and folded his calf leg–sized arms in front of his chest.

Dan ignored this and then turned his attention to the schoolteacher.

"Miss Vendetti," Dan said, "I also do not understand why my son is supposed to be punished for defending himself. That is not fair at all, and the Constitution of the United States guarantees all of us the right to defend ourselves. So does the Good Book. Can you explain this to me?"

She immediately displayed a haughty demeanor and, hands on her hips said, "Marshal Cooper, I most certainly can explain why. Joshua struck him very hard with his fist, right in the face. It was horrible. There was blood everywhere."

Pointing at the bully, she said, "Yes, Billy acted out first, and we talked about it. However, even though he was wrong, he only shoved Joshua. He did not strike him with a fist or even attempt to."

Dan laughed out loud.

"So, ma'am," he responded, "you feel that shoving a person does not constitute an assault on a person, any person?"

"That is absolutely correct, Marshal," she said angrily. "It pales in comparison to fisticuffs."

"So," Dan said, "a person shoving another cannot hurt the other person?"

"Indeed not!" came the terse reply.

Dan walked slowly over toward Whitney, and when he got near him their size difference became quite obvious, as Whiney towered over the six-foot-one-inch lawman and was twice as large as the older man. He stiffened up a little because Dan had come within a few feet of him, but he kept his arms crossed.

Joshua wondered if his pa was at a loss for words, as he had not replied.

Suddenly, without any warning, in an explosive flash of movement, Marshal Dan Cooper launched himself forward, bringing all his weight to bear, and his hands shot out, striking the blacksmith on both shoulders and shoving hard. The 250-pounder, off-guard and off-balance, flew backward, the weight of his body sending him unceremoniously through the one- by twelve-inch pine-board wall two feet behind him, with a thunderous crash. Whitney landed with a thud on his back in the schoolyard and lay there unmoving, knocked out when his head hit the wall.

Dan smiled and gently grabbed a beaming, proud Joshua by the scruff of his neck, saying softly, "I am proud of you, son, for defending yourself against a bully. Miss Vendetti, tomorrow one of my deputies and I will rebuild that wall, and I will bring new lumber and nails to do so. In the meantime, Joshua is taking the day off from school, and he and I are going fishing. Do you have any questions?"

She stared, mouth open, at the unconscious blacksmith and then back at the marshal.

"No, sir," she replied. "You made your point quite emphatically. I will see you tomorrow morning, Joshua. Have fun with your father today."

Dan grabbed her fire bucket from next to her desk and stepped through the gaping hole in the wall amid the crowd of awestruck children. He poured the water on Whitney's face, and the big man sat up suddenly, sputtering and shaking the water from his head. Dan handed the bucket to Joshua, who, grinning from ear to ear, ran to the well and filled it before returning it to its resting place next to Miss Vendetti's old desk.

Whitney looked around in a daze, shaking his head. Dan grinned and stuck his hand down. The big man took it and was pulled to his feet.

Dan grabbed his arm and said, "Are you okay, Whitney?"

Shaking his head again, the burly man said, "I guess. What happened?"

Dan just patted him in the back and chuckled, then turned and walked away.

Joshua followed his stepdad through his gathered classmates, his chest puffed out like a peacock's, and they walked back toward Dan's office. The boy had never been so proud.

"Thank you for standing up for me, Pa," Joshua said.

"Never start a fight, Joshua, and do not strike first unless you can tell the other guy is about to strike. And when you do get in a fight, you win, and you do not take water or give up ever. Understand?"

"Yes, sir."

"Good," the lawman replied. "This is a tough world, and a man has to be tough to survive in it. As tough as you might become, though, you treat every lady you meet like she is fine china and make sure others treat all women that way, too. Understand?"

"Yes, Pa. I give you my word," Joshua said solemnly, and the weight of this commitment hit him squarely.

Although kids talked about the traumatic and exciting event for weeks, none of the adult participants ever mentioned the incident again.

Strongheart decided he would indeed take a room at the McClure House, and he headed there, less than a block away from the restaurant, and registered, getting a room facing the back of her café.

Joshua's head was spinning because of exhaustion. He had to get some sleep and certainly had not the night before. Anytime Belle had not been giving him her full attention, he was doing that for her, staying awake and alert and getting up several times to look out windows.

He walked into the café later, and she beamed when she saw him enter. She rushed over to the door, threw her arms around his neck, and kissed him passionately. He quickly explained about getting a room at the McClure House and why, and she protested a little but was also relieved. Like Joshua, she thought: Why give the tongue-waggers something else to talk about? They would create enough on their own.

"Is Deputy Vaughn here?" he asked.

"Yes, he is at the far northwest corner table drinking

coffee," she answered. "He seems very diligent. He tried to bring a chair in the kitchen here, but you have seen me zip around when the café is busy, and I shooed him out to the dining room."

Strongheart was glad to hear that the big lawman truly had her welfare at heart. He gave her a kiss and told her he was going to go flop on his bed and just sleep, so he could be fresh and refreshed.

Belle grinned at him and flirtingly said, "Well, my dear future husband, I may come over to that nice new hotel and knock on your door."

Joshua grinned, saying, "Sweetheart, I love you more than life itself, but as tired as I am, if you do that, I will put six Colt .45 slugs through the door."

She laughed and went back to her cooking, while he entered the dining room. He spotted the big deputy and went over to his table. Both men nodded, and Joshua sat down across from him.

He said, "Deputy, everything under control?"

Vaughn said, "Please call me Steve. Yes, sir, all is good so far. I just cannot figure out how she stays so busy in that kitchen and then smiles so much and stays friendly with every customer."

Strongheart said, "Don't call me Mr. either, please. It's Joshua or Strongheart. Belle is an amazing woman, amazing. She does bring in help sometimes when she gets really busy, but she still does the work of ten women. Now, about this Blood Feather. He is so brazen, so cold, so cunning, and is obviously very mad. Do not take any chances with him."

Steve said, "Joshua, listen to me, partner. One thing I can do is shoot, and if any seven-foot-tall Indian walks through that door, I will light him up like a church Christmas tree and apologize later if he is the wrong seven-footer."

Strongheart started chuckling. Then his head started swimming again.

He stuck out his hand and shook, saying, "I have a room at the McClure House, so if you have any problems, give me a shout or fire a shot. I got a room looking at the back of the café. You take care of that woman. She is going to be my wife soon, you know."

Steve winked and said, "Yes, I heard. Congratulations."

Strongheart went to the hotel, and into his room, and fell asleep on his bed, only taking his gun and knife off first. He still had his boots on, and he slept the sleep of the dead for hours. It was dinnertime when Joshua awakened. He freshened up and headed back to the café, and got a wonderful shock. There was his friend Chris Colt, the scout he'd become partnered with at Fort Union, and his boss, Lucky.

He had barely sat down with both men before Belle was bringing out plates of large steaks, baked potatoes, and fresh bread for the trio. She was busy, but she sat down briefly at their table, after taking a plateful to Deputy Vaughn.

"Chris," she said, "Joshua told me all about you and your adventures together. I was just thinking. He said you were going up north to be a chief of scouts for the Seventh Cavalry?"

Chris said, "Yes, ma'am."

She said, grinning, "Don't you ma'am me, Chris Colt. You call me Belle or Annabelle."

He said, "Okay, Belle."

Belle said, "If you ever get to Bismarck in Dakota Territory, my first cousin, Shirley Ebert, owns a restaurant there and is the best cook in the West. She is a woman to latch on to, and I have a hunch if you two would meet you would want to latch on to each other."

Little did she know how prophetic her words were, because in just over a year, Chris Colt would indeed meet, fall in love with, and marry her cousin Shirley.

"So," Joshua said, "what brings you two to Cañon City and how did you meet?"

Lucky said, "We met at Fort Union because we had some other business zere."

Chris said, "I had to come back to pick up two scouts for the Seventh Cavalry who had been instrumental for us down south in the Apache campaign. I sent them on with the train. Lucky heard my name and told me he felt he knew me, because you had written such good things about me in your report on Quanah Parker."

Strongheart grinned, saying, "Got caught lyin' again. You headed back to Chicago, Boss?"

"*Oui*—I mean yes," Lucky replied, as always trying to catch himself and stick with English and not lapse into French words.

"Are you okay?" Lucky said.

Joshua said, "What do you mean?"

He said, "I read your telegraph and heard from the sheriff, and from Annabelle, about all you have been through saving that little girl. How badly deed you wound that keeler?"

Joshua said, "I hit him good on the arm and probably broke some bones, but a wound like that won't slow that man down. He is very touched in the head, Boss, and the toughest I have ever faced."

"Well, I have a new assignment for you, but right now, Mr. Pinkerton wants everything, all resources, behind you to get thees man," Lucky replied. "He wants all men to know you do not kill a Pinkerton man and get away weeth it. But you must be exhausted. How are you?"

"He is not going to tell you," Chris said, holding a forkful of steak in front of his lips, "He'll make it work."

He ate his food and grinned.

Lucky said, "How do you know?"

Strongheart grinning himself and said, "Because that is what Colt would do. He understands."

The men gave each other a knowing look, they were so much alike.

"Why don't I put you both up at the hotel I am staying at?"

Lucky said, "No, thank you, Joshua. We both agreed to take thees queeck side trip to see you, but we both have deadlines."

Colt said, "Yeah, I sent those two trackers on ahead, and I don't want them to get near Fort Robinson and then get lost. It might make me look bad."

Joshua and Lucky chuckled.

Belle came out from the kitchen and gave Chris and Lucky big hugs, telling them good-bye. She insisted Joshua saddle up and escort them to the train depot to see them off, so he did. Their train left in an hour.

The sun was getting close to the mountains, waiting to tuck itself in for the night behind those rocky sentinels. As he rode along the river road, Strongheart spotted a familiar house almost overgrown with beautiful fragrant flowers. He dismounted and left Gabe outside a white rose-covered wooden trellis and entered the gate.

The door was opened by a very slight and bent gray-haired woman with hands that were gnarled from years of hard work and whose leathery wrinkled skin creased her face like an old mining trail map. Although her grin was half-toothless, it was very pleasant, and Strongheart could tell that maybe fifty or sixty years earlier, she had probably been quite the looker.

He doffed his hat, saying, "Ma'am, sorry to bother you. I live here and my name is Joshua Strongheart."

She laughed, saying, "Oh hell, I know who you are, young man. How could I miss you?"

She then laughed at her own joke, and he grinned broadly.

She added, "That's about like saying, 'Hello, ma'am, I am one of those mountains over there.' You are the most famous man in the territory. Now, what kin I do fer ya?"

"Well," he said, "I just got engaged and was wondering if I could purchase a dozen red roses from you."

"Just a minute," she said and disappeared into her house.

She reappeared right away with a dozen long-stemmed red roses and handed them to him, explaining, "I just picked these right before ya came. So ya finally asked the Widow Ebert? Good fer you, young man. You jest love her and be yourself, and you two will stay hitched a long time. Now, shoo."

He reached in his pocket for his money, saying, "How much do I owe you, ma'am?"

She turned from the door and threw her hand up in the air, saying, "Pshaw!" Then she walked into the little house.

Strongheart chuckled, shaking his head, and mounted up. He would give the dozen roses to his love and then get his saddlebags and bedroll and move them to the McClure House.

Strongheart rode the short distance to the café with thoughts about his life together with Belle, and he pictured them having little children. Missy was such a precious and brave little thing, she really impressed him and made him wish for daughters. He was determined to make sure Belle was well guarded and then go out and find Blood Feather and kill him. He had to eliminate that threat from her life, as well as his own. Any threat after Blood Feather would pale in comparison to the danger he presented both Joshua and Belle.

He tied Gabriel up to the hitching rack on Main Street and went in the front door of the café this time. Although it was getting late, there were still several customers. Strongheart's eyes went immediately to the far corner, and Deputy Vaughn was not seated there. Joshua figured he must be in the back, and Joshua wanted to be alone when he handed Belle the roses, but he went into the kitchen anyway.

Belle was not there, nor was Stephen Vaughn, and Joshua's

heart dropped. All he could picture was Blood Feather bra-
zenly coming into the café and kidnapping her away just to
intimidate him. Although the killer was clearly insane Strongheart could now figure out some of the things he would do,
and that would fit right in. Joshua could hear his heart pounding in his ears, and his forehead felt like it was on fire. The
back door to the café was standing wide open.

Suddenly, a very large figure burst through the door, gun
in hand, and Strongheart's Colt Peacemaker was out of his
holster and cocked, pointing center mass at Deputy
Vaughn's chest. Joshua uncocked the gun and reholstered it.

Vaughn explained, "I have been watching and being
careful. A couple customers started complaining that their
food was taking too long, and I knew she sometimes would
stay back there if she had several orders to fill at once, and
then bring them all out at one time steaming hot. I decided
right then to come check on her. Then I went into a panic."

Joshua could tell the big man was already beating himself up, but even as scared as he was, Strongheart knew
there was only so much you could do. He looked around
and saw two steaks burned on the stove, and he went over
and removed them.

Joshua then saw that the big Navajo throw rug Belle kept
on the kitchen floor near the door was gone. He knew immediately that Blood Feather, maybe dressed like a cowboy or a
local, had come in the door, probably knocked her out, and
secreted her away rolled up in the rug. But, he wondered,
where would he take her? The most obvious choice would be
her house. Then Strongheart's hope soared. Maybe she had
received an emergency message to go to her house for something and run out.

Strongheart put his hand on the big deputy's shoulder,
as the man looked like he was near tears. "Look," Joshua
said, "I saw you, You were being careful. Don't start whipping yourself over this. We have to find her. I am going to

ride to her house. You start questioning everybody you see. Somebody saw something."

Joshua ran out, praying already in his mind, and leapt into the saddle doing a running mount. Gabriel knew something was amiss. He had him to Belle's house in just minutes. Strongheart jumped off, ground-reined the horse, and drew his gun as he ran into the house. The second he hit the door, his heart almost exploded. There was blood.

"Oh no, God no!" he said aloud as he followed the blood trail to the bedroom.

"Please God, please God protect her!" Joshua pleaded as he opened the door to the bedroom, and almost fainted.

There she lay on the bed, arms spread out wide, naked, staring at the ceiling. He saw the blood everywhere, and the hole in her chest where her heart had been, and a lone eagle feather drenched in her blood was on her face.

Strongheart dropped to his knees and wept, and then bawled. He screamed a primal scream and dashed out the door and around the house looking for tracks. The neighbor saw him.

"Joshua, is Annabelle okay?" the neighbor said. "I saw a big cowboy in a slicker driving a buckboard pull up, carry a rolled-up rug into the house, and he left a few minutes later. It just did not seem right."

Strongheart only shook his head. Stifling tears, he said, "How long ago?"

The man said, "No more than twenty, thirty minutes. Is she okay? Is everything all right?"

Strongheart said, "Belle is dead."

The man screamed and ran around in a circle beating his legs.

Strongheart went back into the house. He returned to Belle and covered her naked, bloody body. Then he removed the eagle feather and kissed her face. He sat there on the edge of the bed where they had become one the night before and held her hand, looking past the blood. He did not want to remember her like this, but as she had been. Tears streamed down his face, and then came a pounding on the door. He wiped all tears away.

Strongheart went to the door, and there was a crowd outside the house, and the sheriff and Vaughn were standing there. Both were obviously out of breath. They came in at Joshua's signal and followed him to the bedroom, spotting the terror on the way. The sheriff put his hand on Joshua's shoulder.

"I am so very sorry, Joshua. We will get this killer," he said determinedly. "I give you my solemn word."

Strongheart said, "No, you won't, Frank. I will."

The way Strongheart said those words made the sheriff not even consider arguing. He just nodded his head. Then he collected himself.

The sheriff became lawman again, and consoling friend, saying, "You do what you have to do. I will take care of the funeral arrangements, the coroner. I'll call Lucky, make sure her plants and flowers are watered. We will see to everything."

Joshua grabbed his rifle, bedroll, and saddlebags out of the corner and walked from the room. The neighbor came up immediately outside and shook his hand offering condolences, and Joshua could not help but notice that every woman in the large crowd was weeping. He mounted Gabe and headed to the McClure House, then checked out and rode right back to the house. More deputies had arrived and a doctor.

Strongheart said, "Sheriff, please keep folks out of the kitchen a few minutes. I have to get ready to leave."

The sheriff said, "Sure. But I have to ask. Where was the feather?"

Joshua said, "On her face, and she was naked. I covered

her and removed the feather. I did not want anybody to see her that way."

"Of course," the lawman replied.

Joshua said, "I am going to leave a few things here in the living room closet. Somebody needs to tend to Belle's horse.

He handed money to the sheriff and said, "I sometimes have paid the kid next door to do chores. Give that to him for feed and care."

He slowly removed his hat and put it in the closet, then retreated to the kitchen.

12

VENGEANCE

One half hour later, Joshua Strongheart emerged, and the house was filled with every type of person imaginable, and everybody just stared. Strongheart had his antelope-skin fringed shirt on, which stretched tight over his bulging muscles. His gunbelt and knife were around the shirt at his thin waistline, and he wore a Lakota breechcloth with decorative porcupine quillwork and beadwork. He had cut the sleeves off the shirt at the shoulders, and at the top of each bicep a leather band with a few ornaments was tied tightly, making the already-large muscles bulge even more so. His legs were bare and nothing but muscle upon muscle except for the many scars he bore. On his feet were Lakota soft-soled quilled moccasins. His hair was parted in the middle and braided Lakota style. Around his head he wore a beaded leather headband with a golden eagle feather and two bald eagle feathers hanging down and off at an angle. Strands of colored horse hair and several other decorations hung down across his neck. He wore a thick fur necklace adorned with each of the giant claws of the grizzly he had killed and that had left fresh claw and bite scars on his legs. What made jaws drop was his war paint, and the look on his face. He wore war paint that was black and covered the lower half of his face and a red raccoon-type mask painted across his eyes and temples. A vertical red stripe went from his hairline down his forehead, across his left eye, and down his cheek, all the way down to his neck.

In his hand was his powerful small hunting bow, and he wore his quiver of arrows on his back. Eyes straight ahead, Joshua walked past all the staring eyes, tied Gabriel's tail in a knot, and mounted up.

Everybody was seeing Strongheart the warrior, not the Pinkerton agent or the tall, handsome multiracial cowboy who quoted Shakespeare. They were seeing the son of *Siostukala*, Claw Marks, the late Lakota warrior, and in his eyes there was clearly a look of determination and passion. This was a man on a mission who would not be denied, and it clearly would be a mission of revenge.

The sheriff ran out while the crowd still watched spellbound.

He offered his hand to Joshua, who was already in the saddle, saying, "Good luck, Strongheart. My men found the wagon. He rode west out of town along the river road and had a large draft horse tied there. He abandoned the wagon and white man's clothes. He rode west."

Strongheart said, "He will go north."

The sheriff said, "Are you sure? How do you know?"

Joshua said, "I know how he thinks. That deputy is a good man and did nothing wrong to cause this. I think he is blaming himself."

The sheriff said, "Do you know when you will return?"

Strongheart looked ahead, saying, "You will know when you see Blood Feather's scalp hanging from my saddle horn."

With a simple "Thank you, Sheriff," he squeezed his calves to Gabe's sides and galloped toward Pikes Peak to the north.

It did not matter to him that it was now past dusk. Joshua Strongheart had a man to hunt down and kill. Finding him would be easy. Killing him would be tough, but Joshua did not care if he was killed himself doing so. Blood Feather was going to die.

He decided he would head north out of town through Red Canyon, so called for its obvious rock walls and monoliths. Then he would continue on up Shelf Road toward the southwestern slope of Pikes Peak. After skirting around Pikes Peak to the west, he would head northwesterly through the South Park area until he cut the giant's trail. Until then, he knew he could make camp in the rocks and have a nice fire and sleep, which he had to catch up on to take on such a killer. It would also give Strongheart many days of solitude, which is what he sorely needed. There was no doubt in Strongheart's mind what route *We Wiyake* would take.

Joshua galloped and fast-trotted Gabe through the lingering dusk, deciding he would have to make the northern part of Red Canyon, where there were many herds of mule deer and elk grazing because of the lush grass, as there was good water there fed by many springs and Four Mile Creek. He made camp there with simply a small fire hidden among the rocks and curled up with his head on his saddle. He let Gabe graze all night in a nearby pasture.

Joshua lay by the fire warm as toast and dreamed about the woman he loved. The dream was very realistic because it was a memory less than two years old. Belle had been kidnapped by the hombre Strongheart was after, Harlance McMahon. The man intercepted the stagecoach on Road Gulch Road, not far from the base of the mountain where Joshua had been mauled by the grizzly bear.

Joshua heard the distant creaking and rattling of the traces and wooden workings of the big red Concord stagecoach. He moved from his hiding spot beneath the branches of a stunted cedar and climbed into the saddle. Looking through the trees

with his telescope, he saw Harlance finally untie the thong
from the carbine barrel and remove it from Belle's head. He
had taken her away by tying the thong to his carbine and
around her neck, so even if Joshua shot him from afar the gun
would put a bullet neatly through her brain.

Holding Annabelle with his left hand, he stepped into
the road and held the cocked carbine with his other hand.

Again, he appeared to be in his wide-eyed panic mode.
The stage came into view, and the driver slowed the horses
to a stop, holding his hands high in the air.

Harlance yelled, "Toss the express gun down!"

The driver carefully grabbed the double-barreled
sawed-off shotgun at his side and tossed it into the road,
then raised his hands again.

He yelled, "I ain't carryin' no strongbox, mister!"

Harlance ran to the side of the stage and yelled inside,
"Everybody out, now!"

Five passengers, three women and two men, got out,
hands raised.

Harlance had started to shove Belle up into the coach,
when the driver decided to grab for his Russian .44 in a
cross-draw holster. Harlance shot and the women screamed.
The driver, dead, fell off the boot and released the brake.
The movement made the coach lurch and knocked Harlance
forward into the stage, landing on top of the rifle, which he
now grasped in both hands. The stage horses bolted and
started running in a panic down the winding Road Gulch
Stage Road, driverless. Annabelle, seated in the coach,
slammed both feet down on the rifle barrel, pinning Harlance's hands underneath it, and his legs hung out the door of
the stage as it raced down the dangerous road. Harlance
started cursing and threatening her, and she kept her weight
on the rifle.

She looked up and saw Gabriel racing along parallel to
the stagecoach, dashing through and around trees and

boulders. Just as she feared that the mighty horse would trip over a branch, log, or rock, and both would go tumbling down, Joshua looked over at her, smiled, and winked. It took her breath away. This man was her hero for the ages.

Gabe came off the ridge and ran alongside the stage in the road, coming up next to the lead horses. Strongheart tried to reach over and grab their reins but could not. Belle still put her weight on the rifle as Harlance screamed, kicked, and struggled. She screamed as Joshua suddenly leapt from his saddle over the back of the right lead horse and landed on the wooden shaft running along under the inside traces between the six-horse team. He started to rein the horses in, but just then Harlance broke free, left the rifle there, and leaned out firing his pistol, hitting Strongheart in the back of his left shoulder.

Joshua fell beneath the horses, and Harlance grinned, holstering his pistol, and crawled out the door, up onto the roof, and into the box.

In the meantime, Joshua was underneath the center shaft, walking with his hands down one by one as he slid underneath the stage, his heels dragging in the dirt, his butt held off the ground. Watching carefully he walked his hands down the undercarriage of the stage, grabbed the leather thoroughbraces, and swung his legs up from the underside of the luggage boot in the back. He pulled down with his knees, grabbed the boot, and pulled himself up onto the back of the coach.

Harlance saw him and slammed on the brake lever while he pulled hard on the reins, yelling, "Whoa! Whoa! Settle down!"

He got the stage stopped and spun around with his pistol firing wildly at Strongheart. Inside the coach, Belle had stopped crying. Joshua was alive! Now, she could feel him moving behind her.

Strongheart reached for his gun and it was gone. Harlance sensed it and stood up on the roof.

"Lost yer gun, dint ya, ya damned blanket nigger! Go haid and pop that little red face up again."

Joshua popped up and back down as a bullet flashed right over his head. Then he popped back up while Harlance cocked the pistol.

Strongheart's upraised right arm whipped forward, and his father's big knife flipped over once in the air, and buried itself in Harlance's hip. He screamed in pain, and Joshua knew this was his chance. He pulled himself up quickly onto the roof, and Harlance raised the pistol, grinning evilly.

"Whoopsy daisy, huh, buck?" he said tauntingly. "Now yer gonna find out ya ain't so tough. Where ya want it, half-breed, in yer haid or yer gut?"

Joshua said, "How about in you?"

He was just trying to joke in the face of certain death, but suddenly something exploded through the roof of the stage and both men heard Harlance's rifle fire below them in the coach. A bright spot of crimson appeared in Harlance's stomach, and he looked down at it in horror. Then Belle could be heard cocking the repeater, and she fired again. A second bullet exploded through the coach roof, smashing into Harlance's chest. He dropped his pistol and in sheer panic tore his shirt open, sticking his fingers in both bullet holes.

Strongheart said calmly, "The fingers won't help, McMahon. You are going to be dead shortly. Killed by a tiny, pretty woman who bested you. Take that to hell with you."

Joshua laughed.

This realization hit him, and Harlance's face turned from white to bright red in anger. He started to speak, but when he did, blood spewed from his mouth, and he only gurgled. His face again turned white, ghostly white, and his eyes rolled back in his head. His body went limp, and he folded like an accordion, falling off the roof headfirst onto the dirt stage road. He did not feel it. He was already dead.

The door of the stagecoach flew open, and Annabelle, tears streaming, leapt out, smiling broadly. She looked under the stage and saw McMahon's lifeless body and dropped his rifle.

Joshua said, "You sure saved my bacon."

She said, "Get down here now, redskin!"

They both laughed, and he climbed down, and she threw herself into his arms. They kissed long and passionately and were in that embrace when the stage passengers came running around the corner. One was carrying Joshua's pistol, and another the shotgun, and they were all cheering. The couple stepped back and looked at them and then at each other, smiling.

Strongheart suddenly saw the giant figure of Blood Feather, bloody knife in hand, diving off a large boulder at roadside, and his leap would send him crashing into Belle. Joshua sat up suddenly, heart pounding, breathing in deep pants. He looked all around and saw he was in his little camp at the north end of Red Canyon. He saw a few gray streaks in the eastern sky.

By daybreak, Strongheart was back in the saddle, bypassing breakfast. He had a man to find and a mission to accomplish.

Gabe ate up the miles as they slowly climbed through the canyon on the road, which would soon become a stagecoach toll road. There was also Phantom Canyon Road, which climbed up through another high-walled, narrow, rocky canyon, but it began on the east side of Cañon City.

That night, after pushing Gabe hard, Strongheart emerged on the western slope of Pikes Peak, where he would make another small, hidden, and relatively safe camp. On his backtrail he had figured the giant killer might try several ambushes, as he might not even be as far north yet as Strongheart. This time, Gabe had plenty of graze in and around the aspen grove that Strongheart camped in. Here he was able to let his guard down some, and he would get another good night's sleep, for the next day he should cut the monster killer's trail. But for now there was no reason to believe Blood Feather was within ten miles of him.

He had spotted a few deer earlier coming into the aspen grove, so he set up an ambush and took a two-year-old buck with an arrow. He would have fresh meat. He made camp, and it was warm and not visible very far because of the screen of trees. Strongheart was dead tired but was almost afraid to go to sleep. He finally did though and was very comfortable in this camp.

The general was appraising the tall Pinkerton agent as well. He could tell the man had been traveling hard for many miles. He read the dispatch from the War Department and the President's endorsement and smiled.

Then he simply said, "Glad I didn't hang the son of a buck yet."

Joshua chuckled.

Davis went on, "I will send a dispatch back by wire and military courier stating I got your dispatch and will comply. No need to make you stick around for a trial. There is no doubt that Captain Jack and his owlhoots will hang, but I will keep Washington apprised up until they do. The orders make sense."

Strongheart had traveled to the northwest to personally deliver a dispatch to General Davis directing him not to hang the notorious Modoc chief Captain Jack.

Joshua said, "General, I think I will resupply at your store and head on back to Colorado Territory."

"I think it will become a state in a few years maybe.

Heard some talk of it," the officer replied. "Did you have much trouble getting here with the dispatch?"

Strongheart chuckled to himself. "Nothing I couldn't handle, sir. The Pinkertons deliver."

"Surprised they hired a redskin, no offense."

Joshua grinned. "None taken, General. They hired the white half of me. The red part tagged along."

The general chuckled and then guffawed.

He escorted Joshua to the door and warned, "I have some men with pretty strong sentiments right now. I hope you understand."

Strongheart said, "General, men shot down and killed under a flag of truce is not something any red man of any upbringing condones. We have honor, too."

Davis stared at him and extended his hand, saying, "I believe you, Mr. Strongheart."

The general thought about having his first sergeant escort Strongheart to the store and away from the garrison, then he grinned, thinking this man would handle whatever his men handed him.

Earlier, Joshua had been attacked by a big, burly sergeant named Rowdy, and he tricked him and dumped him in a watering tough while the men Rowdy had tried to show off for laughed at him.

Strongheart left the headquarters building and asked directions to the store. Unfortunately, Rowdy and his hangers-on were outside the store. Joshua was going to just leave, but he was already headed directly toward the store when he spotted the troublemaker. He could not just turn tail.

Rowdy came forward, chest sticking out and chin jutting defiantly.

"Well, laddie," he said, "ya think ya bested me 'cause I had a slip. We're gonna change the dance."

Strongheart said, "Sergeant, you are playing the wrong tune. I am tired, just traveled halfway across the country to deliver one letter, and plan to buy my supplies and leave. So step aside kindly."

Rowdy stepped forward and tried to give Joshua a shove with both hands. Joshua's hands shot forward and up, like Dan had taught him, with his palms forward. They went in little semicircles from the inside out, and he grabbed Rowdy's fingers, which naturally made both hands turn palms up, with the fingers bent down toward the ground. Rowdy screamed in pain from the pressure on his wrists and knuckles, which all felt like they were ready to pop totally out of joint, and he stood up on his tiptoes it hurt so bad.

Joshua grinned, whispering, "You said you wanted to dance. How about a do-si-do?"

With that, he marched the crusty old brawler twenty feet to the watering trough he'd swum in before. Suddenly, Strongheart swung him sideways, spinning on his own heels and letting go, laughing as the big sergeant crashed into the watering trough again, while all his men laughed. Joshua walked on to the store, while General Davis chuckled to himself, watching from his outer office window. Even the general laughed aloud as Rowdy came out of the trough cursing and yelling, slipped, and fell back into the water. Suddenly, instead of Rowdy, a bully twice as big sat up out of the water. It was Blood Feather, and he held Belle's heart up in one hand and a large bloody knife in the other hand.

Joshua sat up, heart pounding, blinking his eyes, and looked around. He pictured Belle, and he wept.

"I miss you so much already, Belle," he said. "I will never love another."

He let himself cry for now, but could not afford to tomorrow. Sometime during the next day, Blood Feather would be within range. He knew it. He felt it, but right now he simply grieved until he dropped off to sleep again. He would awaken and have venison steaks and biscuits in the morning, and lots of coffee. Right now, he would simply get the rest he needed.

A plan was developing in his mind. It was daring and bold, but he figured Belle was worth it.

The next day, by mid-morning he was halfway across the wide, grassy, treed valley west of Pikes Peak. Strongheart ground-reined Gabe, and over the widely used road up the valley's middle he searched for tracks revealing the big draft horse and its heavy load. This was one of the few bottleneck parts of the valley, where large rock outcroppings came close together, so all traffic was funneled through the area he was checking.

He had guessed correctly. He was ahead of the big killer. Strongheart started making preparations, hiding in the trees whenever a traveler happened by.

We Wiyake sat in the rocks, his rifle ready, watching at the top of the very long, steep hill on the road northwest of Cañon City. He knew Joshua would have to come this way. In his sick mind, he wondered if it was a wise decision to kill Strongheart's woman. He still wanted to eat the man's heart, and women, in his mind, were not that important anyway. Blood Feather saw a posse coming far down the long hill, but Strongheart was not with them. He lay down and waited, knowing exactly what he would do.

Strongheart had picked his spot. He had ridden around the trees looking, and after half an hour spotted what he wanted. Many feet off the ground was a gigantic nest, over ten feet in depth. It was the aerie of an eagle. Now he ground-reined Gabe again, and walked around under the tree, walking out in circles. And forty feet out he found what he wanted, the discarded tail feather of a bald eagle. He had been looking for the nest of a red-tailed hawk, golden eagle, or bald eagle, but this white feather with brown tip would be even more dramatic.

He returned to the narrows.

Blood Feather watched where there was a patch of road that was very rocky. He had made note of it riding up the hill. He lay down in the middle of the dirt trail and aimed his rifle at the rocky patch. The posse was halfway up the long climb, a Ute tracker in front of them. He waited. Now they were less than ten feet from the rocks, and he started firing and chambering rounds, the bullets traveling down the long hill, ricocheting off the rocks, and slamming into the legs and chests of the now screaming and rearing horses. Several riders hit the ground, and he fired toward them, seeing three get hit by either direct hits or ricochets. None of the posse even fired shots close to him. His concentration of rounds caused the desired effect—wounded men and wounded horses. He knew the white men would take the time to care for their wounded and would be nervous about proceeding, plus half their horses were now useless. He waited, watching while they treated the wounded, and none seemed to want to proceed. There was one who rode off to the west, wide of the road, and Blood Feather figured that one was probably hiding in the trees. Even at that distance, that one looked old and was moving very slow anyway, so he did not concern the killer. Finally, the group turned and headed back toward the south.

Blood Feather was certain that Joshua would have pursued him immediately, and it was bothering him that the Pinkerton was not with the posse. Then, he wondered if Strongheart simply wanted to stay with his woman. *Wasicun* were sometimes weak like that, he thought.

We Wiyake turned and went to the big draft horse hidden in the trees, where he was resting and recovering from the long climb up the evergreen-lined hill. Blood Feather started riding at a trot toward the valley where Strongheart was awaiting him. His arm was throbbing where infection had set in, and he knew he had to find some roots and sap to make a poultice to combat the infection.

Two hours passed, and Blood Feather finally came to the narrowing part of the valley. He now slowed to a walk and held his rifle across his thighs, knowing this was the area where he would make an ambush. He did not like this. Something made him stop, but he did not know what. Then he realized it was something out of place.

To lure in a bobcat or even a curious pronghorn antelope on the prairie, American Indians of most nations knew to hang either a flap of fur or a large bird feather from a branch, bush, or tall plant. Under the long overhanging branch of the closest tree, *We Wiyaki* saw something white hanging, moving with the wind. Then he made a big mistake. He knew about luring in pronghorn or bobcats, but he did not think. He rode forward to look closer, like a giant, unsuspecting bobcat. Blood Feather stopped the Percheron and stared at the feather swinging to and fro with the wind. It was a bald eagle feather, and it was covered with blood.

Whoosh! Blood Feather felt stabbing, searing pain in his right thigh, and he grabbed it. He looked down. It was a Lakota arrow, and it had entered his right thigh, mid-thigh, and stuck out the other side, almost hitting the horse's side. His head snapped up, and he saw Strongheart, in war paint and breechcloth and holding his bow in his left hand. Joshua raised the bow in victory celebration and disappeared into the rock outcropping he stood on. Before Blood Feather could do anything. Blood poured everywhere from the wound. The serial killer could not attack or chase Joshua, as he had to get the bleeding stopped fast. He dropped off the horse and went down with pain when he hit the ground. He knew his thigh bone had been broken or chipped by the arrow. He quickly wrapped leather around the wound and secured it with his headband, which he yanked off his head.

He knew he had to get up again and get back on the big horse.

We Wiyake normally never felt emotion, except after eating the heart of a victim. Normally, he was in charge. He struck terror into the hearts of white men and red men, women and children. But now he was twice wounded and in excruciating pain. More importantly, he was unnerved. He had been outsmarted.

He decided that if he was going to make the spirit journey, this mysterious, powerful half-white, half-Lakota enemy would die with him, locked in battle. They would die together, if he could not kill Strongheart outright. This was something he must do.

Joshua went to his next spot and lay down. He waited. Gabe was well back in the trees. In this place, the trail wound its way through the trees, and Joshua lay behind a fallen log across the trail. The big horse would step over the log, and as soon as he was over, Strongheart would spring up with his father's knife and slice through the Achilles tendon on *We Wiyake*'s left ankle, then run into the trees, using the thick woods as perfect cover.

Two hours passed.

Boom! A rifle went off far to the west in the trees. Joshua was up and running in a moment, and rushing to where he had left the big pinto.

"Oh no!" The words came out of his mouth as he saw Gabriel, his beloved horse, lying still.

Running forward, Strongheart saw the pool of blood and the big crimson hole in Gabe's forehead. The big red-and-white horse did not feel a thing. He had died instantly, but now Joshua's heart broke even more. Another thing happened: His resolve to get Blood Feather had been total before, but now it was well beyond that. It was beyond unbridled passion. It was cold fury.

Joshua stripped what he could from the saddlebags and made himself a pack to carry his provisions. Then he lay across the neck of the big horse.

He quietly said, "Good-bye, Gabe. We were partners."

It suddenly hit Strongheart that he was a sitting duck, and he knew that *We Wiyake* could be sighting him in with his rifle now. He felt a shiver go down his spine, that sixth sense of "knowing" that some warriors have. He jumped to the side, and the little tree just past where he'd been sitting exploded, and then he heard the sound of Blood Feather's rifle no less than a hundred yards south of him. He speed-crawled away from his horse, and then got to his feet and started running through the thick trees in a northerly direction. He had to abandon the horse there and not look back.

No more shots rang out, but Strongheart could rest assured that *We Wiyake* was going to pursue.

He kept on northward at a steady, fast pace, jogging. He knew that a man jogging, if in the right condition, could actually keep on going when a horse could not. He went into the rock outcropping, as he knew the big horse could not follow there. Blood Feather would also be very slow-moving there. He had wounds to deal with. *Crack! Whump!* A bullet flashing by Joshua's left ear made him feel its power. He ducked and snapped his head, barely seeing Blood Feather in the trees. Joshua stood up, which was unexpected to the killer, and quickly took a snap shot with his bow. The arrow sailed rapidly and stuck in a tree right next to the giant's head. He disappeared into the trees.

Strongheart knew the man had to nurse his wounds, so he thought about pushing him, keeping on taking shots at a distance, letting him bleed. Then he thought about his beloved Belle and his horse Gabe, and he decided he would not let it happen that fast. This was not about revenge, he decided. It was about retribution. It was about the riddance and destruction of pure evil.

Strongheart crept back into the woods wearing his pack. He stayed out at a distance and walked a route parallel to the clear path the big draft horse made through the trees.

There were lodgepole pines and aspens here, with a lot of undergrowth. The trail went for a mile, and then Strongheart spotted Blood Feather's horse covered with blood on one side and the giant serial killer lying on the ground next to it. He slowly moved forward, arrow nocked, ready to draw and shoot.

Joshua looked closely at the horse first and saw it was covered with *We Wiyake*'s blood from Strongheart's arrow. He then looked at the murderer. The man was clearly unconscious. Strongheart pulled out his scalpel-sharp knife and held it over Blood Feather's throat. Then he grinned an evil grin and put it away. He pulled out the roll of bandaging he now always carried in his saddlebags. He dressed the leg wound and put a tight pressure bandage on it. *We Wiyake* was still out cold. Joshua looked at the giant's arm and could see angry flesh above and below the leather wrapping. Blood Feather's arm was severely infected where Strongheart had shot him.

Joshua then built a campfire and pulled an eagle feather out of the back of his hair. He soaked the feather with *We Wiyake*'s blood and set it on the killer's face. He then rose and walked away from the camp, pulled his Colt from his pack, and fired two rounds in the air. *We Wiyake* started stirring, and Strongheart ran into the trees, disappearing quickly in the vegetation.

He was killing this man a piece at a time. Strongheart waited a good distance away and watched with his spyglass. After fifteen minutes, Blood Feather was sitting up and looking around. He held the bloody feather and stared at it. He looked down at his patched up leg.

We Wiyake normally had no emotions, but now he was terrified. He looked at Strongheart's bandage and a shiver ran up and down his spine. He looked down at the feather, and things started to register. For the first time in his life, *We Wiyake* was scared. He was terrified. He had thought that if he did the terrible things he did, it would force Strongheart to be an even greater adversary, but the smaller man had bested him at his own game. It unnerved him, and the big killer did not know how to react other than to survive.

Blood Feather shaved off pieces of jerky into water he'd put on to boil. He kept getting the shivers and stared all around him, just knowing Strongheart must be watching. He felt stronger after he ate and drank water from his bison-bladder canteen. There was no sense moving, because he was not mobile now, and Strongheart could easily follow him. He slept and awakened a little after dark and fed wood into the fire. All of a sudden out the woods he heard a loud yell.

It was Strongheart, far off, yelling, *"We Tewaci Au We!"* which meant "Blood will bring blood!"

He repeated it three times, then the dark woods got quiet. Blood Feather was never before so frightened in his life. He had never felt fear, and he hated it.

Strongheart freshened his war paint and moved back to his hideout higher up in the rocks, where he knew *We Wiyake* could not pursue him right now. Maybe the next day he could, and he wondered if he was wise to let the man live for now, even nurse his wounds. He decided that he did not care if it was wise. It was what he felt must be done. This man had killed in the most frightening and horrific manner imaginable, for years, in both the red world and the white world. He was pure evil.

Joshua built a good fire among a jumble of boulders and ate a hearty meal. He thought about the love of his life and cried quietly. He sharpened his knife and arrowheads while he drank coffee and thought about Gabriel and the adventures they had enjoyed and survived together. He had not really used his guns, because this was a Lakota warrior. He wanted to use the weapons of his father Claw Marks.

It would be very easy to simply shoot the man with his

Colt or his rifle. In fact, he could use either or both and shoot the giant killer over and over.

However, as soon as he even thought of this, the words of Dan Cooper rang out in his head: "Joshua, the easy way is not necessarily the best way. Most times, it's not."

In honor of his father and even his mother, who loved Claw Marks her whole life; in honor of his stepfather, who raised him as his own son; in honor of Belle, the woman he loved so deeply and was ready to marry, he wanted to do this the Lakota way. The way of a warrior. Blood Feather, even twice-wounded, was still seven feet tall and well over one hundred pounds larger than Strongheart and all muscle and toughness. Joshua was not stupid. He had already evened the odds a lot, but he might even them even more. He knew that the next day maybe, he and *We Wiyake* would face each other and fight to the death. He did not care how badly he would get hurt. He would show the murderer that, indeed, "blood will bring blood."

Blood Feather awakened in the middle of the night. The fire had dwindled down, and he built it up more. His leg was torn up and his arm hurt worse than any toothache he had suffered, and he'd had two major toothaches years before and hated them. He heated up more soup and ate it. Then chewed on some jerky, knowing the nutrition would help him with the challenge ahead.

For the first time in his life, *We Wiyake* wondered if he was going to die. He lay back down and wondered if Strongheart was just outside the circle of light, preparing to kill him now. Another chill ran down his spine. He slept very fitfully during the rest of the night and awakened with his wounded arm aching. It was almost dawn when he doused his campfire and led the big horse to a group of boulders. His whole life, he'd simply grab some horse mane and swing up on the back of a horse, but now he had to stand on one rock like a step to the next. Then he lay across the horse's back, swung his leg over, and sat up moaning and aching.

As soon as he mounted, he wondered if he could slip away somewhere and hide so he could heal a little more.

That feeling left him immediately when, out of the darkness, he heard the loud voice of Joshua Strongheart yelling, *"We Wiyake! We tiwaci au we! We tiwaci au we!"*

He kicked the big horse into a gallop through the trees in a total panic and felt a limb smack him across the chest. He flew off the horse's back, hitting the ground with a thud, breaking a rib on a small rock. He also got the wind knocked out of him for the first time in his life. He panicked but soon got his breath back.

Every time Blood Feather breathed, there was a searing pain in his lower left rib cage. He'd not only broken a rib, but bruised three others. He lay on the ground trying to breathe and heard the voice of Joshua Strongheart again in the trees, laughing heartily. *We Wiyake* felt he was going to die now for sure, but he had to take this enemy with him. He determined he would push past the pain, ignore the aches, and set himself to kill the much smaller, weaker opponent. Although he was hurting more, his adrenaline was pumping now, and he felt stronger.

The sun was starting to peek through the trees, and *We Wiyake* checked his rifle to make sure it was clean and loaded. It struck Strongheart as funny that Blood Feather had used a white man's weapon during this chase and Joshua had used more primitive Lakota weapons.

Blood Feather got to his feet and followed the big horse for an hour. He walked up to it and the horse did not want to be caught. He pulled his cooking bowl out of his parfleche and put pebbles in it and shook the bowl. Thinking it was grain the big horse came forward. As soon as he got up to the bowl and started to stick his nose in it, Blood Feather reached out and grabbed the lead line the horse had been dragging.

The horse nudged him with his nose, and suddenly the big knife came forward. The strike into the heart was perfect and the horse felt nothing. It died on the spot. Weak and with his arm really aching, Blood Feather quickly started carving meat for himself to eat. He did not care about this or any horse. He was in for the fight of his life, and he knew he had to get some meat into his system. He would kill this man, eat his heart, and then he could go for miles on the spiritual energy of defeating such a mighty warrior. He made a quick campfire and started cooking the meat. He ate pounds of it and was unaware that Strongheart watched at a distance with his binoculars.

Strongheart said quietly aloud, "Eat all you want, but it won't help you, Blood Feather. You may kill me, but you are going to die, too. And first, you will die several times in your mind. This, I swear."

He hid himself among the trees and waited for Blood Feather to move. Joshua was amazed at the killer's constitution. He moved with purpose as he went west into the trees and then turned back north. Joshua knew what he was doing. The giant was actually going to go for the western rock outcropping, hoping to find a hiding place among those granite sentinels. It would be extremely difficult for him to move in that unforgiving terrain, and nothing could have pleased Strongheart more.

Joshua decided to intercept Blood Feather in the rocks and figure out a plan to chip away at the brute's strength once more. He trotted forward with the morning sun still hidden on the other side of Pikes Peak off to his right. The pair of eyes with the binoculars watched Strongheart as he moved up into the rocks, and then he turned the field glasses to his left and saw glimpses of Blood Feather moving slowly

through the trees. The watcher kept looking at Blood
Feather but could not find Strongheart again in the rocks.

We Wiyake was totally worn out and his head was spinning. He climbed slowly up through the rocks. Every muscle and joint in his body ached. He was tired, and he was for
the first time in his life vulnerable, like other people. He
hated how he was feeling. He made it one hundred feet up
into the rocks and slowly climbed farther, one-handed,
limping badly. His strength had dissipated, and with what
seemed like the last of his energy, he pulled himself up
around two large boulders, each the size of a buckboard. He
started to step around one and for a split second he looked
into the red-and-black war-painted face of Joshua Strongheart before the punch hit him full square in the nose and
broke it. He fell back, dropping his rifle, and adrenaline
took over. He reached for the rifle and spun around, bringing
it up. The Pinkerton agent was gone. He had disappeared
into the rocks.

The watcher glassed the rocks and saw the figure of
Strongheart as he punched *We Wiyake*. The beast flew back
holding his nose, which was now bleeding profusely. Strongheart slithered up through the rocks as the watcher kept the
glasses on him; then he disappeared as he moved through
the many rock formations.

Blood Feather held his nose and moved it over with a
crunching sound, trying to make it straight. His eyes watered,
and he pinched his nostrils. He knew he could not afford to
lose more blood. This was the worst experience he had ever
been through.

He lay on his belly and started crawling slowly between
rocks, trying to find a hidden sanctuary where he could rest
and regroup. He only crawled for a few minutes and was so
exhausted and out of breath that he just dropped his head
down on his good arm and tried to relax his breathing and
calm himself down. He lay still for ten minutes and started

rethinking about crawling. *We Wiyake* felt that Strongheart could not see him now and would have to guess his exact location, so maybe it would be worth crawling more. It was just so painful and slow. His breathing slowed down after five minutes, and he decided to set a goal. He would crawl twenty more body lengths and relax. The giant reached down for his rifle and could not feel it. His hand moved around something soft. He raised it up and looked at it. It was a red-tailed hawk feather. He turned, his eyes searching the ground frantically. Blood Feather's rifle was gone, taken right from his side. Then he saw the tracks of Strongheart, sneaking in and sneaking away in just those five minutes. He drew his giant knife out, his eyes going back and forth left and right. He looked behind him. His heart pounded in his ears. His breathing was coming out in gasps now.

Blood Feather tried to calm himself down more. He sat up and leaned against a rock, fidgeting. His right hand went up to his left shoulder and upper arm and rubbed them. His arm hurt so badly he wanted to amputate it. The psychotic killer looked all around him and started hearing the voices of all those he killed screaming in the rocks, their voices echoing throughout the outcropping. He put his hand to one ear and hurt his arm trying to put the other hand up to stop the voices.

Suddenly, he saw the face of Strongheart's woman. It was floating in the clouds directly to his front. Just like when she died, she stared at him defiantly, her jaw thrust forward and teeth clenched, but she had not and would not now show fear. She smiled at him.

Strongheart's voice came into focus echoing among the rocks, "*We Wiyake! We tiwaci au we! We tiwaci au we! We tiwaci au we!*"

Joshua had seen the flash now twice off the watcher's binoculars, and he carefully made his way through the rock labyrinth so he would not be seen. He went from the rocks into the trees and worked his way toward the watcher's position. First, he saw the horse and it was magnificent. Over sixteen hands, it looked Arabian, and it was a pinto, with black and white swirling all over its well-muscled body. The legs looked saddlebred and the head was definitely Arabian. The big gelding held himself proudly and stood patiently waiting for his owner.

Strongheart went silently past the horse, who let out a quiet whinny as the Pinkerton moved toward the watcher ahead of him on a pile of giant hardwood blowdowns. Joshua quietly slipped off his pack, pulled out his gunbelt, and strapped on his Peacemaker and knife. He was not stupid, and this man was holding a buffalo gun—a .50-caliber Sharps rifle, in fact.

The man was Zachariah Banta, and ten feet behind him Strongheart put his pistol away, saying, "Zach!"

Banta spun around, startled, and showed a big toothy grin. He climbed down off the logs and walked up to Strongheart, sticking out his hand to shake.

They shook hands, and Zach said, "Wal, son, you are a might painted up fer war. Looks like yer givin' war to that old boy, too. I was with the posse, and when he cut loose on us I rode that ole paint into the trees and jest kept coming up in the hill."

"Beautiful horse, Zach."

Zach ignored those words and said, "Look, I ain't good at speechifyin' at a time like this, but I am really sorry, Joshua. I loved the young lady like a daughter. I even got her Eagle there, but I guess he's yours now. I got Eagle from my cousin down to Westcliffe, and he was bred just like Gabe, half-Arab and half-saddlebred. That breed seems to fit you right fine."

Strongheart was touched.

He said, "What do you mean you got that horse for her?"

Zach said, "I heered you two was officially gettin'

hitched, so I wanted to give her a nice present. That is one handsome horse. I saw Gabe's body. Sorry about that, too, That son of a—"

Joshua interrupted. "You amaze me, Zach. You live in Cotopaxi and you already heard that fast we were engaged? That is a beautiful horse. I don't know what to say. I can't take him."

Zach said, "You and me never talk that much about God and sech things, but the Good Book tells ya not to turn away a blessing. That is your horse now. He is five years old and all you gotta do is put your foot in the stirrup, and he is good ta go. Ya say anything other'n thanks, you will insult me."

Strongheart stuck his hand out and said, "Thanks, Zach."

Zach said, "Ain't ya worried about that dry-gulchin' varmint gittin' away whilst we're yapping like a pair a coyote bitches?"

Joshua said, "No, not at all. You ever see a cat playing with a mouse after he's caught it?"

Zach said, "Reckon so."

Strongheart said, "Can I take Eagle for now and you wait for me up in the rocks? It is time to end it."

Zach said, "I don't care if ya skin him alive, son. I will be happy to see it. Eagle is your horse. You ride him when ya want."

Strongheart lengthened the stirrups and stepped into the saddle. He started Eagle off at a slow trot, and the horse proudly tossed his mane and tail from side-to-side like a parade horse. It was the smoothest trot Joshua had ever felt from a horse.

Suddenly, he stopped, seeing a crowd of riders cresting the hill from the south. He watched for a minute while Zach raised his binoculars. Several riderless horses followed behind them, a remuda. The posse had regrouped and were still pursuing.

Joshua gave Zach a wave, yelling, "Keep them back. He's mine!"

Blood Feather knew Strongheart had disappeared and had not returned to terrorize him again. He decided he would try to walk up the valley as quickly as his wounds would allow and hope that Joshua had gotten injured and would not follow him. He was now carrying a branch to use as a crutch. The giant heard hoofbeats behind him, as he was now one hundred yards out on the grassy valley floor. He turned and saw Strongheart trotting toward him on a magnificent black-and-white pinto. Strongheart rode right by him, looking down at him as he passed. He went on trotting for the distant trees. Arriving, he left Eagle there and kept his knife, stripping off his holster and gunbelt. He quickly cut and sharpened a wooden peg from a stick. He then grabbed the lasso from the saddle and tied one end around his left ankle and walked forward, knife in one hand and lasso in the other.

Blood Feather's heart was doing flip-flops as he watched his enemy walking toward him, a coldness in Joshua's eyes that would have sent shivers down anybody's spine. Strongheart knew that his father Claw Marks had staked himself out with a twenty-foot leather thong and faced a band of Crow warriors who swept him under, but not before he killed some of their number. Strongheart was going to exorcise that demon, too, this day.

He picked up a rock and pounded the stake into the ground, then dropped the lasso, tied the end around the stake, and tossed the loop out. He was running nowhere, and this, too, unnerved Blood Feather. Joshua Strongheart faced Blood Feather, his father's big knife in his right hand. *We Wiyake*'s knife was twice the size of Strongheart's and would have looked more like a sword in any other man's hand.

The serial killer steeled himself for the combat and

walked up until he was five feet from the smaller warrior. They looked into each other's eyes.

Strongheart said quietly, calmly, "*We tiwaci au we.*"

Blood Feather lunged forward, and Joshua dived to his side, kicking his lasso up with his leg. At the same time, he slashed with his knife and cut across and through Blood Feather's hamstring, on the killer's good leg. He fell to the ground screaming. Strongheart was totally calm.

Somehow, the murderer got to his feet, let out a war cry, and charged Strongheart, knife upraised. This time, instead of diving to the side, Strongheart stood his ground and blocked the downward knife swing by canting his own knife blade down, with the back of his blade along his own fore-arm. The strike itself sent Blood Feather's forearm down, slicing all the way to the bone, and he screamed again. Joshua's arm was like a flash as he slashed down on an angle, with his knife blade tearing a deep gash all the way down the killer's chest, exposing chest and abdominal muscles. But Joshua was still moving, and he spun and plunged the knife backward into Blood Feather's solar plexus.

Joshua said, "That one was for Blackjack."

Blood Feather tried to scream again, but sounds would not come out of his mouth. He had never felt such excruci-ating pain, and he dropped to his knees. Strongheart grabbed the killer's hair with his left hand, jerked his head back, and with a flash took his scalp off. He held the scalp high and gave out a spine-chilling war cry.

He raised *We Wiyake*'s head and in Lakota said, "Here is your scalp. See it before you. I was going to cut out your heart out and eat it, but I am not you, I am better than you. They were all better than you. The coyotes and ravens will eat your heart. That is what you deserve."

He pushed the killer forward with his foot, and Blood Feather fell facedown into the dirt, unable now to move at all. That is how he would die, his blood spilling into the

Colorado soil, knowing he would be consumed by predators and nobody would care.

Joshua walked to his horse Eagle and tied the scalp to his saddle horn. Then he looked at it, and untied it, tossing it on the ground.

He patted the horse, saying, "What I do as a man will not always be what I can do if I want, Eagle. You and I will be together a long time. There will always be men like that, who need to meet the same end. Let's go find them."

He rode toward the rock outcropping where he could clearly see his audience, the posse lined up on the rocks. They had just witnessed the most incredible one-sided fight to the death they could imagine. It was a fight of good triumphing over evil, yet the good man wore a red-and-black mask that represented what many of those men had hated and feared for most of their lives. They each realized that maybe there was good in everything and every situation, if you could just recognize it.

They had just watched the ultimate bully get exactly what all bullies need to get—a taste of justice. And as the proud black-and-white pinto trotted sideways toward them, his tail flipped up and off to the side of his rump, the ultimate warrior seated so well on his back, each man knew he had just witnessed the legend of Strongheart grow even more.

EPILOGUE

The descendants of Zachariah Banta all had a quick wit and a dry humor, and they ran cattle all around the Cotopaxi area for many decades, finally moving the ranching operation to southwestern Texas in the early twenty-first century via Zach's great-great-great-grandson Byk Banta. Byk still runs his ranching operation from the back of a horse.

Sheriff Frank Bengley was the sheriff, in fact, of Fremont County, Colorado Territory, in 1874, one of many in a long line of fine lawmen in southern Colorado.

Quanah Parker ended up signing a peace treaty and in just a few years became a multimillionaire businessman in the white man's world. He kept his three wives and freely went back and forth between both societies the rest of his days.

Except for Belle's café and other obvious exceptions, all the locations and local histories mentioned herein were actual places, and many still exist today. I have ridden my horse over almost every piece of land mentioned in this book and in my other Westerns, so you will know it is real and not a Hollywood movie set. For example, I killed and was charged by a blond-and-cinnamon black bear (black is a breed, not a color) in 1985, within a mile of where Strongheart had his fight with the big silvertip grizzly bear. Please come along and join in sharing with me the rest of the tale about Pinkerton agent Joshua Strongheart in his future adventures, also from Berkley. Strongheart's friend Chris Colt was the hero of ten Westerns I also wrote, for Berkley's parent company. He will be featured in future Strongheart novels, too.

Family illnesses kept this sequel from being published closer to *Strongheart*, but hopefully that is behind us and you will see more of Strongheart soon.

Sadly, my horse of 22 years, Eagle, had to be put down in January, 2013. I will never forget him. He was a once-in-a-lifetime horse that saved my life several times. Strongheart can keep riding him though.

Until then, partner, keep your powder dry, an eye on the horizon, and an occasional glance toward your backtrail, and sit tall in the saddle. It does not matter if your saddle is a computer desk chair, upholstered armchair, porch swing, or deck chair on a cruise ship. Many of us grew up with the spirit of the American cowboy and pioneer woman. It is good to keep a door to our past open, so we know where our strength, courage, and tenacity came from. It is the legacy of honor forged from the steel characters, blessed by God, who created some of his mightiest warriors in the American West. It is indeed the backbone of America.

If you need me, I will be on my horse in the high lonesome coming up with more stories for you. That is where I get my tales. They are up there above the timberline, written on the clouds, and I swear that handwriting looks perfect.

ABOUT THE AUTHOR

Don Bendell is the author of well over two dozen books, with over 3,000,000 copies in print worldwide, as well as a successful feature film. An action/adventure man he is a disabled U.S. Army Special Forces (Green Beret) officer and Vietnam veteran, and two of his sons are Green Berets serving now. He is a grandmaster instructor in five martial arts, and he and his wife were the first couple in history to both be inducted into the International Karate and Kickboxing Hall of Fame. He still teaches martial arts once a week. Don says, "to help keep my sanity as a writer."

Don describes himself as "a real cowboy with a real horse and a real ranch." He and his wife own the beautiful Strongheart Ranch south of Florence, Colorado. He also vacations and writes in his motor home on the side of the majestic Sangre de Cristo Mountain Range near Westcliffe, Colorado, that Don often writes about, in this book, in *Strongheart*, and in others. He owned horses identical to Strongheart's, named Gabe and Eagle, and he rode Eagle over all the ground that he writes about, but Eagle died in early 2013. Hardscrabble Creek, mentioned in both books, runs for a half mile through Don's ranch.

Don and Shirley Bendell travel a lot and enjoy dancing, bow hunting, fishing, and camping with their horses in the Rocky Mountains. Don is the father of six grown children and has eleven grandchildren. He has a master of science degree in leadership from the Ken Blanchard College of Business at Grand Canyon University in Phoenix. In 2011, Don was awarded the first annual Excellence in Western Literature Award by the Read West Foundation.